Taste

Kate Evangelista

www.crescentmoonpress.com

Taste
Kate Evangelista

ISBN: 978-1-937254-55-1
E-ISBN: 978-1-937254-56-8

© Copyright Kate Evangelista 2012. All rights reserved
Cover Art: Liliana Sanches
Editor: Kathryn Steves
Layout/Typesetting: jimandzetta.com

Crescent Moon Press
1385 Highway 35
Box 269
Middletown, NJ 07748

Ebooks/Books are not transferable. They cannot be sold, shared or given away as it is an infringement on the copyright of this work.

All Rights Are Reserved. No part of this book may be used or reproduced in any manner whatsoever without written permission, except in the case of brief quotations embodied in critical articles and reviews.

This book is a work of fiction. The names, characters, places and incidents are products of the writer's imagination or have been used fictitiously and are not to be construed as real. Any resemblance to persons, living or dead, actual events, locale or organizations is entirely coincidental.

Crescent Moon Press electronic publication/print publication: April 2012 www.crescentmoonpress.com

To my writing sister, Angie,
for building me up when I knock myself down.

Chapter 1

Rules

I jerked awake to the first note of the bell in the east tower. The metallic clang of the chorus of the school song reverberated in my gut, causing a burst of panic to explode in my chest. The tolls yanked me from my seated position to my feet like a pair of rough hands *Great, Phoenix McKay! Only you would fall asleep in the library past curfew.*

Without thinking twice, I scrambled between floor-to-ceiling bookshelves toward the entrance of the massive library that resembled catacombs in the dying light, each shelf a final resting place for books long forgotten. The setting sun spread sharp finger shadows through narrow, ten-foot windows. I sprinted, skirting long study tables made to look like autopsy slabs by the growing darkness. My expulsion was imminent. I could feel it in the choking dread in my chest. Barinkoff Academy had one real rule kids followed: Everyone had to be off campus by sundown.

The consequence: immediate expulsion, no questions asked.

It was the easiest rule to follow in the history of rules. No one had ever been kicked out of Barinkoff before. It looked like I'd be the first in the academy's illustrious five-hundred-year-old history.

In an attempt to distract myself from dire thoughts, I focused on the predicament I was in. After the initial melodic tolling of the school bells that announced the top of the hour,

the countdown began.

One. I reached the library's double doors and pulled the handles. The heavy doors protested.

Two. My fingers slipped. I wiped my sweat-slick hands on my skirt and tried again. The doors creaked and opened.

Three. I squeezed through the exit I'd made. I didn't know which hurt more, the burning of my lungs or my heart hammering a hole through my chest. I cursed my propensity to skip gym.

Four. I raced down the west hall that ran alongside the Lunar Garden. The massive columns that divided the garden and the hall resembled half of a giant's ribcage.

I quickened my pace and reached the school's front doors by the sixth chime then stopped when an overwhelming sense of hopelessness flooded my insides. My hands trembled and my knees fought to keep me upright. I leaned my forehead against the door. The wood might as well have been metal; the door was so cold. Bile climbed up my throat. I coughed several times before I covered my mouth and swallowed the sourness. I tried to catch my breath, but no matter how hard I tried, I couldn't bring enough air into my struggling lungs.

Damn. This couldn't be happening. I slapped the door with my palm several times. This couldn't be happening! Not to me. Especially not to me! But the bell had stopped. Its silence sealed my fate. I groaned like a dying animal, wanting nothing more than to wake up from this nightmare. Six tolls told me classes had ended two hours ago. The last bus always left half an hour after the last class, taking all the students back to the dorms. And I'd not been on that bus with them.

"This can't be happening," I whispered through my teeth and pushed my way outside. I walked from the doors to the front steps.

Untouched snow covered the empty courtyard. I whistled a slow, sad breath. Forget scenes of death and destruction. True desolation was staring at an empty parking lot.

The chill in the air sank its teeth deep into me. I'd left my jacket—along with the rest of my stuff—in the library. Smokey puffs of breath escaped my lips. Abject disappointment replaced my previous dread. Of all the stupid things I'd done

~ ☾ ~

in my life, getting left behind after curfew was probably the worst.

Defeated, I slumped down to sit on the top step and cradled my chin in the cup of my hands, elbows on my knees. I blinked back tears. I refused to cry. I wasn't the crying type. For the first time in my life, I didn't want to get kicked out of school and sent home. Not to a father who had stopped talking to me exactly eighteen months ago today. I smacked my forehead as the last rays of light disappeared behind the Caucasus Mountain Range.

Disgusted by the new level of pathetic I'd managed to create for myself, I sighed, deep and heavy. The kind of sigh depressed people heaved. Then I shrugged. No point in obsessing. What was done was done. Not like I could invent a time machine just so I could smack myself awake before curfew. So I stood up, wrung out my now snow-dampened pleated skirt, and assessed the situation.

It took thirty minutes by bus to get to the dorms. I wasn't about to risk breaking my neck by walking down a slick mountain road in the dark. If I was going to get expelled anyway, I might as well get a ride to the dorms, which meant making my way to the administration office. The million-dollar question: who earned the first call?

My father? My heart ached at the thought.

The headmaster? I didn't have Kiev's number. In fact, I only saw him on Assembly Day.

The dorms? A ride back was my first priority, so yeah, the dorms seemed like the best option.

I whirled to face the medieval castle that called itself Barinkoff Academy. It loomed in the pre-evening gloom, like most creepy castles did. Its towers, baileys, battlements, and iron portcullis at the front witnessed my shame. To be expelled for falling asleep…I shook my head at the utter idiocy of it. I strode to the front doors and reentered the hall. The decorative sconces—all lit as if by magic—cast eerie shadows on the floor. I picked my jaw up off the floor and twisted my lips. My job just got easier. If I found the person responsible for turning on the lights, I could hitch a ride. A custodian, maybe? Being found out sooner rather than later hardly mattered. I was screwed either way.

I shook off the castle-of-Dracula feel in the air and turned to the Lunar Garden. The tall pillars acted like a curtain between the hall and the perfectly manicured landscaping. A massive fountain at the garden's center gave the impression of a creature on guard over the stillness of pine trees and stone benches. In a weird way, the fountain reminded me of my mother. She would have liked the design—a young girl reaching up toward the sky, her face looked lost, like she was asking the heavens for guidance.

Voices at the end of the hall pulled my attention away from my internal drama. Maybe I could still salvage the situation and avoid expulsion by coaxing whoever would give me a ride home to pretend he or she never saw me. My eyebrows rose in stages as I got a closer look at the group that rounded the corner. None of them looked like the custodian.

The guys wore baggy pants tucked into knee-high leather boots. Their jackets were cut above the waist, unlike the regulation blazers my male classmates wore. The white shirts underneath had the sheen of silk rather than the flatness cotton. And they had on cravats instead of neckties. Not the typical Barinkoff uniform.

The girls glided in floor-length skirts. Corsets hugged long-sleeved blouses, which was a sharp contrast to my own outfit: short pleated skirt, thick leggings and motorcycle boots, a blazer over a white shirt, and a ribbon at the collar.

What made the whole thing weirder was the fact that they all looked extremely attractive. I felt like I'd walked into a Twilight Zone version of New York Fashion Week. All of them were tall, elegantly slender, with creamy skin and black hair. No one told me Barinkoff had students on campus after curfew. Did that mean I wasn't going to be expelled? Or maybe I wasn't the only one who had broken the rule today? My stomach clenched. It couldn't be the drama club. I knew all the members by face, and this extremely good-looking bunch wasn't them. In fact, if the group approaching me were students at all, I would have known. Heck, the whole school would be buzzing about them. No one *that* good-looking would escape notice.

~ ☾ ~

I mentally stomped on the intimidation their perfection brought into my mind and said, "Excuse me."

The group froze, startled by my words. The girls had their brows raised and the boys stopped mid-speech, mouths agape. They stared at me with eyes the shade of onyx stones.

I smiled and gave them a little wave.

The boy a step ahead of the rest recovered first. His stunning features went from shocked surprise to intense interest. He reminded me of a hawk eyeing its prey. I gulped.

"A Day Student," he said, his eyes insolent and excited.

Something about the way he said "Day Student" made my stomach flip. "Excuse me?"

They snickered. The boys looked at each other while the girls continued to stare, muffling their laughter by delicate hands. I seemed to be the butt of some joke.

"You broke the rule." The boy's grin turned predatory.

The students formed a loose semi-circle in front of me. My gaze darted from face to face. Hunger filled their eyes. The image of lions about to chase down a gazelle came to mind. I mentally shook my head. I was in the mountains not the Serengeti for crying out loud.

I took a small step back and cleared my throat. "Can any of you give me a ride back to the dorms?"

The boy wagged his forefinger like a metronome. "Ah, that's unfortunate for you."

One of the girls pinched the bridge of her nose. "Eli, you can't possibly—"

"It's forbidden, Eli," another boy interrupted, pronouncing the word "forbidden" like a curse.

The nervous murmur at the pit of my stomach grew louder. Six against one. Not good odds. Instinct told me to cut my losses and run. Bad enough I faced expulsion, now it seemed like weird, beautiful people who'd suddenly appeared on campus wanted to beat me up. No, scratch that. Judging from the way they studied me, beating me up wouldn't satisfy them. Something more primal prowled behind their looks.

I definitely wasn't going down without a fight. Years of self-defense and hand-to-hand combat classes had me prepared. While other children from rich and important families got bodyguards, I got defense training. But I think my father meant for my skills to go up against potential kidnappers, not against other students who may or may not be crazy. Oh God! Maybe I stepped into a parallel universe or something when I reentered Barinkoff.

"None of the students are supposed to be on campus," I said. Then, realizing my mistake, I added, "Okay, I know I'm not supposed to be here either. If one of you gives me a ride back to the dorms, I won't say anything about all this. Let's pretend this never happened. I didn't see you, you didn't see me."

"We're not ordinary students," Eli answered. "We're the Night Students."

He'd said "Night Students" like the words were capitalized. I didn't know Barinkoff held classes at night. What was going on here?

Eli smiled with just one side of his mouth and said to the group, "She's right, no one will have to know. We're the only ones here. And it's been so long, don't you agree?"

The rest of them nodded reluctantly.

"What's been so long?" I challenged. I fisted my hands, ready to put them up if any of them so much as twitched my way.

"Since the taste of real flesh passed through my lips," Eli said. He came forward and took a whiff of me then laughed when I cringed.

"Flesh." Yep, parallel universe.

"Yes," he said. "And yours smells so *fresh*."

Someone grabbed my shoulders from behind and yanked me back before I could wrap my mind around the meaning behind Eli's words. In a blink, I found myself behind someone tall. Someone *really* tall. And quite broad. And very male.

I realized he wore the same clothes Eli and the other boys did. Not good. He was one of them. Although… I cocked my head, raking my gaze over him. He seemed born to wear the uniform, like he was the pattern everyone else was cut from. My eyes wandered to long, layered, blue-black hair tied at the nape by a silk ribbon. Even in dim light, his hair possessed a shine akin to mercury.

I looked down. The boy's long fingers were wrapped around my wrist like a cuff. His fevered touch felt hotter than human standards, hot enough to make me sweat like I was standing beside a radiator but not hot enough to burn.

"I must be mistaken, Eli," the boy who held my arm said in a monotone. "Correct me. Did I hear you say you wanted to *taste* the flesh of this girl?"

A hush descended on us. It had the hairs at the back of my neck rising. How was it possible for the atmosphere to switch from threatening to dangerous? Unable to help myself, I peeked around the new guy's bulk. Eli and his friends bowed. They all had their right hands on their chests.

"Demitri, I'm sure you misheard me," Eli said.

So the guy standing between me and the person who said he'd wanted to taste me was named Demitri. I like the sound of his name. Demitri. So strong, yet rolls off the tongue. Definite yum factor.

"So, you imply I made a mistake?" Demitri demanded.

"No!" Eli lifted his gaze. "I did no such thing. I simply wanted to show the girl the consequences of breaking curfew."

"Hey!" I yelled. "Don't talk about me like I'm not here!"

Demitri ignored my protest and continued to address Eli. "So, you threatened to taste her flesh." His fingers tightened their grip around my wrist. "In the interest of investigating this matter further, I invoke the Silence."

All six students gasped, passing surprised glances at one another.

Before I could ask about what was going on, Demitri yanked me down the hall toward the library. But why there? Oh, maybe we were getting my things. No, wait, he couldn't have known about that. Everything was too confusing now.

Eli and the others didn't try to stop us when we passed them. Demitri's cold command must have carried power. Handsome *and* powerful, never a bad combination on a guy.

We reached the heavy double doors in seconds. He jerked one open effortlessly. I'd needed all my strength just to squeeze through that same door earlier. To him, the thick wood might as well have been cardboard. I raised an eyebrow and mentally listed the benefits of going to gym class.

"Why are we here?" I asked after my curiosity overpowered my worry. I'd almost forgotten how frightened I'd been right before Demitri showed up. I wasn't above accepting help from strangers. Especially from gorgeous dark-haired strangers with hot hands and wide shoulders.

Demitri kept going, tugging me along, snaking his way deeper into the library. I had to take two steps for every stride his legs made. I tried to stay directly behind him, praying we didn't slam into anything.

He stopped suddenly and I collided with him. It felt like slamming into a wall.

"Hey," I said, momentarily stunned. "A little warning would be nice!"

He faced me, and I gasped. His eyes resembled a starless night, deep and endless. Their intensity drilled through me without pity, seeming to expose all my secrets. I felt naked and flustered beneath his gaze.

"You could have died back there," he warned.

A lump of panic rebuilt itself in my throat. I forced myself to speak through tightened vocal cords. "How could I have known that? I don't even understand half of what happened back there." I gestured toward the library entrance with my free hand.

He grimaced and pulled me forward again. I tugged at my wrist to no avail. His touch was getting too hot for comfort. Sweat dripped down my wrist to pool in my palm. But Demitri didn't seem to mind. He'd set a merciless pace to wherever we were going, and it was clear we weren't about to stop until we reached our destination.

Demitri paused in front of a wall shelf. He glanced over his shoulder at me and said, "We need to use the library to get to the Chem lab."

"The lab's on the second floor."

He tugged at a large book on the fifth shelf up from the floor. A section of the shelves slid to the right, exposing a dimly lit, upwardly spiraling staircase.

"H-how—"

~ ☾ ~

"I will not risk having other Night Students see you. The danger is too great."

I gave the center of his broad shoulders my best scowl, the kind hot enough to melt butter.

At the top of the stairs, a light fixture like the ones along the west hallway illuminated a dead end. I was about to give Demitri a piece of my mind when he yanked at the sconce and a concealed panel swung open. I yelped in surprise.

Sure enough, the Chem lab that I knew was located on the second floor now sprawled before us. I had to blink several times to adjust my vision. The dimness of the staircase couldn't compare to the brightness of the lab.

After the black spots in my eyes receded, I took in the room. My jaw dropped for the second time in less than an hour. The lab was always left clean at the end of the day, but beakers, test tubes, funnels, and other lab paraphernalia currently filled every table. Liquids of different colors bubbled and gurgled. The Chem geeks wouldn't be happy if they found out someone else used their equipment without their knowledge.

We came to a stop at the end of the room where a boy in a lab coat sat bent over a microscope. He had short midnight hair that stuck out in messy spikes. He was as oddly beautiful as the rest of them. I shouldn't be surprised at this point, but I couldn't help myself.

"Dray, I need the Pill," Demitri said.

The boy didn't move or speak.

"Dray!"

The boy Demitri called Dray jumped, barely staying seated. "Damn it, Demitri! Don't surprise me when—who is that? And what's that smell?" His pale complexion turned ashen while his penetrating eyes studied me. Then he pointed a shaky finger at us. "Is that—"

Demitri blocked me from view. "The Pill," he said.

"Stop doing that!" Annoyance vibrated in me. I wasn't some secret he could keep from the world when he wanted to. I leaned around in time to see Dray flick something the size and color of a pearl at Demitri.

Demitri caught it and immediately popped it into his

mouth. He chewed, producing a quick *crunch* like breaking candy between molars. After he swallowed, he said to Dray, "I trust you to keep quiet about this."

Wide-eyed, Dray nodded.

"Good. And I expect you to be in class when I return." Demitri turned around and led the way back to the staircase. The night was getting stranger by the minute.

"You know, you don't have to keep holding on to me," I said as we descended back down. "It's obvious I'm not going anywhere."

At the bottom of the stairs, Demitri let my wrist go and turned around to face me. I was a couple of steps above him, so we were at eye-level for the first time. I sucked in a breath at how close our faces were. I dropped my gaze and busied myself with wiping my slick wrist on my skirt.

"I cannot risk anyone else getting to you," Demitri said. He grabbed my wrist and ran his thumb over the red welts. I shivered despite the heat of his touch. "I can see that I have made you uncomfortable."

Among other things. I managed to hold my tongue.

He let go of my wrist again. "If you promise to stay close—"

"Where else will I go?" I interrupted. "It's obvious I'm not supposed to be here."

The memory of my expulsion crumpled my heart within itself. And I'd just started liking it at Barinkoff too.

Demitri tilted his head down until vertebrae on his neck popped. Then he shook his head. "Stay close." He whirled around and exited the secret passageway. He waited until I joined him before he pushed the book he'd pulled out back. The shelves slid back into place.

I whistled. "That's so cool. I've spent hours in this library and never thought there'd be a secret passageway."

"This is the only one here," Demitri said as if he wanted to discourage me from further exploration. "Come on, I have to get you back to the dorms."

Not even half an hour later, and after I had insisted we pick up my things from where I'd left them in the library, I found myself inside a black Aston Martin, Demitri at the wheel, headed home to the dorms.

~ ☾ ~

On the steep mountain road, Demitri pushed the car over the speed limit. I said a silent prayer that he wouldn't send us over the mountainside.

The purr of the car's engine reminded me of the time I'd "borrowed" a car just like this one for fun. A secret smile curled the corners of my lips. My father had been presiding over a meeting of prominent businessmen when I'd been nabbed by the Italian *polizia*. When I'd made my allotted call to Dad, he'd refused to leave his meeting and instead sent his secretary to bail me out. Even with everything written about me in the Italian and international papers the next day, he never came to my hotel suite to reprimand me. Never even grounded me. He hadn't expressed anger—just indifference.

My smile faded.

I forced myself to concentrate on the present inside a different Aston Martin in a whole different part of the world with someone I'd met barely a few thousand heartbeats ago.

I flicked on the overhead light switch. Even in the dim light, compared to Eli and Dray, Demitri embodied Adonis. A straight nose. Lush lips. Long lashes that framed intense eyes. A jaw line that could cut. Too good. Too perfect. A dude who underwent cosmetic surgery? All the kids at Barinkoff were beyond wealthy—but perfection like Demitri's usually came by way of a scalpel and loads of cash thrown at a private plastic surgeon.

"Who are you?" I blurted out. "I mean, you're too good looking to be human."

"Not as naïve as I thought," he said, more to himself.

"Spare me the insult."

"Good looking, huh?" His lips curled upward.

A flush burned its way across my face. "Forget I said anything."

"Why were you on campus past curfew?"

Despite his monotone, softness laced his words. I flicked the switch off, more comfortable sitting in darkness if I had to confess my sins. "I fell asleep in the library, okay?" No sense in lying about it. "I sat down in my favorite spot—between mystery and mythology—with my e-reader. Unfortunately, somewhere between Alexander conquering half the known world and Hitler destroying it, I dozed off. When I woke up, I was alone." I paused. The next thing I was about to say would make my situation real. I took a deep breath and exhaled slowly. "I'm going to get expelled, aren't I?"

"Your name, what is it?" Demitri asked.

"Phoenix." I rubbed the back of my neck. "McKay."

"If you promise never to miss curfew again, *and* that you forget what you have seen, then Alek will never have to know, Phoenix McKay."

"Alek? Alek." The name sounded familiar. I thought about where I'd heard it. When the memory clicked, I said, "Aleksander Kiev! You're on a first name basis with the headmaster?"

Demitri shifted in the leather seat.

"What about the Night Students?" I continued. "I assume you're one of them. Why is Barinkoff hiding the fact that other kids go to school there? So what if there are students at night?"

"You do not want to know the answer to that question."

Because of the way he said it, all final and without reproach, the more I wanted to know. But I kept the rest of my questions to myself. There was time. If what he said was true, then I wasn't getting expelled, which meant I could find out answers. For now, I needed to figure out a way to sneak into the dorms without getting caught, and Demitri dropping me off at the front gate where the guard would surely see me wouldn't be the wisest choice. An ember of happiness sparked in my chest.

As the imposing stone walls of the dorms neared, I pointed. "Can you drop me off by the corner there?" I asked.

Demitri obliged, easing the car to a stop. "Have you been to all those places?" He pointed at my e-reader filled with travel stickers.

"This one's my favorite." I tapped the one with the Eiffel tower.

"It must be nice to see what the world has to offer."

"Are you telling me you've never travelled before?"

Demitri pressed the car unlock button. "You better get going."

~ ☾ ~

I gathered my things and opened the door, but before I could step out, he grabbed my hand.

With a blank expression, he said, "Promise me, Phoenix."

I nodded then got out of the car. I balanced all my stuff on one arm and used my free hand to close the door. The Aston Martin made a quick U-turn and sped off. When the red taillights disappeared into the gloom, I shifted my gaze to the stone wall. *How the hell am I getting inside?*

Chapter 2

Curiosity

Sunlight reflecting off snow sucked. My eyes burned from the outside in because of the glare. The heat spread to form a world-class headache across my forehead, made worse by the clomping my boots made on white marble. Each step was like a nail being driven into my skull. Last night, I had been all alone in the west hall, paralleling the Lunar Garden. Today, I waded through a current of annoyed students in the east hall, adjacent to the Solar Garden. At the end of the hall was The Coffee Bar, the oasis where I could mainline life-giving coffee.

I shielded sleep-deprived eyes with my hand and cursed myself for forgetting my sunglasses at the dorm, ignoring the shouts of "Hey" or "Watch it" or the occasional "Get out of the way" from classmates who thought nothing of being up and cheerful at this ungodly hour. With no caffeine buzzing in my system to cushion my increasingly crappy mood, I grumbled, snapped, and hissed at everyone who made the mistake of addressing me directly. Most of all, I cursed my roommate Preya to the deepest depths of hell for wanting to meet at the campus café so early. I had woken up with a Post It stuck to my forehead, and on that small slip of neon pink sticky paper, Preya requested we meet during her first break between classes. I had no morning classes. In fact, I had no classes at all that day. Only loyalty and friendship kept me from turning around and catching the next bus down the mountain. I'd rather sleep than confront whatever she wanted to talk about—my best guess was the fact that I'd slunk into our room well after curfew the night before.

Demitri had returned me to the dorms a little after seven, but I only made it into my dorm room at a quarter past ten. I had to climb a wall overgrown with ivy, get past five guards, dodge two maids, and hide from the dorm master. I had no idea our dorm was so heavily guarded until I had to sneak back in undetected. When I'd finally reached the room I shared with Preya, I removed my boots, climbed into bed, and stared at the ceiling for hours, replaying what had happened with the Night Students and Demitri over and over again. Barinkoff had secrets after sunset that nobody knew about. I immediately discounted the notion of the headmaster being unaware of the mysterious goings-on after hours since Demitri referred to him by his first name. Why wouldn't the headmaster know? He imposed the curfew, after all. But why hide the existence of the strange Night Students?

I stopped and glanced over to the large sundial that dominated the Solar Garden. The sun's brilliance created a shadow over the number nine. I winced and hurried along. Still half asleep, I no longer cared if I bumped into anyone on my way to the cafeteria. Having Preya annoyed at me for being late would most likely be worse than Eli tasting my flesh, whatever that meant. Well, maybe not. His weird joke had creeped me out. I shivered. Who talks about flesh tasting anyway? Maybe someone with a weird fetish?

The café glass doors parted and the scent of Sumatran coffee greeted me with open arms. Formica tables, plush chairs, couches, booths, a menu worthy of an international hotel, and a soda fountain and coffee counter equaled heaven. The checkered blue and white tiles matched the leather on the couches, the napkins, and the mugs. With our uniforms in the same color scheme, students blended in nicely. It wasn't my immediate fashion choice, but what could I do? I imagined the Night Students in the café and wondered why I didn't even think of asking them why they were dressed so...*off*? Well, then again, they were threatening to "taste" my flesh. It always came back to that.

I pushed away my encounter with Eli and swept my gaze

~ ☾ ~

over the crowd. I drew comfort from my normal. The Mathletes argued over a theorem. The Physics jocks huddled together, whispering—a one-liter soda bottle and an air pump on top of their table. And the artists lounged together—painters, musicians, sculptors, dancers. The combined IQ of all the kids in school, not counting the professors that taught us, would be enough to power a small country indefinitely.

I spotted Preya at our favorite table. She sipped her triple espresso with a lifted pinky while leafing through a textbook thicker than the Gutenberg Bible. I sighed heavily and prepared myself. Preya Rachandani had a science pedigree that rivaled most of the kids on campus. Everyone considered her Barinkoff royalty—fifth generation. I suspected she had been accepted into the school upon birth. The bindi on her forehead caught the light and sparkled. She opted to wear crystals in place of the traditional red dot, declaring them more fashionable. A nerd scientist with fashion sense. Who would have thought?

I sat down across from her, and without even a glance away from the text, she slid a steaming coffee mug toward me.

"Double chocolate chai latte," she said. "I don't know how you can drink that stuff. No better than sludge. I figured you'd be late so I ordered it five minutes ago. It should still be hot."

Preya put Shiva to shame by how scary she could be sometimes. I sipped from my mug and let the sweet, warm liquid wake up my nerves. It gave me the courage to speak. I figured if I started the conversation, I could control the information I shared. Little did I know, Shiva—I meant *Preya*—had other plans.

"Preya—" I began, but she cut me off with a raised forefinger. So much for controlling the conversation.

I slouched into my chair and waited, losing the fortification my first hit of caffeine provided. No one deflated a buzz better than Preya. She'd make a fine scientist one day. She could be cutthroat when she wanted to be. Mob bosses had nothing on her.

She closed the book and swung her long braid over her shoulder. "So," she said, tapping her fingernails on the table.

~ ☾ ~

"Mind telling me why you were sneaking into our room at approximately ten last night?"

"Ten fifteen, actually." I raised an eyebrow. "Weren't you asleep?"

"Light sleeper. Don't change the subject, McKay."

Preya's level stare had me cringing. I hadn't received a note from the headmaster, so Demitri must have upheld his end of the bargain. I'd promised him nothing. A nod wasn't a promise in my book. But the decision whether to tell Preya about what had happened last night presented another Pandora's Box altogether.

"You know what? I think I need glasses—" I squinted.

"Spit it out, McKay." She slapped the table. "I don't have the patience for this."

When impatient, Preya's British accent snapped into Indian. I quickly sifted through possible scenarios in my head that she would buy as I made small circular patterns with my fingertip on the table. "I skipped study hall yesterday and ..."

I watched her watch me. I'd left the rest of what I didn't say to Preya's more than capable imagination. I could almost hear the gears in her head turning as I waited to see if she'd take the bait. Because if I told her the truth about Eli and his posse or Dray and his lab or Demitri and his...well, anyway, Preya's natural curiosity wouldn't allow her to rest until she discovered all their secrets. Talk of flesh tasting and secret students of the night made the risk too great.

My lie hung between us—a noose ready to hang me. I sipped my latte and tapped the heel of my boot in a rapid staccato drowned out by the ambient noise surrounding us to release some of my pent up tension.

Preya closed her exotic green eyes and leaned back. "You were researching about your mother's disease again weren't you? Phoenix, what you're doing is dangerous. You know what it will mean if you get caught."

I breathed a sigh of relief. Ever since my father shipped me off to Barinkoff, I'd been obsessed with finding answers. But damn. Why'd Preya have to assume that was what I was doing? I blinked away the tears that rose just at the mention of my mother.

~ ☾ ~

"I miss her every day. Every damn day." I clutched my mug with both hands, its heat providing me a shred of comfort.

She reached across the table and took my hand into hers. "I read the article from *The Medical Journal* about her, Phoenix. There was nothing the doctors could do."

My jaw stiffened. "Of course there was nothing they could do. They were all idiots."

"Don't be like that." Preya pulled back, shaking her head. "I understand that you're still hurting, but your father had the best doctors in the world looking after your mother."

"Don't use your bedside manner on me, Preya." My voice had more bite in it than I expected. I was too caught up in the conversation now to reel myself in. "How could you understand what it means to lose someone without having a chance to save her? Huh? Those 'best doctors'"—I sandwiched the words in air quotes—"couldn't even come up with a diagnosis. She had so many tubes stuck to machines coming out of her, keeping her alive, that it was like I was staring at some sick government experiment. If that's what the best in this world could come up with, then we're all dead."

Without me knowing it, the tears I tried valiantly to blink away overflowed and began streaming down my face. I swiped at them with all the frustration I felt inside. I bit the inside of my cheek to keep myself from saying anything more until I tasted copper and salt.

Preya's expression softened. "I'm sorry, Phoenix." She fished out a tissue from a packet in her bag and handed it to me.

I stared at her offering, wondering if I should take it. I was too angry. But Preya didn't move, obviously willing to wait me out. I breathed in and exhaled all the emotions I didn't know I'd been keeping bottled up. I took the tissue and blew my nose. Preya nodded her satisfaction. All was right between us again. Six months as her friend, and I could never stay mad at her for long.

She beamed a smile at me. "Aren't you glad you got that off of your chest? I keep telling you to talk about coming to grips with your mother's death. I think we're making progress."

I sank deeper into my chair. Whatever Preya meant flew over my head. I just rehashed what she already knew about my mother and the way I felt about what had happened to her. If that was what Preya thought of as progress then we were moving backwards. I never kept what happened to my mother a secret, but good luck getting me to talk about it. The only reason Preya knew had to do with the fact that my telling her coincided with the anniversary of Mom's death. I'd been an emotional wreck. I'd cut class and cried all day in our room. She actually caught me sniffing. I blamed it on allergies, but she kept pestering me about it until I snapped. In a relentless stream of shouted words with a few choice expletives mixed in, I let it slip why I'd been in bed all day with puffy eyes and a nose Bozo the clown would be proud of.

The bell's successive clangs signaled ten minutes to the start of the next class.

Preya picked up her textbook and slung her bag over her shoulder. "No more researching about your mother's mysterious disease. It's not doing you any good."

I sat up quickly. "What I do with my time is none of your damn business."

"If it means saving you from yourself, then it is my *damn* business." She walked away.

One word: scary.

I slumped back into my chair and covered my face with both hands, shaking my head, wishing for expulsion. I may have just made matters worse by keeping secrets.

After a couple of hours of feeling sorry for myself while I crammed for my English test, I left the Coffee Bar and wandered off to the library. Thoughts of Demitri swirled in my head again. I really wanted to know what Barinkoff was hiding. From the way Dray had set up the lab yesterday, he was clearly working on something. If I was right, he would have the same set up again tonight. And from the way Dray paled when he saw me, he would most likely be easier to get answers from than Demitri. Once my curiosity was satisfied, I could go back to my life as a Day Student.

~ ☾ ~

Or so I told myself. I pushed my way into the library, planning to return to the scene of the crime. If they didn't expel me the first time I'd been caught on campus after dark, what would a second time hurt?

"Phoenix." The librarian, Ms. Lipinski, waved at me from within her doughnut-like desk. She had a computer to her left and several book carts behind her. "How's my favorite bookworm?"

I looked around, partially freaked out by the memory of last night that superimposed itself over the sunny interior of the room. I could plot the path Demitri had taken when he'd dragged me to the secret staircase hidden behind the false shelf. I blinked several times, slowly, willing light to come back.

"Slow day?" I asked as the darkness dissolved.

The librarian nodded. "Something I can find for you?"

"Just going to the back for some research." I hated to dash the enthusiasm behind her question since she looked way too eager to help out.

"I'll be here ..."

I moved off, and tall stacks swallowed the rest of what she said.

I weaved my way to the back. Once I reached the area where Demitri had taken me, I scanned for the book he'd used to reveal the staircase. I stood up on tip-toe, gripped the spine, and pulled. It refused to budge. I tried again, but the book remained wedged between two other books in the same family of thickness and faded quality. I studied its spine, the lettering long gone, then folded my arms over my chest. A mulish tome wouldn't discourage me. I just needed to wait it out.

Ms. Lipinski closed up shop at four. The bang of the heavy door marked her departure. Ensconced in my corner, I assumed she'd forgotten about my presence. Or she assumed I'd leave at the appointed time for curfew. Too easy.

Two hours later, the tolling bell bringing with it a sense of déjà vu, a series of clicks, like the opening of locks, startled me. They came right after the sixth chime. I set aside the copy of *The Odyssey* I'd been reading, and stood up. The setting

~ ☾ ~

sun transformed the library into the labyrinth of shadows I'd run out of the day before.

I tugged on the faded book. No resistance this time. The shelf moved aside and revealed the spiral staircase. Without hesitation, I ascended the steps, my heels clanged on the metal. Darkness warred with the glowing sconce beside the concealed panel. I yanked down on the sconce the way Demitri did.

The hairs on my arms stood on end the second the panel opened. Self-preservation held me in place at the top step. The irony of "curiosity killed the cat" brought a frown to my face. Dray didn't seem as malicious as Eli. Twitchy maybe, but not malicious. Even so, that he was "one of them" earned my need for caution.

Curiosity overwhelmed me and I pushed forward. The lab had once again been transformed into the lair of a mad scientist, with beakers bubbling and flames under Bunsen burners. I walked from table to table. The beakers with multi-colored liquids intrigued me. The seriousness of the room's setup told me to keep my hands to myself, like in a store with the policy of "You break it, you bought it." The difference being that here, if I broke it, I might turn into a frog or whatever the liquid inside the glass containers did.

I made my way to the other side of the lab where Dray had sat the night before but saw no one. The cardinal rule of the lab was to never leave an experiment unattended. Heads would roll if the Chem geeks were ever caught leaving experiments alone to bubble and boil.

The *whoosh* of a sliding door prompted me to turn to my left.

Dray, dressed in a lab coat over what I'd come to think of as the Night Student's uniform, entered the room with a distracted expression on his face. He sipped from a dainty teacup, his brow knotted in concentration. He walked to the table with a microscope. After another sip, he lowered the cup on top of the saucer on the table with a small *clink* as china met china—an almost absentminded move that coaxed a tiny smile from me. My mother, when painting, had stayed in the same state of focus. Nothing short of an alien invasion or a

natural disaster could break her concentration.

I pushed away the loneliness that accompanied thoughts of her and wondered if I should draw attention to myself. Not a second after the idea entered my mind did Dray start sniffing the air like a hound on a scent. I held my breath.

He twisted around and gasped. "You!"

"Hi, Dray." I waved like we were friends who hadn't seen each other in years.

"You shouldn't be here," he said.

"Why is that, exactly?"

"Er, because, uhm …" He cleared his throat. "Because …" He paused. His right hand supported his left elbow while he stroked his chin. I waited patiently for him to continue. He seemed like he was on to something. It was a look I knew well from hours studying with Preya.

After a long minute, Dray smiled. "Would you consider trying something for me? I would love to have a human test subject."

I glanced at the beakers filled with chemicals. "Is it safe?"

"Of course. I never do anything dangerous. Well"—he shrugged—"not in a very long time. At any rate, I don't think you'll die. At least, the possibility of it is really low."

My stomach somersaulted at the way he phrased the last part of his sentence, but his smile was so reassuringly sweet that I weighed my options. I might as well find out about Barinkoff's secret while Dray was conducting his experiment. It only seemed fair. "If I agree, I want you to tell me what's going on here."

Dray blanched and ran his fingers through his messy hair. "This is a mistake. A potentially big mistake. But, oh, I don't think I'll ever get a chance—"

The door he used to enter the lab *whooshed* open again.

A delicate girl entered. She resembled a budding rose, fresh and soft. A silver circlet on her forehead held her thick raven hair in place. Silver chains clicked across the front of her corset when she moved. She was by far the prettiest of them all. I had to blink several times to make sure I wasn't hallucinating. The reality of the existence of the Night Students was so unreal that if I hadn't decided to see Dray I

~ ☾ ~

would think I'd fallen asleep in the library again and was dreaming.

"Dray, I need help with my Organic Chemistry." She stumbled to a halt. "Is that what I think it is?" The end of her question came out in a long hiss when she saw me. She held up her hand to forestall Dray's answer. "It's human. It's been a while, but I still remember that smell. What's a Day Student doing breaking curfew?"

Human? What did she mean? Weren't we all human here?

"She was with Demitri—"

"It was *what*?"

Dray waved his hands. "You didn't hear what you thought you heard, Calixta."

The girl named Calixta glared at him. "Tell me what Demitri has to do with *that*?"

I put my hands on my hips and said, "Excuse me, I have a name."

"Please, no violence around the experiments," Dray pleaded.

"Then. Start. Talking. Andrayus." Calixta's words dripped venom.

Like a startled dog barking, Dray explained how Demitri escorted me into the lab and back to the dorms the night before. He spoke so fast that he barely seemed to breathe. With each new detail he gave, Calixta's heart-shaped face shifted from threatening to lethal. As she slowly turned her head to stare at me, her lips pulled back to show perfect teeth. God. A mountain lion about to pounce on an unsuspecting jogger couldn't have been more menacing. Why would she be so pissed about my breaking curfew?

Apprehension, like a deer sensing danger, spread through me. "Did I miss something?"

"Only that you're going to pay," Calixta said.

"Okay …" I surveyed my surroundings quickly. A potential fight in small quarters would hinder movement. I felt sweat dot my upper lip. I had to stop myself from licking it. "But you have to tell me what I'm paying for."

"Catching Demitri's attention."

My hands began to shake. I could feel her growing

animosity from across the room. So it wasn't that I broke curfew. Calixta was clearly pissed that I was with Demitri the other night, but I couldn't understand the intense jealousy.

"I'm going to enjoy killing you," she said.

Kill me? What? How did we get from me paying to me dying?

Dray grabbed Calixta from behind and shouted, "Run!"

"Why?" I pointed at Calixta. She was practically frothing at the mouth. "I didn't do anything to her."

"You have no right to Demitri," she said.

"I didn't say I did." I backed away. "Geez, if you're his girlfriend, then just say so."

A brief moment of shock crossed Calixta's face before her rabid anger returned. "I'm not just his girlfriend you puny human."

"Me? Puny? I'm much taller than you."

"You're dying tonight, human," she said with relish. The determination in the deep, black pools of her eyes actually confirmed her promise. "Nothing gets between me and Demitri."

"Okay, I think you just stepped into insane. And why do you keep calling me *human*, like you're somehow not? Why do you want to kill me? Demitri saved me from expulsion, that's all."

Her pointed chin jutted out. "If you knew Demitri like I do, you'd know he never saves anyone from *anything*. Something else is going on here."

"Phoenix," Dray pleaded. "I can't hold her back any longer."

Not waiting to be told again, and having had enough of Calixta's brand of crazy, I wove around tables until I reached the door that led out into the hall, the spiral staircase to the library completely forgotten. The sharp stab of stiletto heels on marble coming from behind spurred me forward. My height gave me a definite advantage. Thank you, good genes. For every running step I made, she had to scramble twice to keep up. Whatever Calixta did to Dray to get him to let her go made me cringe. I hoped the poor guy was alright, at the very least still able to walk. But as much as I was beginning to like

~ ☾ ~

Dray, I had to set my concern aside and focus on my survival.

I swerved around a corner and flew down the steps two at a time, heading to the first floor. At the bottom of the stairs, I veered left to The Coffee Bar. My heart was pounding loudly between my ears when I dodged between pillars separating the Solar Garden from the hall. The night air cut through me like razor blades. Every breath froze my lungs little by little. I should have listened to Demitri and stayed away from the Night Students. I didn't think him warning me that I almost died last night had any truth to it. I thought he'd been trying to scare me.

Oh, I was scared now. No doubt about it.

I darted deeper into the garden. If I made it to the far wall, I'd be able to reach the gate. Beyond it: freedom. Safety. And access to a flight home because Barinkoff would surely expel me after tonight.

In my panic, I skidded to the right. My foot slipped and I face-planted. All the air in my lungs exploded upon impact. The cold, hard ground didn't yield as I slid and rolled. Ignoring the bruising pain my whole left side had become, I scrambled for a weapon, anything to help me survive until I reached the gate.

With no branch or stone in sight, I clenched my fists. I readied myself to stare death in the face. The thought of my blood on the pristine whiteness of snow had me thinking of my mother and how I would be joining her soon enough. Was that so bad?

Only then did I notice the palpable stillness.

Calixta stood five feet away, staring at something beyond where I lay. "Luka," she whispered.

~ ☾ ~

Chapter 3

Secrets

I sat up and followed Calixta's gaze upward. I rubbed my eyes. I didn't know what I was seeing at first. A statue? My brain refused to snap together coherent thoughts. I didn't realize I'd fallen so close to one of the garden benches until I stared up at the boy that sat on one. He was strikingly beautiful. His tumble of blonde hair curled just above his sculpted cheekbones. He wore a silk shirt and a loosened cravat, like he'd become bored while dressing and decided to leave himself in disarray. His ivory skin and frozen position was what had me mistaking him for something carved from marble by Michelangelo. Then he sighed—a lonely, breathy proof of life. If I had to imagine what Lucifer looked like before he fell from heaven, the boy on the bench would certainly fulfill that image. My brain told me I had to look away, but I couldn't.

"Luka," Calixta said again, her voice unsure, almost nervous. It no longer contained the steel and bite she had threatened me with, which made me wonder who the boy was.

He leaned on his hands and crossed his legs, all the while keeping his eyes fixed on the night sky. His movements spoke of elegance and control. I'd encountered many people with breeding before, but his took on the air of arrogance and self-assuredness of someone used to getting what he wanted when he wanted it.

~ ☾ ~

I only realized I'd been holding my breath when my lungs protested. I exhaled. My heart sputtered and restarted with a vengeance. Luka tore his gaze away from the stars and settled it on me. I'd expected pitch-black irises, like the other Night Students, but blue ice stared back at me.

"Human," he whispered.

He reached out, and with a finger, followed an invisible trail down my cheek. I stiffened. His touch, cooler than Demitri's, caused warm sparks to blossom on my face. He lifted his finger to his lips and licked its tip. He might as well have licked *me* from the way my body shivered.

Luka's curious gaze held mine. "Leave us," he said, but not to me.

"But—" Calixta protested like a spoiled child.

He spoke in a language I hadn't heard before, remaining calm yet firm. The words had a rolling cadence I couldn't quite follow, like rumbling thunder in the distance. They contained a harsh sensuality. The consonants were hard and the vowels were long and lilting.

Footsteps retreated behind me.

Luka reached out again.

It took me a minute to realize he wanted to help me up. I hesitated. He smiled. I smiled back timidly and took his hand, completely dazzled. Even with my uniform soaked from melted snow, I didn't feel cold—all my attention was on him and the way his callused hand felt on mine. Without moving much from his seated position, he helped me stand.

"What's your name?" he asked. He had a voice like a familiar lullaby. It filled my heart to the brim with comfort.

I swallowed and tried to stop gawking. "Phoenix."

"The bird that rose from the ashes." Luka bent his head and kissed the back of my hand. "It's a pleasure meeting you."

My cheeks warmed. My head reeled, not knowing what to think. I couldn't understand why I felt drawn to him. And the strange connection frightened me.

From behind, someone gripped my arms and yanked me away before I could sort out the feelings Luka inspired in me. I found myself behind a towering figure yet again. Recognizing the blue-black silk for hair tied at the nape, relief

washed over me. Calixta hadn't come back to finish me off.

Demitri's large hand wrapped around my wrist. Unlike the night before, no calm existed in his demeanor. He trembled like a junky in need of a fix. The coiled power in his tense muscles vibrated into me.

"What are you doing here?" Demitri asked.

I didn't know he'd spoken to me until I saw his expressionless profile. I sighed.

"Phoenix."

The ruthless way he said my name punched all the air out of me. "You owe me answers," I said with as much bravado as I could muster.

"I owe you *nothing*." He glared. "In fact, you *owe* me your life."

"I don't think so."

Ignoring my indignation, he faced Luka, who'd remained seated on the bench during my exchange with Demitri. "Why is she with you, Luka?"

"I wasn't going to taste her, if that's what you're implying," Luka said. "Although, she *is* simply delicious. I wouldn't mind if you left us alone."

There it was again. Taste. The word that kept coming up between these Night Students and I was connected to it in an increasingly uncomfortable way. To taste meant to sample, but what? My flesh? They had to be joking because the alternative wasn't funny.

"The sins of the father …" Demitri left his sentence unfinished.

Luka's smile shifted into a snarl. "Obey my command." His chin lifted. "Kneel."

Demitri's stance went rigid. His grip tightened around my wrist. I winced.

Okay, weird just got weirder. Why would Luka want Demitri to kneel before him? I thought back to Eli and the others bowing to Demitri when he questioned them, but they didn't kneel. Seriously? Were they all living on a different planet or something?

"*Kneel.*" Luka's detestable smirk made his features sinister rather than angelic. The real Lucifer: a fallen angel.

~ ☾ ~

Without letting go of my wrist, Demitri knelt down on one knee and bowed his head, his free hand flat at the center of his chest. "Your command has been obeyed," he said formally.

Luka nodded once.

Demitri stood up and pulled me toward the school without telling me where we were going. Not having the time to thank Luka for saving me from Calixta, I risked a glance back. Luka smiled at me. His smile spoke of whispers, secrets, and promises to be shared on a later date. Demitri strode on, with me in tow like a small truck attached to a string. We hustled through the north end of the school. A large courtyard used for several activities such as fencing practice, stretched out before us. Beyond lay the rest of the Barinkoff gardens. I didn't visit the north end much. I had no interest in botanical gardens and greenhouses. Or fencing.

Having had enough of being manhandled, I snapped out, "Demitri! Quit pulling me."

In a smooth motion, he let go of my wrist and turned to face me. His arresting expression stopped me in my tracks. He looked about to slap me.

"Demit—"

"Do you know how close you came to dying...*again*?"

My fingers crumpled into tight fists. "Why are you so obsessed with the idea of me dying?"

"You should care more about staying alive than I do." The control he had over his voice didn't match the seething anger in his eyes.

My throat dried up. He had no heat in his tone, which made him seem more dangerous than if he'd yelled it at me. Honestly, I preferred yelling so I could yell back and let out some steam. I didn't know how to react to quiet menace.

"Why are you here, Phoenix?"

"Answers," I said. "You can't just expect me to ignore what I discovered. If you want me to keep your secret, you need to give me answers."

"I thought we had an agreement."

"I didn't promise you anything. I merely nodded."

Demitri crossed his arms like a bouncer refusing entry to a

club. Again that intense gaze drilled into me.

A corner of my lips twitched. "Last night, I couldn't stop thinking about what happened. What did you save me from? Who are the Night Students, Demitri? Why can't we know that you go to school here?"

He shook his head. "You humans and your need to know. Positively annoying."

I frowned. "Why do you guys keep saying 'human' like you're not?"

"You are in way over your head, Phoenix."

I ignored his statement and plowed on. "And how did you find me anyway?"

He rubbed the bridge of his nose. "More questions?"

"They won't stop until I get some answers." I put my foot down. No matter how menacing he looked, I wasn't about to let him intimidate me. Although my stomach quivered.

Demitri's lips disappeared into a white line. His stare traveled from my face to my shoulders, breasts, hips, and legs, before returning to my eyes. I honestly felt naked for a second before he said, "The fire in you will eventually burn you. Obviously, you have no idea what you are up against so let me enlighten you: I could kill you without a second thought and eat your flesh for dinner."

My heart stopped. I couldn't move, couldn't breathe. I rubbed the sweat that coated my suddenly damp hands on my skirt. Did he just say what I thought he said? Did flesh tasting really mean actually *tasting* flesh? Bile rose up my throat at the thought of being eaten. I swallowed, shaking uncontrollably now.

Demitri unfolded his arms. "Good. Finally some sense in you. You should be frightened."

"I'm not scared." My voice trembled as I spoke, which earned me a raised eyebrow from Demitri. "Th-th-the curfew. That's why it's enforced. Because you Night Students would actually eat the Day Students?"

"Humans." He hissed out the "s" the way Calixta did.

I closed my eyes and banished the memory of Calixta threatening to kill me. To anchor myself, I gripped the hem of my skirt with my hands and opened my eyes. "You won't."

~ ☾ ~

"What?"

I sucked in as much of the cold night air as I could, shocking my lungs into some semblance of calm once I exhaled. The trembling subsided some when I said, "Eat me."

"And why not?"

"Because you wouldn't have saved me if you didn't care."

His expression grew unreadable. He moved as if to speak, but the bell's din cut off his reply. He looked around, uncertainty in his features. Then without another word, he took my wrist again.

"Can you stop doing that?" I yanked away so hard that I thought I'd dislocated it. My annoyance replaced my fear.

"If you want answers, follow my lead." He moved forward in ground-eating strides.

Cold sweat dotted my forehead as I scrambled to catch up to him. I was still slightly afraid. Who wouldn't be faced with flesh eaters? Could I seriously believe what Demitri had said?

"So," I said, licking my bottom lip, "where are you taking me this time?"

He glanced over his shoulder and said, "The solarium. The Night Students never go there. You need to hide until I figure out what to do with you."

That wasn't what I'd expected. What did he mean by figuring out what he needed to do with me?

My silence apparently prompted him to continue, because he added, "Needing to save your life all the time is a habit I want to break. Last count is three in less than forty-eight hours."

"Three?" I scratched my head. That number couldn't be right. "It's just Eli and Calixta, right?"

"Luka."

"He didn't seem all that bad. Actually, I think he saved me from Calixta."

Demitri spoke without looking at me. "You should stay away from him. Luka does not do anything without a purpose."

His words hit me like a slap in the face. The easiest way to get me to do something was to forbid me to do it. Now I *had* to know more about Luka. I groaned internally. I was putting

myself in harm's way left and right. Whatever happened to my self-preservation instincts?

Soon, we reached the octagonal, glass building of the solarium. It gleamed between four greenhouses. Fruits and vegetables grew in two, while flowers and herbs grew in the other two. The secluded location of Barinkoff forced the campus to be sustainable. Deliveries could take weeks at a time. So, to ensure the food supply remained constant, the students and faculty developed an elaborate farming system. Everyone took reduce, reuse, recycle to another level of environmental protection around here. I'd even heard about a barn and a milking shed somewhere on campus, but I never really had the time or the impetus to locate them.

The solarium, on the other hand, had no other use than to be decorative. With the lights on, it resembled a large crystal with plants inside. We entered the structure and I relished the warm air, rubbing my freezing hands together. Demitri strode to a marble table with cushioned iron chairs at the center of the octagon surrounded by ferns, orchids, and other potted plants and flowers. A hammock and an empty birdcage were on the far right. While to the left, a rattan bookcase held an assortment of novels. Soft light bathed everything golden yellow. Why hadn't I found this place sooner?

"This is amazing," I said.

"Is this your first time here?" Demitri asked.

"I'm strictly a library girl."

"If you had kept your promise, this predicament would never have happened. Now, I have to find Calixta and see what kind of damage control I have to perform. No one can know you are here."

"Are you going to use the Silence?"

His eyes widened a fraction at me. "You recall?"

"Duh. I'm not senile." I rolled my eyes. "So, what is it?"

"You are not afraid anymore. This is bad."

He was right. I was starting to realize it was hard to be scared when Demitri was around. He made me feel safe, like nothing could harm me because he would maim it first. I dropped my gaze and shrugged in response to his comment.

~ ☾ ~

"Ever heard of ignorance is bliss?"

"Too late for that," I said.

His brows came together to make the perfect picture of consternation. "The Silence is a command someone with authority can give to subordinates to keep information to themselves upon pain of death. Eli and the five others with him will not speak of what happened last night without my consent."

I quickly connected the dots of what he implied. "You're a higher rank than them?"

"Out of everything I have said you deduced that?" He pinched the bridge of his nose and exhaled. "Why do you have to be such trouble?"

"Admit it, you like it that way," I teased. Definitely wasn't afraid anymore. Maybe I was in shock or something.

"Dray will wait with you until I return."

"Why didn't you just bring me to the lab then, save him the trip?"

Demitri just stared as if I should know the answer to my own question.

I scowled. "How long do I have to hang out with the twitchy mad scientist?"

"Not more than two hours."

I had to grimace at the thought. What was I going to do for two hours? My gaze landed on the bookshelves. "Fine, but when you get back, you need to answer the rest of my questions."

He raised an eyebrow at me. "Why am I finding it hard to believe that you will actually stay put?"

"I think I've had one too many threats against my life for one evening." I crossed my heart. "I promise to stay here and wait. There? Satisfied?"

He waited a moment before he nodded and left the solarium without a backward glance. I studied the entrance for a long while, imagining his broad-shouldered frame filling the doorway. I had never met anyone quite like Demitri. He seemed to exude a cold and threatening persona, yet something deep seemed to simmer just below the surface.

Twenty minutes later, the clinking of china wrenched me

away from the thriller I'd ended up reading. Dray walked into the solarium with a tea set on a tray. I dog-eared the page and looked up.

Dray trembled uncontrollably.

Concerned for the safety of the elegant blue-and-white-trimmed china, I stood up and took the tray from him. All his nervous energy made me nervous. Geez! The guy had to take a chill pill and relax.

His smile wobbled. "Thank you."

"Why more twitchy than usual?" I placed the tray on the table.

"Too much coffee maybe." He plopped down onto a cushioned chair and stretched like a sunbathing cat. He seemed sweet in his own way, like he couldn't hurt a fly—unless he wanted to. My eyes darted to his face then to the table. If he wanted to hurt me, he would have done so in his lab. But the thought brought with it little relief as I poured tea for the both of us. I had no way of knowing who to trust.

Dray took the cup I handed him and stared at the amber liquid thoughtfully. With my own cup in hand, I settled into my chair.

I wanted to banish the ice of uncertainty. I usually flew by the seat of my pants, deciding what to do as I moved forward. My plans went down the drain the moment Calixta threatened my life. The annoyance I felt for Demitri's overprotectiveness kept me on edge. And Luka? I didn't even have words to describe what I felt when I remembered him. I took a sip and ignored the burn on my tongue. The tea had a distinctly floral aftertaste with a hint of spicy-musk.

"Darjeeling?"

Dray's face drained of color when he shook his head.

"It tastes familiar, though there's a difference I can't quite pinpoint," I said.

"It's a special tea. Its leaves are grown in our gardens."

"Your gardens?"

"Yes, where we live."

A fuzzy dizziness came over me. I heard what Dray said, but I couldn't quite understand what he'd meant. Where they lived? My brain fogged over. I dropped my cup when the tea set on the table swayed. Dray swayed, too. The cup shattered, spilling its contents on the roiling floor. When did I get on a ship?

"Why aren't you drinking?" The last of my question came out slurred. My tongue refused to cooperate. The solarium spun like a top—first slowly, then faster and faster, until everything around me faded to black.

~ ☾ ~

Chapter 4

Obstacles

Shaking. Lots of it. The kind that rivaled most San Franciscan earthquakes. I slapped away the hand on my shoulder attempting to wake me. I rolled to my side to try and find a more comfortable position. Somehow my bed had morphed into a hard slab, but I chalked it up to still being half asleep. Anything that involved me today had to do with lying in bed. My body felt too heavy to even want to move. Damnable light pierced through the darkness behind my eyelids, so I reached for my head. Where had my pillow gone off to?

"Phoenix, you have to wake up," a female voice urged.

The shaking continued.

"Preya, if you don't stop shaking me, I swear I'll put toothpaste in your shoes," I threatened in a gravelly voice. A metallic tang coated my sandpaper tongue. I worked up as much spit as I could to wash away the taste, but my dry throat wouldn't let me.

The voice gasped. "Well, I never!"

Several giggles and a few laughs greeted my slowly waking ears like an annoying birdsong. People. As in plural. Wait a freakin' second. I lifted one eyelid to peek at who wanted me up so early. But the bright morning light forced me to shut it again. I pushed myself up to a seated position. No sheets hampered my rise. Normally, my bedsprings would give a little *creak*, but no sound came. I scooched up effortlessly. I

~ ☾ ~

brought the heels of my hands to my eyes and rubbed the sleep out of them. Then I stifled a yawn, stretched my arms above my head, and finally opened my eyes.

Sunlight streamed in from the large windows. I found myself sitting on top of a long study table located at the center of the library. Along with Ms. Lipinski, several students crowded the table I sat on like they might observe bacteria growing in a Petri dish.

"What am I doing here?" I blurted out.

"That's what we'd like to know," Ms. Lipinski said, her brow as wrinkled as a prune.

My gut sank. *Oh God.* I finally managed to swallow. The metallic taste made me want to gag. Dray and Demitri must have drugged me. But why would they leave me in the library instead of bringing me back to the dorms? Then the realization of why I had been left to sleep in the library for all to see crashed on top of me like a monster wave. I didn't use the word imbecile lightly, but I thought it appropriate for my current position. I'd been tricked and hung to dry.

"Ms. Lipinski," I said with great trepidation. "By any chance, does the headmaster want to see me?"

My question had all the students stepping away from the table. They made the connection between finding me and the mention of the headmaster. It only really meant one thing. And as if a stink bomb had exploded, they scattered.

"Why, as a matter of fact—"

I didn't wait around to hear the rest of what Ms. Lipinski said. I hopped off the table and ran for the door. Luckily, two girls opened the door just as I reached it, saving me the trouble of struggling with its impossible weight. I elbowed my way past them, much to their annoyed protestations. I didn't care. I had more important things to figure out.

Outside, I made a right and scrambled to the nearest bathroom. My lungs felt tight inside my chest, hungry for every breath I struggled to take in.

I stumbled into the blue and white girl's bathroom and slammed the door shut. If Demitri went to great lengths to expose my breaking curfew then it meant what he said about them tasting my flesh was true. He kept saving me from all the Night Students, insisting they could kill me without a second thought. He would actually see me expelled just to keep their secret?

A girl with thick glasses had just stepped out of a stall. She stared at me for a second before she ran out, completely forgetting to wash her hands. I leaned on the door to keep anyone else from coming in as the bell gonged eight times. I wanted to damn Demitri to a slow and painful death for putting me in this situation. But after a couple of deep breaths, the realization that I'd dropped myself at the doorstep of my own destruction all by my sorry, pathetic self hit me. I should have realized the trap. I should have been prepared for it.

I stopped the pity party. How could have I anticipated Demitri's cunning? Even dragging Dray into it. He couldn't face drugging me, so he had someone else do it for him. The coward.

My heart pounded in my chest so hard that I felt it in my head as I made my way to the row of sinks. I gripped the porcelain in front of me and stared at the drain before looking at my reflection in the mirror spanning the entire wall.

A toilet flushed. I whirled in panic. "Who's there?"

The door to the last stall opened and Preya came out. "What are you doing here so early?" she asked.

"Preya!" I bit my lip to keep from using an expletive. "What are *you* doing here?"

She blinked her cat-like, green eyes at me. "Isn't it obvious?"

I heaved a great and heavy sigh, using the sink for support. "Give a girl a break."

"You look like crap." She glided to the sink beside mine and proceeded to wash her hands. Her braid slid over her shoulder to dangle precariously close to the draining soapy water. She looked neat. Tidy.

"Did you sleep in your uniform?" she asked.

I looked down at my rumpled self. "Long story."

"In fact, you didn't make it to bed last night. You weren't out researching again, were you? That's actually counterproductive, you know."

~ ☾ ~

"Are you asking because you're concerned?" My words sounded harsh in the acoustics of the bathroom. I winced, but knew I couldn't take back what had come out of my mouth.

Preya paused for a second before continuing to soap her hands. "I resent that," she said softly.

My heart broke a little. "Preya, I—"

My friend raised a soaked hand, which splattered water droplets on my face. I didn't wipe them away, letting them stream down my cheeks like tears. Preya pushed the tap down and moved toward the hand dryer, placing her palms underneath it. A leaf-blower-like *whirring* drowned out her next words.

"What did you say?" I yelled over the sound.

"I said," she yelled back, "you really need to stop being this reckless, staying out all night researching. You're practicing avoidance. I get that you think it sucks that your father shipped you off here without even consulting you, but you can't keep hating him for that. You wouldn't have met me if he didn't."

"Oh, Preya." My stomach sank to new depths as the hand dryer eased off. "You don't know my father like I do. After my mother died, he just ..." I couldn't finish my sentence. It hurt too much to think about. "I don't want to talk about this anymore." I gripped the sink until my knuckles hurt. I had too much going on to think about my father. Discovering a flesh-eating race hiding their existence was one of them.

"If it makes you feel any better, I think if there's anyone who will find answers, it's you."

"No, it doesn't." I shook my head. "Sometimes, I wonder why we're even friends."

Preya gave me a syrupy smile. "Because you need help in Bio Chem."

"*Bull.*"

"Because of my infinite charm?"

"Keep going." I fought hard not to smile at her.

"Because I can easily freeze your bra with liquid nitrogen while you sleep?"

"Figures."

"What?" She tilted her head to the side.

~ ☾ ~

"That you'd use my curiosity against me. Can you really freeze my bra that way?"

Her laughter bounced off the walls like a merry tinkling of bells. Since starting at Barinkoff, I'd never had any friends other than Preya. We shared a room, so close proximity made our friendship inevitable. Wait. Scratch that. I had tried at first to avoid making friends with her. But something about Preya's personality drew me in whether I liked it or not. At some point, her presence stopped annoying me and we'd started hanging out. She'd managed to attach herself to my life like an exotic orchid attaching itself to a tree.

"But seriously," she said when she sobered up. "You look like crap."

The reflection I'd seen in the mirror confirmed her assessment. My hair was frizzy. I had bags under my eyes. My lips were cracked from being too dry. I licked them to ease some of the discomfort. Whatever Dray had added to my tea had dehydrated me. A lot.

"Here, use this." Preya fished out a Chap Stick tube from her pocket.

"Seriously?" I scowled at her.

"Oh, don't be such a tomboy. It's not lip gloss." She pulled off the cap and dabbed some of the cherry-scented wax on my lips. It burned a little.

"Okay, okay." I raised my hands as if to push her away. "Enough."

She pouted. "You really need to work on your personal space issues."

"Will it make my dad like me?"

An awkward silence passed between us until Preya said, "I'm sorry for bringing up your father. I know how sensitive that subject is to you."

I squeezed her shoulder and forced myself to smile. "Forget about it. I'm just having one of those days."

"Want to go grab coffee and talk further about why you didn't make it to bed last night?"

The coffee I wanted badly. The talk, not so much. Then I remembered where I had to be. "Can't," I said. A sense of renewed urgency made my stomach churn. "I have to go."

~ ☾ ~

After giving Preya a quick hug and promising to meet up with her later, I ran all the way to the north end of Barinkoff castle, which housed the administration offices. Three rooms side by side. The secretary, registrar, and staff occupied the first room. The records room sat at the center. And at end of the spread lay the office of the man I'd been handed to on a hard, wooden table.

Demitri had played me, and now I had to pay. He'd promised I wouldn't be expelled if I didn't show up after curfew again. Well, I'd broken my end of the bargain because of a misplaced sense of curiosity. I'd found out more than I bargained for, and now would be getting expelled. I wanted to kick myself—if only it were anatomically possible.

I couldn't bring myself to enter Kiev's office. The massive door with its gold nameplate that spelled out HEADMASTER in black letters seemed to mock me. It looked too formal, too highbrow. If the wood had a face, I was sure its eyebrow would be arched as if to say "You deserve what you're about to get in here."

There was no point in waiting any longer than I should. I twisted the knob and pushed my way in. At the other end of the room stood a tall man gazing out of bay windows that offered up a view of the northern courtyard. Below, students hustled from one end of the courtyard to the other to get to class. The headmaster had mink-colored hair, a clean-shaven face, broad shoulders, and long legs. I would have thought of Aleksander Kiev as handsome if the concept of good-looking hadn't changed forever for me. Meeting Demitri, Luka, and the rest of the too-attractive-for-their-own-good crew messed with the bell curve for everyone else.

"I have been waiting for you, Ms. McKay," Kiev said in his Russian-accented English.

I flinched. He regarded me with a neutral expression, his hands clasped behind his back. Nothing seemed worse than someone who didn't wear an angry expression. Screaming, shouting, reprimanding I could handle. But calm silence reminded me too much of my father, and it put me on edge.

"I took a detour," I mumbled, intent on staring at my boots.

~ ☾ ~

"What detour?"

"Bathroom."

"I see." He sighed. "Please take a seat."

I looked up at him then. He had moved from the windows to his oxblood leather executive chair. His cherry-wood-paneled office had a wood burning fireplace, reading chairs, a wall filled with books, and a painting of a line of miners carrying picks over their shoulders. It hung over the mantel. The plush carpet reflected the Barinkoff colors, which made the room darker than it should be.

"I'll stand, thank you," I said. I couldn't be sure of what Kiev knew. If anything, Demitri had already spoken to him.

"Alright." He laid his hands on the armrests of his chair. "I assume you know why you are here?"

I shrugged. Feigning indifference always helped determine the wrong committed without accidentally confessing to a different crime.

Kiev studied me for the longest time. "Ms. McKay, you have been caught breaking curfew."

"Headmaster, I can explain—"

"Twice," he interrupted without changing the cadence of his voice. "As you know, Barinkoff does not impose many rules. The students who attend classes here are specifically chosen for their academic achievements. They work hard and are good at what they do. They study to the best of their abilities, which does not leave much room for disciplinary offenses."

In short, we were all nerds. We liked stability. We liked to study. What more could someone ask for?

"How is this connected to my breaking curfew?" I asked.

"I was just getting to that, Ms. McKay," Kiev answered in an even tone.

I briefly wondered how rude I would have to get to bring out the anger inside him. It didn't take much to piss off someone. The only person I'd tried and failed to get riled up barely spoke to me unless absolutely necessary. I bit my lip hard for slipping into thoughts of my father again.

"Normally, I would be signing your expulsion papers right about now."

~ ☾ ~

A ray of hope parted the storm clouds above me. "But?"

"You have friends in high places." He gave me an all-knowing smile. The kind I hated because it took away any control I had over a situation. Meaning—no matter what I said or did—the other person already had the upper hand. But I wanted the upper hand.

"What are you hiding here at Barinkoff, Kiev? Who are the Night Students?"

His expression went from neutral to serious in less than a second. "For your own safety, Ms. McKay, I suggest you forget about the existence of the individuals you have recently come in contact with. It is a miracle that you are even standing before me...alive."

Tell me about it. Then the first part of what he'd said clicked.

"Is that a threat?"

"Only if you make it one."

My palms suddenly felt damp. I ignored the urge to wipe them on my skirt. "So, why not expel me? It's the easiest thing to do."

"Like I said, you have friends in high places." Kiev reorganized his features to the neutral mask he'd previously worn. "For now, you are being put under disciplinary probation."

I couldn't stop the sigh of relief that left my lungs.

"Thank you," I said.

"You are not getting off that easy, Ms. McKay."

I waited for the rest of what Kiev had to say. It hardly mattered to me since I wouldn't do anything to jeopardize my stay at Barinkoff. Not anymore. Demitri was right. It was too dangerous to keep digging. I didn't want to risk being anyone else's dinner.

"You will not break curfew again. You will attend all your classes and report to me every day before you leave campus. And you most certainly will not mention what happens on campus after sunset to anyone. If you do, I assure you that I will not only expel you, I will expel everyone you have told. No one, and I mean *no one*, will be able to stop me. Am I making myself clear?"

~ ☾ ~

I had so many choice comebacks for the authoritative way he doled out my punishment, but I stopped myself. Instead, I said with a smile, "Crystal."

Chapter 5

Rendezvous

    Every student I passed the second I entered Barinkoff after a well-deserved shower at the dorms stepped out of the way like I had a communicable disease. Every time I looked at someone, he or she moved in the other direction. I'd only been gone an hour and already the news about my probation had spread. My suspicion was confirmed when I attended my first class. My professor kept calling on me to answer his questions as if my IQ had decreased by fifty points since the last question he'd asked me not two minutes before.

    I couldn't care less that I'd been put on probation. As far as punishments were concerned, I'd gotten off easy. Kiev hadn't even suspended me. But then again, a suspension would have meant time away from my classes. For a school that focused on academics, keeping a student out of class seemed like a big no-no. If I was right, no one had ever been suspended at Barinkoff. Did they even give out detention?

    After my last morning class, I made my way to the Coffee Bar to meet Preya for lunch. The glass doors parted and a momentary lull in the conversation accompanied my entrance. I glanced around the room to catch at least half the eyes in the place focused on me, but nobody had the guts to meet my stare. Then, like flipping on a switch, the whispering continued. The different cliques huddled together, talking all at once to each other.

    I hurried to Preya's table and sat down, dumping my bag

on the floor. "Preya?"

She fiddled with the tip of her braid. "It's going around that you're on academic probation."

"Disciplinary," I mumbled.

"What?"

"It's disciplinary, not academic."

Her eyeballs almost fell out of their sockets she'd opened her eyes so wide. "That's worse. Far worse. They finally caught you didn't they. That's why you were so haggard this morning. I knew you couldn't keep researching your mother a secret for long."

A fiery blush spread across my face, prompting me to avoid Preya's direct gaze. "This wouldn't have happened if I didn't fall asleep in the library."

There was a brief silence followed by laughter so hard I thought she'd fall off her chair. "Was that where you were last night?" She slapped the table several times.

"Shhh!" I grabbed her shoulders. "Will you keep it down? It's embarrassing enough as it is."

Preya continued laughing at me. Normally, I'd be forcing her to stop. But the fact that she'd bought my story like a cashmere sweater on sale without asking any further questions gave me some needed relief. I knew Kiev would make good on his threat of expelling anyone else who found out about the Night Students. His hard stare had confirmed it.

"Oh, will you stop it already." I rolled my eyes at her and slumped into my seat.

She smiled. "You hungry?"

I returned her smile. "Starving."

After Preya's chicken vindaloo and my salmon patties arrived, I gave her an update on my pariah-like experience when I arrived at school today. With every bite of patty, I got more and more wound up by the smug expression on her face.

"What?" she finally asked.

"You make me want to pinch you. *Really hard.*"

"Oh, stop it. I told you researching late into the night would be counterproductive. Worse, you were cutting curfew because of it. Be lucky they didn't expel you." Preya scooped another spoonful of rice into her mouth. She chewed thoughtfully, swallowed, and then added, "Besides, you're a rebel now. Although I doubt any of the other students will be following in your footsteps considering what's happened to you."

"You make it sound like an achievement."

"Even if everyone is giving you a wide berth because of it, many of them admire you for being the first ever to break curfew. You'll go down as a legend."

I dropped my fork and knife on my plate and sat back. "I honestly don't want to be a legend." I hoped Preya was right when she said no one would follow in my footsteps. If they knew what lurked in the halls of Barinkoff at night ...

I'd realized my mistake too late when Preya said, "But you're not stupid enough to get caught breaking curfew for researching about your mother's sickness. If you weren't doing it to gain legend status among the nerd population, why did you get caught?"

"I *really* did fall asleep, Preya. Nothing more," I said.

Her crystal bindi caught the light when her brows came together. "Fine."

Putting on a fake frown, I nodded. The less I said the better.

Preya reached for my hand and squeezed. "How are you feeling now? I'm sure being on probation isn't easy. What can I do to make it better?"

"I dare you to run around campus naked." I resumed eating.

Preya threw a crumpled paper napkin at me. I swatted the ball way, and we laughed. We finished our lunch while chatting about other things not related to my disciplinary probation. After parting ways with my best-friend-slash-worst-enemy, I muscled my way through the library doors. Then I sneezed. Twice. Loudly. The sound actually bounced off the walls. My gaze landed on the outraged Ms. Lipinski. She had her finger to her lips. I wasn't getting on her good side anytime today it seemed. I mouthed "sorry" and hurried to the history section, ignoring the exasperated stares other

students beamed my way for disturbing the sanctity of their study time.

I wanted to get a head start on a few of my assignments. I didn't want professors breathing down my neck because of a little thing like disciplinary probation. The phrase stung now that I had time to process what it really meant for me. Not that I didn't deserve worse. I'd figured Demitri was who Kiev had been referring to when the phrase "friends in high places" came out of his mouth.

The tall bookshelves I slipped between muffled out all sounds. Even the soft *whirr* of the temperature control disappeared. I stopped for a moment, reveling in the utter and complete silence. Not even the thud of my heartbeat could be heard. I veered right and followed the descending letter plates stuck to the side of the shelves until I reached the shelves I was looking for then began pulling out large books that smelled oh-so-old. I took a long whiff and smiled. E-readers were a great convenience, but nothing could beat the smell of a library and old books. I had pulled a third book free from the shelf when clear blue eyes greeted me on the other side.

I yelped. The books slid from my hands and hit the ground in a series of loud *thumps*, eliciting a sharp "shhh!" from a student somewhere close by. I stumbled and tripped, falling against the opposite bookcase. I grabbed a shelf to steady myself while my heart attempted to leap out of my chest.

"Geez!" I said, leaning away from the shelf and dusting off my skirt and blazer. I sneezed a couple times. The corners of the eyes watching me crinkled.

"I apologize for startling you. It was never my intention," a very sexy, very familiar voice said.

I looked up and my jaw joined the books on the floor. Goose bumps rose along my arms. The one Night Student I didn't expect to see again electrified my senses.

"Phoenix?"

"What are you doing here, Luka?" I whispered, afraid someone might overhear us. "It's day time."

A soft chuckle. "We didn't get a chance to talk last night."

"But, but …" I paused. "You're not supposed to be here."

~ ☾ ~

"I'm not?"

"No!" I insisted. "You're a Night Student. Won't being in the daylight…" I stopped myself as I realized how insane my words sounded.

"I can go out during the day, Phoenix. It's just frowned upon. That's all."

"That's all? *That's all*?" Frustration rose up my throat like an angry mob. "I almost got expelled because of you!"

"Me?"

"Well, not you directly." I glanced around, checking for other students. "I mean I almost got expelled because I found out about the Night Students. I admit, it's kind of weird for the headmaster and whoever else is involved in this to be keeping it a secret. But that's over now. I'm not curious anymore," I rambled on. A golden eyebrow rose in response to my words. "Okay, that's a lie. But I really don't want to get expelled. And you being here can get me kicked out!"

"You're not getting expelled."

"Right. Like that's going to happen." I picked up the books I'd dropped and moved away. I heard his footfalls at the other side. I stopped. He stopped. At the end of the row of shelves, a guy wearing an orthodontic headgear passed by, nose stuck in a book.

I turned to where I thought Luka stood and said, "You have to leave!"

"Not until I get to talk to you," he insisted.

A searing blush crept across my face. "What do you want to talk to me about?"

"I'm curious about you."

I stared dumbfounded at the books blocking Luka from view. "I didn't expect that answer."

"It's the truth."

My own curiosity hummed in response to his. Would he actually answer my questions? The temptation made my hands sweat. The books I clutched to my chest seemed to weigh nothing in the split second I made my decision.

"This way," I whispered.

I hurried to a secluded corner of the library near the archives section no one ever used. Too much paperwork

involved in getting in. Plus, the books in circulation rivaled most national libraries, so students pretty much stayed in the main room. I figured we'd be far enough from anyone to be safe from being overheard.

I whirled around so quickly when I reached the corner that Luka almost slammed into me. I hadn't heard him approaching. He stopped abruptly, and with reflexes rivaling someone with a black belt, he stepped back without losing his balance.

"Nice ninja trick," I said, impressed and a little disturbed.

"I beg your pardon?" Luka cocked his head to the side.

The late afternoon light made his curls look like a halo of golden flames. A hint of uncertainty entered those too blue eyes. I swallowed hard.

"Phoenix?"

I clutched the books like a security blanket until my arms ached. "You came all this way just to say you're curious about me?"

"I wanted to get a glimpse of the girl reckless enough to break curfew," he said. "And I wanted to see the girl who was ready to confront such a strong opponent even when she had no hope of winning. I wanted to know more about that girl. Plus, I must admit, I had nothing better to do."

I felt my blush spread from my face to my neck and roots of my hair. "Forget that girl. She's currently on disciplinary probation because of breaking curfew. And you being here can make things worse for her."

His lips twitched downward. "I apologize. I didn't intend to cause you undue stress."

"Well, leaving me asleep in the library for the whole school to find can be considered a stressful situation."

"I had nothing to do with that." Luka's stare turned serious. "I would have taken you back to the dorms had I known."

"Bull," I said, harsher than I'd intended.

"Believe what you will. But I had nothing to do with what happened to you."

The sincerity in Luka's tone became difficult to ignore. Yet a nagging feeling in the deepest part of my gut said I shouldn't trust him—them.

~ ☾ ~

"I asked Demitri this already, but he didn't answer me. Well, he did, but he didn't give me enough of an explanation. So, I'll ask you: what are you exactly? I'm done fooling myself into thinking you guys are human. All the secrecy is just insane for nothing out of the ordinary to be happening here at Barinkoff at night."

The unexpected happened. Luka smiled the kind of smile that melted hearts and brought peace to the world. A reassuring smile. One that said everything would be fine. It drew me in with the promise of comfort. I lost my train of thought in a snap.

"What did you say?" I asked. Apparently, that smile made me deaf, too.

He shook his head, a rueful grin replacing his gates-of-heaven smile. "To know what we are is to believe in the unbelievable."

"*Oo-kay.* I'm not getting a straight answer from you, either. Great." Impatience punched my chest. "Can you be even more vague and cryptic?"

"Simply put, we're flesh eaters. Human hunters." His brows twisted. "Well, not any longer, but we do eat flesh."

A familiar chill ran down my spine. Not because of Luka's words, but because of the way he said them—with such certainty. With such confidence. Memories of Demitri confirming his people could eat my flesh surfaced. Luka stepped forward, but I didn't step back. He traced a finger up my arm, the coolness of his touch melting me.

"You're colder than Demitri," I blurted out.

"I beg to differ."

"No." I gathered my thoughts. "I mean your temperature. You're cooler."

He shrugged as if what I'd said had no consequence. "He and I are of different clans."

"I don't get it." I shifted the books in my arms to ease some of the growing strain. Luka took them from me as if they weighed nothing more than autumn leaves gliding to the ground. I shook my arms in relief. "Thanks."

"My pleasure." After a pause, he continued, "This is what you need to know: we're strong. We can heal. We're fast. And

we live longer than most things on this planet."

I couldn't believe what I was hearing. The stuff of myths and legends. "God complex?"

"Hardly. Just long lived."

"Then how do you die?"

He laughed. A melodic sound incomparable to anything I'd ever heard. "How do *you* die?" he threw the question back at me.

"We get sick, we grow old, we get into accidents. A million different ways." I crossed my arms in front of my chest, feeling my heart thud. "You're messing with me, aren't you?"

Luka regarded me with chagrin. "I assure you, I have no interest in 'messing with you.' I'm simply having fun."

"Fun? You think this is fun?" I stared at him skeptically. "If you consume"—I swallowed, a part of me still slightly skeptical—"human flesh, doesn't being here with me make you hungry?"

What little humor Luka had on him disappeared. "I'm on the Pill."

"Contraceptives?"

He made a circle with his thumb and forefinger. "A sphere about this big."

It dawned on me. "Dray gave Demitri one of those."

"I procured one for myself."

"Which makes you not want to eat me?" It sounded more like an uncertain question than a statement. My hands shook and my mouth had gone dry. The urge to bolt got stronger by the second. This must be what being prey felt like.

"The Pill staves my craving for flesh. It's what allows me to be in your presence without the overwhelming need to taste you."

"Then why keep your existence a secret if you can just take the Pill and go to school during regular hours?"

"It doesn't work when there's too many of you. It's like being in an all-you-can-eat buffet when you haven't eaten for days."

It made sense. In a roundabout way.

"How do I smell to you right now?" The question came from a morbid place.

~ ☾ ~

He breathed in then said, "To me, you smell like—"

The east tower bell interrupted him. We glanced toward the direction of the sound. I counted four peals. Panic bubbled up my neck from my chest.

"I have to go," I said, backing away.

Luka stood still and studied me, holding three heavy books in one hand. Something about his stance screamed silent predator. I matched his stare with one of my own, but the last bus left at 4:30 and I still had to show myself to Kiev. I looked down, then up.

Luka had disappeared like a dream that faded with the morning's early light.

~ ☾ ~

Chapter 6

Plea

Luka's cryptic and confusing explanations haunted me all night and well into the next day. Thank goodness for multitasking because I had to hand in my assignments, attend my classes, and figure out what Luka had meant. Add trying to keep a low profile to that. Well, as low a profile as rumors about probation permitted. I believed I'd become the first school delinquent Barinkoff has had in its halls. If other delinquents had come before me, I surely hadn't heard anything about them.

By the time my morning classes ended, my brain had staged a massive strike. The pounding felt like a thousand East Germans with sledgehammers tearing down the Berlin Wall. I needed coffee. Or food. Or both.

At the Coffee Bar, I quickly ordered chicken soup. The waiter winced when I sneezed after he had set the steaming bowl in front of me. I couldn't enjoy the smell. My nose had stopped working. As clogged as a drainpipe. I tried to sniff, but it magnified the pain in my head.

"You look terrible," Preya said the second she saw me.

"Thanks for the reminder." I lifted a spoon filled with chicken-y goodness and blew on it.

Preya set her books down and slid into her usual seat. "Well, it begs repeating."

I let the heat of the soup burn its way down my throat. "I'm fine."

~ ☾ ~

"I don't believe you." She observed me like a cat watching fish in a bowl. "You're a walking infection right now. What possessed you to come to school anyway? You should've stayed in bed."

I dropped the spoon into the bowl and rested my burning forehead on the coolness of the table's surface. I groaned. "I had to hand in my assignments today. I didn't want to attract any more attention than I already have with my probation."

"Phoenix, making yourself sick from the stress won't help you."

I gnawed the inside of my cheek before I blurted out that stress had nothing to do with my cold. Fleeing blindly through the snow with a psychotic flesh-eating chick in hot pursuit, then being drugged and left to sleep it off in a cold library was enough to make anyone sick. I just groaned again in response.

"Okay, that's it." Preya slapped the table. "Finish your soup and I'm taking you to the nurse."

"I don't need to go." I switched from my forehead to my cheek so I could see Preya's livid expression. "I have classes this afternoon."

"Like hell you do."

I grinned. "You said 'hell.'"

"You're skipping all your afternoon classes," she continued.

"Look at you, making me skip class. You're a bad influence."

"Phoenix?" She blinked at me.

"Yes?"

"Shut up."

I bit my lower lip to keep from laughing. My head would explode if I did. Besides, Preya wasn't above hitting a sick person.

She sighed then said, "We'll get the nurse to give you something so you can sleep. Then I'll come for you when my class is over."

"I'll just go home now. Why wait?"

"Because I don't want to leave you alone in your condition." She glared. "Now, quit whining and eat up."

~ ☾ ~

I sat up and stared at the bowl. I picked up the spoon and brought it to my lips. Preya stared at me the whole time, growling when I paused longer than ten seconds to eat. She made sure I swallowed every bite.

In the minutes after leaving the Coffee Bar, the walk to the clinic became a harrowing experience. My stomach sloshed from the chicken soup Preya had forced down my gullet. I wanted to scream at her, but I felt too nauseated. It took all my strength not to puke my guts out.

My legs felt like rubber by the time Preya opened the door to the clinic and pulled me in. The nurse stood up from her desk and hurried to my other side. She put my arm over her shoulder and wrapped her arm around my waist, and then she and Preya moved me toward the beds.

"Sink," I mumbled.

"What?" the nurse asked.

"I think she said 'drink,'" Preya said.

"Sink!" I yelled.

They hurried me to the small washing area near the rear of the clinic just in time for the stainless steel sink to catch the chicken soup that refused to stay eaten. I heaved and heaved until I had nothing left to heave, and then some. Preya held up my hair while the nurse rubbed circles on my back. My entire body convulsed. After the trembling stopped, I lifted the tap and washed out my mouth.

"When did I eat carrots?" I faced Preya, and she shrugged.

"Come on, Phoenix," the nurse said. "You should lie down."

I refused their offer to help me behind the privacy curtain. With one careful step after another, I made my way to the bed nearest the window. If I had to lie down for the rest of the afternoon, I at least wanted a view of the Lunar Garden and the sky.

I passed out sometime after the nurse took my temperature and gave me something for my cold. I vaguely remembered Preya mentioning something about coming for me before the last bus. When the oblivion of sleep chased away the incessant pounding in my head, I hardly cared about anything else.

Visions of Demitri hauling me around campus

~ ☾ ~

interspersed themselves with images of Luka carrying my books in the library and sitting with Dray in the solarium. I must have been half delirious because the imagery sped past my line of sight so fast that my nausea returned. I saw myself running away. A sense of overwhelming fear pushed me along a dark hallway. To stop meant death. I had to keep moving. I glanced over my shoulder. Nothing. Just endless darkness. When I faced forward again, I slammed into a marble wall.

I opened my eyes and gasped for air. Sweat slid down my temple to my cheek. The winter afternoon sun cast the room in gray light. In my periphery, I caught sight of a figure sitting beside my bed. Dray.

"Oh, geez!" I squawked out and scrambled to the farthest corner of the bed, pulling the blanket with me. "What are you doing here?"

"Phoenix, you have to lie down," Dray urged. The grayness of the room made his pale skin look even more ashen than usual. "I'm not here to hurt you."

"Easy for you to say." I rubbed my chest. "I thought I was about to have a heart attack."

Dray studied me. He gripped his fingers together on his lap, as if in prayer. I noticed a hint of desperation hidden behind the relative calm he portrayed. I saw it in the urgency in his eyes and the tight line of his lips. A muscle on his cheek jumped. His stillness and a dizzy spell prompted me to take his advice and lie down. I stared at the ceiling for a while to keep the room from spinning.

"I can't seem to get rid of you," I said.

"I resent that." The stool Dray sat on squeaked.

My eyes traced a hairline crack on the plaster above me. "The last time I saw you, you drugged me."

"Demitri made me do it," he said. "I wanted to keep you around, but he insisted you be returned."

"Why leave me in the library?" I looked at him then.

Dray stared at his entwined fingers. "He said you needed to be taught a lesson."

"Some lesson. The most he did was get Kiev to put me on probation. If he really wanted to teach me a lesson, he should have had me expelled."

~ ☾ ~

"I believe that was me."

I raised an eyebrow. "You mean Demitri doesn't know I'm still here?"

He nodded then his fathomless black eyes pinned me down. "I requested that you remain a student here."

My mouth opened but no words came out. Even if my face felt hot from fever, my hands turned icy. The temperature in the clinic seemed to have dropped a few degrees in the last minute. I gulped away the tightness in my throat.

"The nurse," I said. "Won't she—"

"No," Dray cut me off. "She's currently being detained."

"You didn't—"

"No! Oh my, no!" He shook his hands at me. "She's in Kiev's office. I had a hard time locating you today."

"Does Kiev know you're here?"

"Yes. But he doesn't know why, and I don't care to explain myself to him."

"Friends in high places," I joked.

"I beg your pardon?"

Fatigue sat like an elephant on my body. I needed rest. I needed to hurry along what Dray wanted to talk to me about. He wouldn't risk discovery for nothing. I smiled to myself, he wasn't Luka.

"What are you doing here, Dray? Why don't you want me expelled?"

"Maybe this isn't a very good idea after all," he whispered.

I threw an arm over my eyes. It eased some of the sting brought on by the gray light.

"Don't back out now, Dray," I said. "You seemed to have gone through all this trouble to keep me here at Barinkoff. What do you want from me?"

"I need your help." A palpable pause. "We need your help."

"Who are *we*?"

"My people."

The desperation I observed in his manner finally entered his voice. I lowered my arm and searched Dray's face. He betrayed nothing, returning my stare with a blank one. I felt sorry for him a little. I didn't know why. I just did.

~ ☾ ~

"I know this is going to sound cliché, but I have to ask it anyway: why me?"

A crack in his expression revealed sadness. It had fear and uncertainly mixed with it. I sighed, long and hard, prepared to listen to what he had to say. He'd come all this way. Plus, I felt too sick to leave.

"You already know about us. And it seems like you're curious enough to want to know more. Don't you want to find out what goes on at Barinkoff when the sun sets?"

"What about the headmaster?"

"Kiev doesn't act without confirmation from any of us."

"And Demitri? When he finds out, who knows what he'll do."

"After what I'm about to do to you?" Dray's brows inched up a notch. "He won't have a choice but to keep you with us."

My eyes narrowed. What he was about to do to me? A suspicious tingle climbed my spine when I sat up. "I don't like the sound of that."

"Are you going to help us or not?"

"With that attitude, I don't think so."

"Stop this, Phoenix." Dray rubbed the back of his neck. "I'm being serious."

The coming together of his dark brows said as much. I was being serious as well.

"What's in it for me? What do I get out of helping you?" I countered. I knew I sounded selfish, but I needed to have an idea of what I was getting myself into before I agreed to anything.

"You'll become one of a chosen few who knows what we really are," he said.

Luka's words in the library pinged inside me. Believing the unbelievable. The hairs on my arms rose.

"You're going to tell me what you are?" I asked.

A ray of hope shone in Dray's eyes when he said, "Better yet, you get to live with us for a while."

"But wouldn't that be dangerous for me? From what Luka said, you hunt humans."

Color drained from his face. "You spoke to Luka?"

"Yesterday. In the library." I studied his stiff posture.

~ ☾ ~

"Why do I get the feeling that wasn't supposed to happen?"

"What did he tell you about us?"

"You're fast, you're strong, you heal, you can live a really long time, and you eat flesh. Demitri told me about the flesh-eating thing, too. But no one's said exactly what you all are." I narrowed my eyes at him. "So? What are you?"

"Never mind that for now. You wouldn't believe me anyway if I told you right at this moment." Dray shook his head. "Are you going to help or not?"

"Why is it I don't seem to have a choice in this matter?"

"I read your file."

Anger sparked in me. "You what?"

"It says there that your mother died of an unknown disease, that the doctors couldn't do anything for her. There are notes in your file that show how desperate you were to find a cure to save your mother. Phoenix, without your help, my people will surely die. We're sick—like your mother, we need a cure. And I'm on the verge of discovering one, but I need a human to help."

I thought about Dray's offer for a minute. He used another one of my weaknesses against me. I didn't like the tactic, but I knew where he was coming from. Memories of my mother surfaced from the depths of my subconscious. Her frail body bogged down by so many life-support tubes. Her translucent skin. Her perpetual state of slumber. She'd wasted away from a disease no doctor could find a name for, let alone a cure, until nothing of her remained. Emptiness ate at the edges of my consciousness every time I remembered her.

If I could have done anything to save my mother I would. The doctors were useless. Now here was Dray, desperate to save his people. He was giving me an opportunity to make a difference. I didn't know him well, but I felt a strong urge to say yes to his request. My father, when he still loved me, taught me to be selfless. Would he respect me if I agreed to Dray's request? I shook my head. That was the wrong question to ask. Help should be given freely and unconditionally, my father told me once. So many nights I wished someone would save my mother. I couldn't let the same thing happen to Dray and his people.

~ ☾ ~

"What do I have to do?" I asked, making my decision.

Dray's face relaxed into a smile. He pulled out a hypodermic needle from the pocket of his lab coat and pulled off the safety cap. He grabbed my wrist so fast I didn't have time to struggle before he plunged the needle into my arm. The pain came instantaneously. First came the prick, then the needle's contents emptied into my arm. It felt like oil going in, thick and dreadfully torturous. Dray pulled the needle away and let go of my arm, which I grabbed, then curled into a fetal position.

The pain pulsed. It traversed my whole body.

I screamed.

Dray replaced the safety cap on the needle. "It's okay. Everything's going to be okay."

"It hurts!" I howled at him. "What did you inject me with?"

"Here, Phoenix." Dray shoved a rolled up face towel into my mouth.

I groaned, attempting to spit out the thick cloth.

"It's so you don't bite off your ..."

The rest of his words were lost to me as my eyes rolled back into my head.

Chapter 7

Hunger

A few years ago, I had contracted meningitis. I'd woken up one morning in my room feeling like my head would explode. My mother found me groaning in bed. I must have blacked out from all the heat and pain inside me because the next time I'd opened my eyes, I was already at the hospital.

In the darkness, I now felt the same heat and pain from that time. I had lava in my veins. A massive headache had my brain in its clutches and refused to let go. My heart pumped fire all over my body. My stomach roiled; its contents an angry sea attempting to escape. I wanted to scream except my mouth wouldn't open, seemingly sewn shut by barbwire.

"Phoenix," a rough voice whispered.

My eyes scanned the inky blackness for the person who had spoken. What I wouldn't give for a scream-at-the-top-of-my-lungs moment. I thought that if I screamed then maybe the burning pain would go away. If I was having a dream, now was the best time to wake up.

"Open your eyes, Phoenix."

I followed the voice's command. My eyes fluttered open. I blinked to clear my vision. Soon I recognized a canopy of gauzy fabric looming above me. My agony receded in degrees. It started in my head and drained from my body like a bucket of scalding water with a hole at the bottom. Every breath eased the soreness until none remained.

After a moment of disorientation, I realized I lay on a large

~ ☾ ~

four-poster. I tried to remember what had happened. Images fragmented in my brain too fast for me to piece the puzzle together. So I let my gaze roam until they landed on familiar onyx eyes, severe in their scrutiny.

Demitri sat facing me on the bed minus his blazer and cravat, leaving only his billowy silk shirt loosened at the collar. He leaned closer, maintaining a stone cold expression.

My stare settled on the exposed flesh of his neck. Saliva filled my mouth and my stomach churned. I lifted my arms and sat up like a corpse rising from a coffin. He froze, his eyes alert, his muscles tense. I swallowed and ran the tip of my tongue over my lower lip. I could almost taste him. On impulse, I wrapped my arms around his neck and touched the corner of his jaw with my lips.

Demitri's quick inhale excited me. Anticipation for what I wanted to do to him curled my toes. A hunger so deep, so encompassing pushed away any logical thoughts I might have had. My entire existence revolved around a need I couldn't quite understand.

Like obedient prey, Demitri remained still. Not pushing me away even though he certainly could. That he refused to pull away as I moved my mouth across his jaw meant nothing to me. A purr rolled up my throat. I wanted more, so down his neckline I went until I reached the juncture where his neck ended and his shoulder began. I slid his collar away to reveal the broad expanse of his shoulder. I nuzzled him, appreciating the scent of his skin.

Demitri smelled of morning dew on a spring day. Lovely. Fresh. Absolutely delectable.

My lips parted. My teeth grazed his skin, traveling across the width of his neck. He trembled. A moan of pure pleasure escaped my lips. I swirled my tongue on his exposed flesh, teasing and tasting. Then I bit down like I did with a succulent apple. The muscle on his shoulder twitched. A sudden rush of euphoria filled my body, reinforcing the pleasure brought on by the contact my teeth made on his skin. Heat pooled in my gut, causing me to squirm. I wanted to get closer. I needed a connection. The act of biting his flesh brought a kind of high I'd never experienced before. It was the weightlessness just as a rollercoaster took the plunge.

Overwhelming lust, longing, and desire boiled below the surface of my skin. It scared me. And like a rubber band snapping, my mounting fear broke the heat-filled intoxication that allowed me to take pleasure in biting Demitri. Dread, like a wave of black tar, crashed over me. I jerked away from him. My shoulders slammed against the headboard. The sting of the impact jarred my senses to reality.

I had bitten Demitri.

Not to draw blood or to feed. It was more an act of claiming, of possession. I covered my mouth with the back of my hand as drool trickled from my lips down my chin. I whimpered in disgust and hastily swiped at the trail it created.

"I ..." I swallowed the next wave of saliva. "I didn't mean to."

A pink crescent-shaped mark rose on Demitri's flawless skin before he readjusted his shirt to hide the evidence of my bite. His eyes seized mine completely, for the first time showing real emotion other than a deadpan blankness. I saw hunger and it called to me, begged me to continue what I'd forced myself to stop doing. My stomach rumbled like I wanted to throw up. A deep part of me felt frustrated, like I'd deprived myself of an essential part of living—something that wanted release. Demitri broke eye contact first and reached for a white sugar cube thing with the texture of tofu from a bowl on a side table. He lifted it to my mouth.

"Here, this will help," he said.

I turned away.

"You must be starving."

As if in response to his words, my stomach consumed itself.

"Come on, Phoenix. Eat this and the discomfort will ease. Trust me."

I turned to Demitri and considered the perfect planes and angles of his face. He sounded almost gentle. So unlike the forceful, bossy robot I'd met a few nights ago. I tentatively parted my lips and let him place the white cube on my tongue. It tasted like sweet yogurt, and when I found the

~ ☾ ~

courage to chew, a squid-like texture presented itself—rubbery, but not tough.

"More," I begged after I swallowed.

Piece by piece, Demitri fed me like I was an eager chick waiting for its mother's attention. In my appetite for more, I reached out for whatever he fed me. I wanted to stuff the cubes into my mouth like popcorn. He grabbed the bowl and held it out of my reach. I scrambled forward and he settled me into a seated position by pushing down on my shoulder.

"Let me feed you," he said.

"Or what?" I blurted out. My anger over Demitri withholding food was completely irrational, but I couldn't stop my spew even if I gagged myself. "You'll have me drugged and expelled? How did that work for you the last time?"

"I will not apologize for something I thought was for the best at the time." Demitri's brows came together. "If I let you eat on your own, you will end up overeating and make yourself sick."

He deflated my anger by ignoring my words. I crossed my arms and glared at him. He met my stare with a patient one of his own. When I no longer moved to take the cubes from him, he returned the bowl to the nightstand. I considered his point. The cubes seemed to stifle the hunger, but not completely satisfy it.

"What are they anyway? Some kind of flavored tofu?" I asked.

"Not exactly." He took a silver goblet that sat beside the bowl and handed it to me.

"What's this?"

"Spring water."

I sniffed the clear liquid before taking a sip. What little passed my lips tasted harmless enough. I took a bigger gulp to wash down the sour aftertaste of the cubes. As the cool liquid slid down my throat, memories of the nurse's office resurfaced.

"Dray," I growled.

Demitri wrenched the goblet from my shaking hand.

I blinked at the now crumpled metal. "That was straight, right?"

~ ☾ ~

"Yes."

The goblet's stem was now bent, with four distinct grooves. I looked at my hand and curled my fingers. "I did that?"

He nodded and twisted away.

"What happened to me?"

"You should get dressed," he said.

I wondered what he'd meant and glanced down. The blanket previously covering me had pooled around my waist. Blue lace covered my breasts and nothing else. The image didn't click until after my cheeks burned. I panicked, hastily covering myself with the blanket.

"Where's my uniform?" I asked.

Demitri stood and tugged at a cord hanging from the ceiling.

A woman in a French maid's uniform entered the room. Her hair, in a tight French braid, matched her gray eyes, but she appeared no older than twenty. She placed her hand at the center of her chest and bowed. Demitri inclined his head. She straightened and went to the large armoire on the other side of the room. Having another female in the room eased my nerves. I felt less naked, less insecure. But still wary.

I eyed her skeptically. "What's she doing here?" Okay, that came out a little rude. I cleared my throat and tried again. "I mean, why is she here?" Okay, still too rude. My emotions vied for attention inside me. I went from angry to cautious to annoyed to rude to calm to frustrated. It was worse than PMS.

"Her name is Deidra," Demitri said, gesturing to the woman. "She is here to help you get dressed."

I gathered the blanket around me and slid off the bed.

Demitri strode to the door. "Oh, before I forget—she can't speak."

"Why?"

No one answered.

My gaze went from Deidra to Demitri. I watched the door close behind him. A nip of loneliness caught me off guard. Even with Deidra in the room, I felt alone without Demitri there.

~ ☾ ~

In an effort to keep myself from asking him to come back, I returned my attention to Deidra. Every detail in the lace trimming of her apron jumped out at me. The clarity, which I'd only noticed when I'd focused on my vision, almost sent me stumbling back. A few days ago, I thought I needed glasses. Now, I had eyes like a hawk.

The cloying scent of lavender on her skin stung my nostrils. I stifled a sneeze by lifting the blanket to my nose. The crispness of thousand-thread count cotton saturated each inhale. I tilted my head and heard Demitri's steady breathing outside the room. And if I concentrated hard enough, I could even hear his heartbeats. And no matter how silently Deidra moved, I still made out her shuffling.

What was going on with me? First, a cold that rivaled meningitis. Now, an emotional rollercoaster to rival a manic-depressive. And hyperactive senses a superhero might envy. I squeezed my eyes shut and shook my head to awaken myself from this dream.

In my struggle to figure things out, I didn't notice Deidra, with her simple yet pretty face, glide toward me. She grabbed an end of the blanket I'd wrapped myself in and tugged, startling me out of my internal debate.

"Hey!" I yelled, slapping her hand away. I gripped the blanket tighter around my body.

Even when alarmed, Deidra made no sound. She just stared at me wide-eyed.

"Let her dress you, Phoenix." Demitri's muffled voice came from behind the door.

"I can dress myself," I barked back.

"With the clothes the ladies wear here? I do not think so. You need someone to help you into the skirt, not to mention the corset. The lacing is tough to tighten alone."

"Then return my uniform! And where's my phone?"

"Stop fussing or I will command Deidra to forcibly get you into that uniform."

I gaped. The stern quality in his voice actually convinced me he'd make good on his threat. I glanced at Deidra, who nodded and handed me a pair of midnight blue stockings. I glimpsed a hint of compromise in her eyes. Defeated, I let the

blanket fall to the floor. Unless Deidra hid something in her skirt different from what I hid in mine, I had nothing to be embarrassed about.

I sat on the edge of the bed and tugged on the thick stockings. "So, you really can't speak?"

Deidra smiled.

"I guess it's useless to ask you why?"

She pointed at the door.

My gaze fell to my stocking-covered thighs.

A finger tilted my face upward. Gray, concerned eyes met mine. The corners of Deidra's lips curved up. My own attempts at a smile faltered. I was more confused than afraid at this point. Dray made good on his promise to reveal his world to me. I stood in the middle of it now.

Deidra moved away, then grabbed the blouse hanging from a chair. I raised my arms and allowed her to dress me.

The blouse chafed, the corset pinched, and the skirt's weight threatened to buckle my knees when Deidra had finished. The only things still mine in the whole ensemble had to be my boots and my underwear. The rest were all Barinkoff Night Student standard issue.

Deidra beamed at the final product. She led me to the vanity, sat me down on the cushioned stool, and picked up a brush. I suffered her tugs on my suddenly rich chocolate hair, mesmerized by my reflection. Gone was the dull brown hair. A touch of pink stained my cream-colored skin. My face didn't seem to have pores anymore. My lips were plump and rosy. And my eyes matched my hair. Behind their hazel specks was a vibrant sparkle. If I didn't know any better, I would think I actually looked beautiful. How was that possible?

Oh, God.

Panic erupted like a volcano in my chest. Every breath became shallower until finally I screamed. The door slammed against the wall, barely staying on its hinges. Demitri's towering form filled its frame. He searched the room for signs of danger then relaxed when he found none. In her surprise, Deidra fled the room quicker than a discovered thief.

"What happened?" Demitri asked after stepping out of Deidra's way.

~ ☾ ~

With deliberate care, I stood up and faced Demitri. My fury expanded like a balloon filling with water.

I bared my teeth and said, "What *happened* to me?"

"Only Dray can fully explain," he answered.

What little control I had snapped. I moved closer to Demitri, adrenaline coursing through my veins. My muscles coiled as I raised my hands to his chest and shoved. Hard. An animalistic snarl escaped my throat.

Demitri slammed into the wall, causing a hairline crack to run up from where his head smacked into marble to the ceiling. With preternatural speed, he flung himself at me until I hit the opposite wall. He secured my wrists above my head with powerful hands. His lips twisted into a grin I'd never thought him capable of. I licked my lips and matched his expression with an obstinate smirk of my own.

I opened my mouth to speak but was interrupted by Demitri's searing kiss. I moaned my surprise. I felt every nuance of Demitri's lips on mine. The soft friction from each touch sent waves of tingles rushing through me like sparklers underneath my skin. In an instant, I lost track of what I had wanted to say. He tilted his head to the side and brought the kiss to a new level of perfection. I wanted more and more until I drowned in it. In no time, Demitri became my anchor, my legs refusing to carry my weight any longer.

He groaned. Its intensity stirred a need in me different from the gnawing agony I'd gone through earlier. No end came to the dizzying heat that swirled in me. Wave after wave of delicious sensation washed over my body. When Demitri finally broke the kiss, I gasped. He stared at me with unfocused eyes. If he would let go of my wrists, I'd snake my hands around his neck and force him to continue where he'd left off.

"Why is this happening?" I said, thumping my head on the wall in an effort to clear it. The kiss had ignited a yearning that scared me.

"Phoenix." Demitri closed his eyes and breathed. "Shut up for a second, will you?"

"Why? I'm the one disturbed by what just happened. *You* kissed *me*."

~ ☾ ~

"I said shut up. I need to think."

I had participated in my share of make-out sessions before. Some messy. Some sweet. Some utter disasters. But in all my encounters, feelings never entered the picture. I'd kissed someone because I wanted to. Because I'd let them kiss me. Unlike those occasions, I had no control here. Demitri had taken without mercy. Yet he actually left me wanting more instead of feeling violated.

"You are a smart girl," he said, interrupting my attempt to make sense of it all. "You would not have been accepted into Barinkoff if you did not have the academics to back you up. But, no matter how much I think about it, I cannot fathom what possessed you to say yes to Dray's harebrained experiment."

I shrugged. I didn't want to get into the real reason. "What was I supposed to do?"

"Clearly, you were not thinking of the consequences."

"He put together a really convincing case," I admitted. "But I didn't think he'd inject me with…whatever it was. I thought all he needed was my blood or something."

He leaned further away without letting my wrists go. The hard line of his mouth spoke of control, but his eyes showed no signs of regret. The passion within those irises sent delectable quivers through me.

"If I let you go, will you promise not to attack me again?" he asked.

No chance of that happening now. My body felt too limp to even call up the anger I'd previously felt, so I nodded. More space between us meant the possibility of thinking straight.

Demitri moved to the other side of the room and tangled his fingers in his hair—an action that betrayed his agitation. He could show a range of emotion after all. Imagine that.

I remained propped up against the wall. If I tried to move, I'd surely melt into a puddle. My knees shook badly while I counted every breath until the air coming in and out of my lungs resembled normal breathing again. He was just a boy, I reminded myself. I ran my tongue over my lips and recalled the sensations he'd left behind. Who was I kidding? He wasn't just a boy. No boy could kiss like him.

~ ☾ ~

Demitri faced me with a reconstructed mask of seriousness. He'd managed to reset himself. I wished I had his ability to calm down in a snap. Sweet tremors still ravaged my stomach just from me looking at him.

"We should go see Dray," he said. "At any rate, I think it would be prudent if we leave this room."

He glanced at the bed, a blatant hint at what he was thinking. Afraid to even consider what would happen if we stayed in the room, I pushed myself off the wall and ran for the door.

~ ☾ ~

Chapter 8

Transformation

In my rush to get away from the feelings Demitri had awakened in me, I didn't notice the opposite wall of the hallway until I almost plowed into it. I dug in my heels and screeched to a halt just in time and rested my hands on the smooth surface before me. I straightened and tried to get my bearings, gulping in several calming breaths, willing my heart rate to stabilize. I searched for another point of escape.

The white, so bright and blinding, canceled out my depth perception. What I thought was a way out opened to a corridor stretching the length of a football field. No other doors marked other rooms, just smooth, white walls from left to right. And above, the illusion of an endless ceiling, stretching to infinity.

"Where am I?" I asked the empty air.

"The palace."

I jumped at the sound of Demitri's voice behind me. I whirled around so fast that I wobbled slightly. My lips trembled at the sight of him exiting the room—a dark contrast to the pristine whiteness of the hallway. If I thought he was handsome when I first met him, now, with my magnified senses, it almost hurt to look at him head on.

"The academy?" I hoped.

"Not exactly." Demitri's eyes avoided mine. He turned left and walked without checking if I followed. "Come, Dray's lab is this way."

~ ☾ ~

I stood there in mute disbelief. The sudden detachment he demonstrated confused the desire out of me. Yes, he normally acted unemotional, but at that moment, he acted as if the passion we'd shared not five minutes ago meant nothing. The thought of him having his way with me propelled my legs forward. Anger, the twin sister of betrayal, convinced me to grab Demitri's collar from behind and slam him against a wall. I clutched fists full of his shirt and lifted my knee onto his midsection, shifting all my weight to keep him in place.

I bared my teeth like an incensed feline ready to hiss and spit at anything that crossed its path. Demitri's steady gaze punctuated my anger. I wanted him to react to my sudden aggression. I couldn't comprehend why I suddenly wanted to pick a fight, but I sure as hell wanted one. Yet he remained uncooperative. What did I expect? Did I want him to whirl me around and kiss me into oblivion again? I shook away the image—it caused my insides to become molten liquid.

"I don't know what's going on inside me, but I'm not the best person to mess with right now." I pushed my knee in harder. My strength cracked the wall behind him.

"Phoenix," he said, not showing any signs of pain.

The way he said my name sent shivers through me so strong, I was sure he felt them too.

"What you are experiencing right now has something to do with biting me. If what I suspect Dray did to you is right, your bite released chemicals in your body akin to a combination of endorphins and aphrodisiacs. The lust, the wanting, the desire—those are all urges caused by the need to mate with me."

His last sentence transformed the heat inside me into ice. "Excuse me? Did I just hear you right? Did you just say I want to *mate* with you?"

"The bite created a connection between us." Demitri continued to stare at me stoically. "Believe me when I say that if we stayed in that room, we would be finding ourselves in a compromising situation right about now. I feel the same pull you do. From the way you managed to run out of the room, I say you still have some modicum of control over yourself. I suggest you keep it that way because I intend to practice the

same restraint. And accomplishing that would be challenging if you do not cooperate and stay away from me."

"Urges? Is that what you call me wanting to fling myself at you every second I'm near you? Huh." I clucked my tongue. The red mist of anger receded from my vision. "And you promise to stay away from me, too?"

"Yes."

I quickly let go of his shirt, lowered my knee, and stepped away. If what Demitri had said held some truth behind it—not that I completely trusted him—I would absolutely kill Dray. After he reversed whatever he had done, of course. I couldn't be one hundred percent sure of keeping my raging desires in check. I didn't sign up for finding myself in bed with Demitri just because Dray had slipped me the alien equivalent of Spanish fly.

"Let's get going," I said.

Demitri motioned for me to follow.

Dray's lab disappointed me in that it looked exactly like the Barinkoff Chem lab. I'd expected the place to be bigger and more sophisticated.

"I thought it would be more...well, just more," I said when the sliding door *whooshed* open.

"Bigger than it looks," Demitri whispered as an aside while Dray hurried toward us, an excited gleam in his eyes.

"You're awake," he said in greeting. "I was getting worried. In fact, I was just about to pay you a visit."

Of its own volition, my fist connected with Dray's jaw. The once happy mad scientist flew across the room, thudded into a table with an array of test tubes atop it, and knocked it over. Tubes shattered. Dray shrieked. For a second, Demitri's face showed awe before he covered it up with indifference. I stared at my fist and grinned. Super strength rocked! Then I sobered, realizing what I'd done. I wasn't generally a violent person, but Dray had it coming, with or without my crazy mood swings. Regardless of wanting to help his people because of my love for my mother, what he did to me was unthinkable. As soon as I found out what it was that he did to me and made him reverse it, I was walking out.

~ ☾ ~

Carefully, Dray picked himself up from the floor. Viscous liquid stained his lab coat green.

"I think I deserved that," he said, looking balefully at the destroyed set up. "I'll clean that up later. You're lucky it wasn't anything explosive."

"That's for stabbing me with a needle," I said.

"Phoenix." He faced me with pleading eyes. "You agreed to this."

"You could have at least told me what I was signing up for. I want out. *Now*."

"I'm sorry. That's not possible."

My surprise knew no bounds. Dray's apology had no remorse behind it whatsoever. He reminded me of Preya when she came close to a breakthrough. She remained relentless from beginning to end, a crazy look of determination on her face. No matter what, results outweighed all other considerations. It frightened me then, and it continued to alarm me now as I watched Dray's expression change from one of pleading to one of complete resolve. I swallowed, losing all my previous fight. I was trapped. Whether I liked it or not, he was right. I had agreed blindly. Had not asked any questions. Just said "yes." As if that "yes" could have brought back my mom.

"Come. Sit." Dray pointed at a table with a blood pressure kit, tongue depressors, and other medical paraphernalia. "I need to take a blood sample."

Unable to think of a reason why I should say no, I took a seat on a metal stool. "Just so we're clear, what did you do to me, exactly?"

Dray sat on an identical stool in front of me and proceeded to draw blood from my arm. I ignored the initial needle prick by watching his face grow shades paler. He pulled out the needle and pressed a cotton ball on the wound.

"Apply pressure to that," he instructed.

I bent my arm, squeezing my finger over the cotton ball in the crook of my elbow, waiting for him to answer my question.

"What I did wasn't that bad, when you think about it."

"This is complete bull—" I reined in the rising fury by

biting down hard. The pressure between my molars was such that I thought I'd break my teeth if I kept at it. So after a labored breath, I said, "Before I start ripping heads off, please answer my questions. You turned me into one of you. Why can't you just turn me back?"

"Don't answer that yet," Demitri said to Dray. "I want an explanation. What did you give her?"

Dray rested his hands on his knees and sucked in a lungful of air. Some color returned to his ashen features. "I'm working on a formula with the ability to transfigure the physiology—"

"In layman's terms—"

"Give me a break." I interrupted Demitri's interruption. "Like you said, I'm not in Barinkoff for nothing. I understand what he's saying. Speaking of which…school? Kiev must be freaking out by now."

"I took care of it," Demitri replied simply.

"You took care of it?" I stood, then sat back down. "Of course you did."

"If you had stayed away like I told you to …"

"How dare you—" I rushed him, but Dray wrapped his arms around my waist in time.

"Phoenix, calm down," he said. "Demitri just needs to be in control of things. It's for your own safety."

If I wasn't in a hopeless situation, I would have followed through with my attack. Demitri had it coming too, but the steam from my initial emotional outburst dissipated. To avoid transforming into a homicidal maniac, I needed to make the best out of the lemons life had given me, and all because I fell asleep in the library. I stood limp in Dray's arms until he let me go.

"Where's my phone?" I asked.

He handed me the black device he'd fished out of his lab coat. "Not that you'll get cell reception here."

I tapped the screen. The missed call icon blinked. I clicked on the icon. Preya's number flashed across the screen. I'd forgotten about her. She said she'd come get me at the end of the day. She may be scary sometimes, but she did worry. What must she be thinking by now? I slumped down on the stool. My life was steadily becoming more and more complicated. How was I going to lie away all this—I scanned the lab—to her?

"Can we continue our previous conversation now?" Demitri inquired.

I sighed and nodded.

"I injected Phoenix with a formula that basically allows her body to become like ours," Dray said.

Demitri cursed under his breath. "That explains much. She has the strength, the hunger, the *urges*."

Dray rubbed his chin. "Has she eaten the *yusha*?" He watched Demitri dip his head once before Dray faced me. "Did it help with the hunger? Are you sated?"

"You mean the white cube thing that tastes like yogurt? Yes." I moistened my tongue by moving it around my mouth. "I'm full, but not satisfied."

"That's to be expected." He smiled. "The hunger can only be truly satisfied by real flesh. *Yusha* is only an approximation of the nutrients flesh provides. It's synthetic."

My stomach clenched. "When you say flesh, you mean …"

"Human flesh, yes."

"Oh, god." Images of Demitri's exposed skin and my biting him flashed before me. I gagged.

"But not anymore," Demitri said.

Dray nodded matter-of-factly. "It's been forbidden to taste human flesh for over six hundred years. I'm surprised you didn't take a bite out of Demitri."

"Actually—" I began, but stopped when Demitri raised a finger to his lips and shook his head at me. Not really knowing what he meant for me to do, I scrambled for a lie. "As if I'd want to take a bite out of *him*."

"Odd." Dray tilted his head to the side and clutched his elbows.

A worrying question occurred to me. "Does this mean I'm not human anymore?"

"The formula is far from perfect." Dray shook his head. "You're still fundamentally human, only with more perks. You're faster, stronger, and you can heal. Think of it as an upgrade."

~ ☾ ~

I removed the cotton from my arm and not a trace of the puncture wound remained. Put that way, it didn't sound so bad. Well, besides the weird hunger. And the increased libido. I cringed, then remembered the superhuman strength. I thought of Calixta and grinned. The idea of a smack down between her and me made up for the fact that I had to be careful around Demitri.

"So, whatever this is will wear off?"

"Yes. Although, I cannot say when, exactly."

"You just had to conduct this experiment before the Winter Solstice Festival," Demitri interjected, disgust in his tone.

Dray's expression hardened. "I had no choice."

"We always have a choice, brother!"

"Whoa!" I raised my hands. "Back up a sec! *Brothers*? As in, we share the same mother, brothers?"

No one paid attention to me anymore. They stared at each other like two dogs about to fight. I thought the lab would explode from all the testosterone in the air. I leaned on the table and let the stare-down play out. Boys. Why did they always have to solve everything with violence?

"Not the point," Dray said. "I needed a test subject. I didn't want to waste—"

I merely blinked and Demitri already had Dray by the lapels of his lab coat. Impressive, since Demitri had been standing all the way across the room. He shoved his brother so hard that I suspected they would have gone through the opposite wall if Dray hadn't planted his feet on the ground.

"*Brother.*" Dray switched to a beseeching tone. "It's for the good of our people. You have to trust me on this."

A rich, throaty growl reverberated from Demitri. Then he said, "Your little experiment can jeopardize *everything*. I have worked too damned hard to have you derail my plans."

Dray stood firm when he said, "It won't. Her contribution to this experiment will help us take steps forward. I'm on the verge of something important here."

"Know that if anything happens that I cannot control, I will hold you responsible. And you know what we do to those found wanting," Demitri threatened through his teeth. He let

~ ☾ ~

go of his brother's lapels, shoving Dray in the process.

Dray took a moment to smooth out the wrinkles of his coat before he spoke again. "She needs constant supervision."

"I know," Demitri grumbled.

"I need to see her every five hours for tests." Dray moved toward me. "I'm not sorry for putting you through this, Phoenix. I hope you understand."

"I understand," I said then I slapped him. My stinging palm made me feel a whole lot better. More so than the punch earlier.

"Is this something I can expect from you every time we see each other?" Dray rubbed his cheek and grumbled. "Just let me know so I can prepare myself for future abuse."

"Don't tempt me." I crossed my arms. "So, are you going to tell me what you are? You're certainly not human."

"Maybe a step up from being human. We're an ancient race called *Zhamvy*... we're akin to what you humans call zombies. Just not ugly and mindless. Humans have bastardized who and what we are, but if you've ever wondered where the mythology of eating humans came from...well, that's us."

"Wait. Wait. Wait. Wait!" I held my hands up as if to brace myself. "You mean to say you're like, eat-my-brains zombies? You've got to be kidding me!"

A silent moment passed between Dray and Demitri.

"A bastardized way of describing us. We merely consume flesh, not brain matter or any other organs," Demitri explained.

"But, you're not dead. Or at least you're not the walking dead, right?"

His expression returned to its emotionless state. "What part of *bastardized* escapes your understanding?"

I pouted. "So, all those things about zombies—"

"Pure Hollywood, my dear." Dray tsked. "You humans are queer creatures. You get the names right, but you get the mythology wrong. *Zhamvy* actually means supreme deity when translated from our language to yours."

"You're gods?" My jaw popped from having been dropped to many times in the span of a few minutes.

~ ☾ ~

"Only when we used to rule your lot. Some of us like to think of ourselves as being at the top of the food chain, that's all. Apex predators if you will."

"Are you done with her, Dray?" Demitri asked.

Dray looked me over. "For now, but if there are any changes, rush her back here."

Demitri came to my side and a prickling blush bloomed on my cheeks. My heartbeat jumped a couple of notches higher than normal. And my mouth went dry. I stifled a groan.

"Oh, before I forget," Dray said. "Take this." He placed the same white pill Demitri had asked for the other day into my palm. "It'll help control the urges and mood swings. Wouldn't want you humping anything on two legs, now would we?"

I cringed, reminded of what *almost* happened with Demitri. Then I twisted the pearl-like ball between my fingers before popping it into my mouth. "Peppermint?"

"Close enough." He grinned, looking too proud of himself for my comfort.

"Come along," Demitri said as he led the way out of the lab.

I scrambled to follow before Dray decided he had other tests he wanted to perform on me. Even if I agreed to help Dray out, it didn't mean being a lab rat made it to my list of top ten enjoyable things to do. Grief gripped my heart as I recalled my mother, emaciated on a hospital bed. I hated hospitals and labs and experiments, but if the doctors had told me I could help in making her better, I wouldn't have hesitated to say yes.

I pushed away memories of her and stomped along the ultra-white hallway beside Demitri.

"Sooo," I said.

"So," he echoed.

"You're a Zhamvy. The mythological equivalent of a zombie."

"Were you hoping I was something else? A vampire perhaps? Or a werewolf maybe? I hear they are popular these days."

"A joke? Huh, the robot knows how to tell a joke. Imagine that."

~ ☾ ~

Demitri gave me a sidelong glance. "I'm sensing animosity from you."

"It's just…you're so stiff sometimes. You need to loosen up a little. When you grabbed Dray at the lab, that was the most emotional I've seen from you. Except for that impromptu make-out session, of course."

"I have emotions."

"Could have fooled me." I went back to my earlier thought, figuring I'd get nowhere with Demitri when it came to talking about feelings. "I'm assuming your race is old."

"You may assume."

"How come humans don't know you exist?"

"On the contrary, you do. You just relegate us to monster myths. Remember what Dray said." His gaze took on a faraway quality. "At one time, we used to rule over humans."

"I'm sure you liked that." I tapped my chin. "The headmaster knows."

"He does, as do several others. Aleksander comes from a few families that have kept our secret for generations."

I considered his words. A small part of my heart wanted to trust this inhuman—flesh eating—guy. But my mind screamed no. I had treaded into unknown territory the second I'd agreed to Dray's little experiment. My stomach coiled.

The sound of heavy footsteps distracted me from my mounting uncertainty.

A group of men strode toward us in a phalanx—seven in all. Six men in black-lacquered breastplates, three in a line on both sides of a seventh man in a dapper gray suit. He had short, glossy-black hair and deathly pale skin. I suspected these Zhamvy people saw very little sunlight. When Luka came to see me at the library he said it was frowned upon for them to come out during the day, it made sense they would be so pale. Some of the guards had long hair while others wore theirs in a crew cut, but all had the same shade of caramel. Their stolid faces were reflections of each other. What was it about the Zhamvy and their weird clothing choices? Except for the guy in the gray suit, I'd say most of them didn't know what century they currently lived in. Armor? Seriously?

~ ☾ ~

Demitri shoved me against the wall.

The jarring impact made me bite my tongue. "I'm getting so tired of you—"

"Whatever you do, keep your head bowed and your gaze on the floor," he interrupted. "And for the love of everything sacred, only speak when spoken to."

Chapter 9

Throne

Following orders had never been my strongest quality. In fact, I naturally rebelled against being told what to do. Once, after I'd bonded my math teacher to her chair with super glue, the guidance counselor had explained to my parents I had authority issues. In my defense, my math teacher had it coming. She'd made me write one hundred on the blackboard, so I wrote one, zero, zero in words since one hundred consisted of those numbers. Because she hadn't been specific in her instructions, she'd berated me for being a smart aleck. The whole class had laughed at me. The next morning, they had to cut her out of her chair.

Years later, standing in a blazing white hallway, I realized I still hadn't changed. The moment Demitri turned his back on me to face the approaching group of men, I lifted my gaze. Well, maybe I had changed somewhat since I maintained a half-body bow like I'd seen my father execute for Japanese businessmen.

My curiosity wouldn't let me avoid staring at the group with their all-business-all-the-time expressions. My father had the same appearance. I only needed to recall his face when he'd told me about Barinkoff. Perversely, I wondered how he'd react if I told him the school hid secrets like flesh eating zombies. Would he have me committed?

Compared to my father's cold features though, the man in gray held on to a hint of self-importance in the slant of his chin, the narrowing of his eyes, and the lift of his brow, like he was above everyone else. He had the features of a GQ model and the aura of an evil dictator. World domination 101: look the part. Having his eerily identical lackeys by his side fulfilled that requirement, too.

Demitri's tension affected me. His pose seemed unnatural, bowed head and all, hands plastered to his sides. The hard line of his back and the stiffness of his shoulders oozed a barely leashed aggression. It made me nervous, and I hated being nervous.

Dictator-man raised his hand, and the phalanx stopped. I had to refrain from recoiling because of his tannery smell. He reeked so much that the urge to wrinkle my nose almost overpowered my common sense. Thankfully, the rest of his entourage smelled like a candy store: cherry, peppermint, chocolate, caramel, banana swirl, and toffee. I froze when he gave me a quick glance, then his gaze landed on Demitri. He placed his hand on the center of his chest and inclined his head slightly.

"My prince," he said in a stick-up-the-butt voice.

Prince? Demitri? My eyebrows twitched. I played connect the clues: A prince, a palace. Whoa.

"Prime Minister Vladimir," Demitri answered as he mimicked Vladimir's gesture before straightening from his inclined position.

Vladimir. Very dictator-ish. And a prime minister to boot. Definitely not in Barinkoff anymore, Toto.

"I trust you will attend Parliament today." Vladimir lifted his chin.

"Of course." Demitri remained impassive, with only a slight tightening at the corner of his lips. "After my last class of the day."

"How are things with my ward?"

"I beg your pardon, Vladimir." Demitri let his hand fall to his side. The tip of his forefinger twitched. "I have yet to see her. Maybe in class today."

"I see. We shall remedy the situation. You two need to spend more time together."

"I will abide by what you believe is for the best, Prime

~ ☾ ~

Minister." Demitri tilted his head like a maître d' at a five star restaurant about to leave the table. "Would that be all?"

"Who's this?" Vladimir's gaze fell to me, and I dropped mine to the floor. "She's unfamiliar to me."

"An exchange student from the north. The king requested—"

The armored guards tapped their breastplate once and said, "Hail the king!"

"Yes, hail the king," Vladimir repeated.

"As I was saying," Demitri continued, "I have been asked to escort her while she familiarizes herself with the palace."

"Very well. Carry on." Vladimir raised his hand again and the group continued their procession down the hall.

Demitri waited until they rounded a corner before facing me. He spoke through his teeth once again.

"You were looking at him."

I leaned on the wall, my palms flat on its smooth surface, hopefully absorbing the sweat that had accumulated there. "Forget that for a minute and answer me something: you're a prince?"

His severe expression reminded me of the time I'd spilled milk on the table. My father had slapped me. From the irritation in Demitri's eyes, I could tell he came close to doing the same.

"You can hit me," I said. "I know you want to."

"I refuse to hit a woman, Phoenix, no matter how annoying she gets. Violence solves nothing." Finally, he opened his eyes. "Perhaps I should have told you that staring directly at the prime mister when your presence is unacknowledged is punishable by death?"

My brows crinkled. "I resent that."

Demitri cracked his knuckles by clenching his fist. It sounded like popping bubble wrap.

"Honestly, why do you have to be this unmanageable?"

His words hurt—each one an ice pick to my heart.

To cover up my vulnerability, I said, "Well, we can't do anything about that now. I'm still alive, so let's lead with that."

Demitri wiped all emotion from his face and stepped back.

~ ☾ ~

"Understand this: no one can find out about you. We need to keep you safe until the formula wears off, so you can return to the academy. You have no place here, Phoenix."

"Ouch." My face fell. I couldn't meet his gaze anymore.

Sighing, Demitri placed his finger underneath my chin and tilted my face up until I met his gaze. "Do not misunderstand. This world is no place for a human, even one who is currently mimicking our physiology. Our kingdom is a very dangerous place."

I couldn't tell which affected me more, his sudden detachment or his words.

"But Dray said—"

"Whatever Dray said matters little if you fall into the wrong hands."

My eyes widened. "Vladimir?"

"Especially Vladimir, along with anyone from the Traditionalist party. Calixta—his ward—is bound by the Silence from telling anyone you're human, but that hardly keeps you safe from her."

"Why would the Traditionalist party be a danger to me?"

"If you follow what I have planned then you will not have to find out why."

My tongue stuck to the roof of my mouth.

"Calixta does not know you are here and I would like to keep it that way. She will not speak of you; however, she can still kill you if she had a mind to."

I understood then. The Zhamvy had kept their existence a secret for centuries. Hence the automatic expulsion rule set for anyone who broke curfew at Barinkoff. Not only because of the danger flesh eaters presented, but also because the world wasn't ready to find out about them. Unfortunately for anyone except Dray, I stood in the middle of it all, a human who might endanger their existence.

I mustered all my resolve and promised, "Won't happen again."

"Good." Demitri turned toward the end of the hall and left me to follow him.

After so many right and left turns through similar white corridors, annoyance crept up my throat. I wanted to scream.

~ ☾ ~

Too much walking and very little talking made me grumpy. He refused to answer any of my questions...*again*. So what if I'd messed up with the whole prime minister thing? It didn't mean he should punish me by shutting up. I hated not knowing what happened next.

"Dem—"

He shushed me.

I gaped. *The nerve!*

Before I could argue, we stopped at a T intersection with floor to ceiling velvet drapes where the dead end should be. A man in a sleek suit who smelled like freshly brewed coffee stood to the right of the navy curtains, a clipboard in his hand. His obsidian eyes widened.

"Prince Demitri," he said with a stiff bow. "Shouldn't you be—"

"I know, Lev. " Demitri pointed at the drapes. "Is he in chambers? I need a moment with him."

Lev eyed me. "I'll see what I can do."

When he disappeared behind the curtains, I pulled on Demitri's arm until he tilted to the side.

"I guess now is the right time for this," I said. I cleared my throat, and as if sensing what I was about to ask, Demitri's jaw ticked. I didn't care. I asked anyway. "You're a *prince*?"

Demitri straightened, adjusting the sleeve of his shirt and said, "Really not important at all."

"Oh, so you'd never tell me? Is that it?"

"Not exactly."

I snorted. "More like if keeping it a secret was no longer an option." I slapped his arm. "Is there anything else I need to know about you?"

"I promise," he said, his gaze locking on mine, "I will answer all your questions after this."

Lev slid out from between the curtains. "He'll see you now."

"Alone?" Demitri asked.

Lev nodded. "Make sure to hurry. He has an important meeting with the captain of the Vityas in a few minutes."

"Demitri, what's going on?" I tugged at his sleeve.

His uncomfortable stare didn't help settle my nerves. "I

need to introduce you to my father—the king."

"Hail the king," Lev responded without looking up from his clipboard. I imagined a printout with a neat schedule on it. Add wire-framed glasses and he'd have the complete ensemble of a chic personal assistant.

"So, what brings you here?" Lev asked after Demitri disappeared behind the curtains.

I didn't know how to answer Lev's question. Demitri said to keep my presence a secret, but he didn't say to what extent. Lev worked for the king—Demitri's dad—so could he be considered trustworthy?

I'd waited too long to answer because Lev said, "Right. You won't tell me. I understand. But to have the crown prince introducing you to his father," he raised an obnoxious eyebrow, "that's big. *Very* big."

The way Lev said "very" made me cringe. I stared dumbfounded at the navy fabric Demitri had pushed through. I was about to meet Demitri's dad. No! Oh no, no, no! I studied the marble floor, following the dark veins with my eyes. Why couldn't he have been a normal Zhamvy? Why did he have to be a prince? A crown prince, no less. Heir to the throne. Future king to a race that could possibly enslave and eat the human population if they had a mind to.

I suppressed the urge to rub my temples. I'd managed to land in a pretty deep pile of crap. And the how of digging myself out escaped me. Demitri returned before I worked myself up to the point of hyperventilating.

"Come on," he said.

My hands grew damp. I'd never done the whole meet-the-parents thing before. Seeing that I wasn't about to make a move, he grabbed my hand and dragged me forward. I locked my knees, but the marble floor didn't provide enough traction to stop our momentum. In fact, it didn't even seem like he struggled with my weight. When he wanted to, he could easily overpower me. Something I often forgot.

"De—I'm—will you wait a sec!"

He stopped in a dim partition between two sets of velvet curtains. "Now, before we see him, I want to warn you about something."

~ ☾ ~

The gravity of his tone changed my stomach into tumbleweed—prickly and upending on every bounce. I made a mental note not to disobey, even if my natural instincts said to rebel. I didn't need the king's ire added to my lengthening list of misdeeds.

"Spit it out," I said.

"Do not stare."

Was he joking?

Demitri tugged me through the curtains and I gaped. Understatement of the year: massive. The word "huge" seemed too small. Running out of adjectives, I settled for cavernous. The room resembled a marble cave, or so I thought as I tried to wrap my mind around what stretched out before me. The builders had kept the walls and high ceiling rough while smoothing out the floor and throne. Blue velvet curtains on the far wall opposite where Demitri and I had come in and on both sides of the throne lent warmth to a pretty much barren room. My arm hairs stood on end. The faux bravado I always walked around with vanished, almost as if I had become an insecure little girl who wanted her mommy.

Above the throne hung a massive shield taller than Demitri and three times as wide. Painted on its surface was a unicorn on its hind legs standing on a bed of roses with large thorns. The animal's horn pierced through a crown. The words *Scientia est lux lucis* carved in curly script hovered above the image. *Knowledge is enlightenment.* Why would the Barinkoff motto and symbol be on a shield in a Zhamvy throne room?

On the smooth stone sat a Zhamvy in rich, cobalt robes with gold trim over a dark suit. His blue-black hair, much like his son's, swept off his brow and fell over his shoulders. He wore no crown. In my opinion, he didn't need one. The regal air in the way he placed his hands on the armrests combined with his straight shoulders and stiff posture more than made up for the lack of a crown. He exuded power, even if his expression was compassionate. His eyes, black as the darkest night, watched me, irises reflecting my wonder. He had the same striking features as his son. His only flaw—if it could be considered that—were silver crescent scars that created intricate lace-like patterns over every exposed surface of his pale skin.

I forced myself not to stare when I bowed.

The smoothest honeyed voice with the hint of grandfatherly sternness filled the room. "Did my son think he was being funny by telling you not to look at me?"

I peeked. My heart sputtered.

"Father," Demitri said, "may I present Phoenix McKay, a Day Student of Barinkoff Academy."

"Welcome to the Barinkoff court, my dear." The king raised his hands in greeting.

"Phoenix," Demitri said, ignoring my glare at having been tricked, "I present my father, King Darius Excelsar Barinkoff of the Barinkoff Dynasty."

"Barinkoff?"

"Yes, my dear." King Barinkoff—Darius?—smiled graciously. "I founded the academy."

"You own the *school*?" I pointed at Demitri since it felt too rude to point at the king.

The king hooted and slapped the armrest over and over in a rapid drumbeat that punctuated his laughter. Definitely just Darius. I couldn't imagine mentally calling someone a king when they were laughing like a baboon.

Demitri remained impassive.

"Don't think this is over, Demitri." I squinted at him. "I'll get you for almost giving me a heart attack."

"My son has kept things from you." The king swiped at a stray tear that fell from the corner of his left eye. "Forgive him. He's modest, if not secretive."

"Father!" Demitri's careful composure splintered.

Darius waved dismissively at his son. "How are you feeling?" he asked.

Only when Demitri switched from embarrassed to pissed did I get Darius meant me.

"I'm fine," I said. "At least, I think I am, considering Dray's experiment."

"Hide nothing from my father, Phoenix," Demitri urged. "Be completely honest with him. He needs to know everything."

"Sir?" I looked at the king.

~ ☾ ~

He raised a hand. "In private, you may address me as Darius," he said. "Despite your current state, you are still fundamentally human, thus unbound by the customs of our people. In public, 'your majesty' is usually appropriate."

"Darius," I said and he dipped his chin once. "I don't understand what Dray did-"

"Yes, he should have given you a choice."

"I don't see it that way." I shook my head. "Not anymore, at least. I'm pissed, don't get me wrong, but being able to walk among you is fascinating. It's not every day you get to discover a super-secret race."

"Phoenix," Demitri chided, staring at me.

"Right." I took a deep breath and let it out slowly. "What I'm trying to say is...Dray believes my transformation"—for the lack of a better word—"would be helpful."

"My youngest son can be impulsive when it comes to his work." Darius rested his cheek on the palm of his hand.

"He was wrong to drag Phoenix into this." Demitri said.

"I understand your concern." The king's gaze brimmed with empathy. "Believe me, I do. Especially given these uncertain times, but we cannot undo what has already been done. I must beg for your forgiveness, Phoenix."

"There's nothing to forgive." I fidgeted. "Who wouldn't want super strength and perfect eyesight?"

"But the hunger and the urges must be difficult for you."

The moment Darius said "urges," Demitri stiffened.

"It's a challenge, but I'm trying my best to control them." I touched Demitri's arm. I wanted to let him know, even if by touch alone, that I was alright. I hoped he got my message.

"Are you sure you're aware of what you're saying, my dear?" Darius raised his brows.

"I don't really know what I've gotten myself into." I doubted myself for a second. "But I'm willing to ride it out until the formula wears off."

I'd lied, for sure, but it was my best option. Freaking out was a complete waste of time. The way I see it, why not enjoy my stint as a Zhamvy? Not everyone could admit to having that experience. Oh, who was I kidding? A small part of me was still freaked.

~ ☾ ~

My words brought on a cordial smile from the king.

"I like her," he said, wagging a finger at me. "You're welcome in our kingdom, but for your safety, we'll continue the ruse my son started."

"With your hair and eye color, we cannot pass you off as royalty," Demitri said. "If anyone asks, you are a merchant's daughter from the northern clans."

My doubts fled. Enthusiasm flushed my skin with warmth. I'd never had to hide my identity before. I'd always been Phoenix McKay, daughter of a pharmaceuticals magnate. But in this kingdom, I'd have to be someone else, just like in spy movies. How exciting!

"Should I change my name?" I asked.

"I do not like how eager you sound about all this." He glanced at his father as if he didn't want to be associated with the laughing monarch. Only the slight upward curve of his lips said otherwise. Then he resettled his potent stare on me. "You can keep your name. The northern clans are less traditional than we are. In any case, you will stay in your room until Dray's experiment wears off."

All my thoughts of espionage and mystery flew out the window.

"But—"

"No excuses, Phoenix." Demitri cut me off. "I have no time to school you on our society's rules. My family is one thing, but others are less tolerant—"

"*Demitrius*," Darius warned.

"I have to attend class, and then Parliament." Demitri paused. "Lev will have to take you to your room."

"Alright, *geez*!" I said. I looked toward Darius.

"You've made the right choice, my dear." The gravity in Darius's gaze made him look more like a king in that moment than when Demitri and I had first entered the room. "Even I cannot protect you if something were to happen. We follow protocol written several millennia ago. Even if we fight for change, it doesn't come on swift wings."

~ ☾ ~

Chapter 10

Light

Despite how thin and uptight Lev looked, he sure knew how to effortlessly steer a struggling girl out of a throne room. We walked through both sets of heavy curtains like they were confetti rain. I hadn't even agreed to stay in my room the whole time yet when Lev arrived to take me away. I'd gone from accomplice to prisoner in five seconds. But I'd be damned if I'd let them handle me this way. I sneezed from the dust kicked up by the rustling drapes. Rubbing my nose, I decided I'd had enough of Lev's particular brand of escorting. I yanked my elbow out of his grasp the moment we entered the hall.

"Either you're very good at what you do, or you like pushing people around. I'm willing to bet on the latter," I said.

Lev studied his fingernails like he'd chipped his polish. He grimaced theatrically. "I like what I do. Not anyone can work as close to the king—hail the king—as I do."

"I think we started off on the wrong foot here. The last thing I want is to annoy the..." I gestured at him.

"Royal liaison."

Translation: pain in the ass, total pushover, lapdog. I lifted a fist and pretended to cough into it to hide my smirk. "Royal liaison. Right. Up in the north ..."

I didn't need to finish my sentence. Lev's nod said, *I understand. You country folk know nothing of the city.*

~ ☾ ~

Zhamvy or not, personal assistants all possessed the same self-important air.

"Forgive me, but you don't sound like you're from the north." He looked down his straight nose at me.

"Speech therapist." I gave him my best fake-sweet smile. I inched closer to him, and as expected, he leaned in. "Between you and me, my father sent me here to learn proper decorum. I was becoming a little heathen, if you know what I mean."

Lev clucked his tongue in fake sympathy and tapped the top of my head with his clipboard. It took every ounce of control I had not to snap his arm off. Some lines didn't need to be crossed. And maiming the royal liaison was one of them.

"I understand completely," he said. "So, what did you discuss in there?"

"Oh, the king—"

"Hail the king." He motioned for me to continue.

"He just wanted to welcome me to the kingdom and asked about my father." I pursed my lips.

He couldn't hide his disappointment.

"Oh, don't mind that. *Booooring*!" I pretended to giggle. "I like your suit, by the way."

He picked off invisible lint from his jacket sleeves.

"Hugo Boss?" I kept my voice airy.

"Armani." He proceeded to walk down the hall, straight with arrogance, as though he really had a rod rammed straight up his butt. "Come along. I have too much to do today to waste my time babysitting you."

Fluff self-important assistant's ego, check. Make a complete fool of myself, check. Resist incredible urge to snap said assistant's neck, check. I counted to ten silently then followed.

"Is the palace always this empty?" I asked, putting every bit of enthusiasm I didn't really feel into my question.

"Everyone's busy preparing for the Winter Solstice Festival. The queen—bless her beauty—has the Silent running around like crazy. I even have this meeting to attend just for assistants. I swear…they have so little respect for the King's assistant. Hail the king."

~ ☾ ~

My ears perked up at the mention of the festival. Demitri had commented on Dray's experiment coinciding with it. What could be so important about it? Why did Demitri worry about Dray's experiment overlapping with the festival? I puzzled over all the information I'd gathered so far and…nothing. Too many loose ends to make definitive connections. Lev mentioned the event so casually that it sounded like he expected for me to understand what he'd meant, so I gave him my best "Uh-huh."

"What about *you*, Lev? What are *your* responsibilities?" I asked, the need to get out from under Lev's supervision becoming my first priority.

"You wouldn't believe what I have to do on a daily basis around here."

"Try me," I urged.

"Well, not only do I prepare the schedule, but I also coordinate with other assistants to make sure communication runs smoothly between the Royals. It's a pain when the other assistants don't print out their schedules on time. Hundreds of years old and still incompetent."

"It must be so hard working with people not as good as you."

"If you only knew …"

Lev launched into a self-important narration about himself. If I knew personal assistants, and I did, he would be talking about himself and complaining about his work for a while. He wouldn't notice me gone until it was too late. And surely, fearing for his job security, he'd never rat me out for disappearing.

I let him round a corner before I rushed back to the throne room. I looked from left to right to make sure no one saw me enter through the curtains, then I parted them to one side and slipped through the gap. I took a quiet breath and pulled the second set of drapes aside an inch.

Demitri stood where I'd left him. His broad shoulders shook slightly, his large hands balled into tight fists, like he wanted to punch someone.

"I understand your concern, my son," Darius said.

"No, Father." Demitri lifted his chin. "What Dray did not

~ ☾ ~

only endangers Phoenix, it threatens our family's safety, too. The Traditionalists will never stand for what Phoenix has become. You know what will happen if they get their way."

I pressed a hand to my chest, preventing my heart's attempt to burrow its way out. How could the royal family be in danger? It didn't make any sense. At least to me it made no sense. If living with my father taught me one thing, it would have to be that people in power always had threats against them. But surely the Barinkoffs had people protecting them. What threat against the Barinkoff family could possibly agitate Demitri so much?

Darius lifted a frail hand. A few minutes ago, he'd looked strong, dignified, filled with regal presence. Now, he resembled a tired old man reaching the final season of his life. Dried husk replaced his smooth skin. How had he changed so quickly?

"That's where you come in, Demitri. Your presence at Parliament will lend support to the Reformists. You know I can no longer intervene with our party. But you, my son, can give them the support they need. But watch what you say. We have reached a precipice." Darius took one rasping breath, held it, and then exhaled slowly. "I have held this throne far too long. It has started to chafe."

Demitri dropped his gaze to the floor.

"Say what's on your mind, my son," Darius urged.

"I have absolute respect for the throne you sit upon, Father, but ..." Demitri met his father's gaze. "But what about what I want? It's been so long since I've seen the world outside these castle walls. I crave—"

"Remember your responsibility to your people, Demitrius," Darius cut off his son. "I understand the pressure you must be feeling. Believe me, I want to give you your freedom, but we are not so fortunate. I feel rather tired of late."

A part of me wanted to run out from my hiding place and shelter Demitri in my arms. That was why he had pointed at the stickers on my e-reader the night we met. For the first time since I decided to return to the throne room I felt like I shouldn't be listening in on something so personal about

Demitri. He was baring his soul because he thought he was alone with his father. Guilt ate at me a little. In front of his father another side to him emerged. He softened, voicing his concerns with care.

"Father," he said, "you cannot let go. Not now. Your people need your guidance to usher them into a new age."

Darius waved away his son's concern. He sat up and took another deep breath. This time, on the exhale, a change happened. In a blink, the frailty disappeared like a wilted flower returning to full bloom. His wrinkled flesh smoothened and showed off the silver crescents once more. I covered my mouth with both hands to keep from gasping. How was that possible? There was more to these Zhamvy than they'd led me to believe.

"I may be at the end of my life, but I haven't reached my deathbed yet," Darius said.

"I do not want to find myself burdened, father. Not yet." Demitri rolled his shoulders. He snapped a few cricks out of his neck and flexed his fingers.

The king chuckled.

"Your shoulders are strong enough for this kingdom's woes, my son. You've grown worthy of this seat. The Barinkoff Dynasty lives on in you and your brother."

Placing his hand on his chest, Demitri bowed.

A hand touched my elbow. I spun around and punched without thinking. Long fingers covered my fist. I narrowed my eyes in the gloom to make out rumpled blond curls, marble-like skin, and blue-sky eyes.

Luka still wore his uniform disheveled. Although, this time, he had the jacket over his shirt sans cravat. If Barinkoff handed out demerits for improper uniform, Luka would certainly get ten for his just-climbed-out-of-bed ensemble.

"You jerk. Don't sneak up on me like that," I whispered. "I thought you were Lev."

He brought his forefinger to his lips.

"What are you doing here?"

He answered with a mischievous wink.

Footsteps came from the other side of the curtain.

Luka seized my wrist and yanked me into a corner. He

covered my mouth with one hand and wrapped his other arm securely around my waist. He slowly backed us into the gloom. He didn't exactly exert any force. If I'd wanted, I could have stepped away from him. Except...I didn't. I was too captivated by the sweetness of honeysuckle surrounding him. It helped relax my tense muscles and soothe my impulse to shy away from the intimate contact.

Demitri glided through the first set of velvety fabric. He knew Lev was supposed to have escorted me to my room. If he saw me now, with Luka no less, who knew how he'd react? The scowl on his face spoke of the mother of all bad moods, and I would not be a willing recipient of it. I held my breath and felt Luka do the same.

"What are you doing here, *villyat*?" Luka whispered into my ear after Demitri cleared the second set of curtains.

I tried to speak, but his hand muffled my response. He laughed and let me go.

"Will you keep it down," I whispered, shocked by his reaction.

"You bring joy into my life, *villyat*. You really do," he said.

"Why do you keep calling me that word? What does it mean?"

"Translated into your language, *villyat* means little cat," he said, leveling those blue eyes at me. "You're too curious for your own good. Just like a little cat."

"So what?"

He inhaled then said, "You smell different."

"It's the scent of not showering for more than a day," I said, hoping to cover for my transmutated state. The prickle on the back of my neck said otherwise.

"Alright."

Surprise and confusion collided inside me. How could Luka accept what I'd said without feeling the need to ask more questions? If I were him, questions one after another would be leaving my lips right about now. Among all the Zhamvy I'd met, Luka acted casual, even playful. But my gut told me not to trust him. A pretty face like that hid lies behind it like a conman who lived on a smile.

"I need to follow Demitri," I said as I moved to the outer

set of curtains and pushed into the hall. Maybe Demitri was right. Maybe I should stay away from Luka.

I froze mid-step and Luka plowed into me from behind. I stumbled forward.

"Watch where you're going, will you?"

"But it felt nice bumping into you," he said. "You're so serious."

I faced him. "You confuse me."

"Good. Where are we going?"

"*We* aren't going anywhere. I'm going to follow Demitri to Parliament. *Alone.*"

"Why would you want to do that?"

"Something's up. He said the royal family is in danger. And if I'm the cause—" I stopped myself. I'd said too much. Luka's disarming nature had unhinged my jaw and made my tongue wag far too much.

"Oh, but he's not going to Parliament." He wiggled his eyebrows up and down.

"What?" I looked at him. "Darius just said Demitri needs to attend—"

"He will. But he needs to be somewhere else first. And since you're already here, I want to show you something."

Before I could ask him what he'd meant, Luka grabbed my hand and dragged me back to the throne room. I had no time to react or pull away.

"Luka, the king—"

"Hail the king!" he playfully interrupted.

"Why does everyone say 'hail the king' every time I mention Darius?"

"Tradition." He winked at me from over his shoulder. A grin stretched my lips.

"So, if I say king—"

"Hail the king!"

I tried again, "King?"

"Hail the king!"

"King."

"Hail the king!"

"K—"

"Stop it!"

~ ☾ ~

I laughed for the first time since I'd decided to invade Zhamvy central. It felt good. And it felt even better because Luka laughed with me. He strode through both curtains without hesitation, like the room belonged to him. Fabric engulfed me again. Panic didn't even have a chance to settle into my chest. Darius no longer sat on his throne.

Luka didn't spare the empty seat a glance and just kept moving, taking me with him. He parted another set of curtains.

Sudden blindness had me closing my eyes. I didn't know what happened. First, I stared at the throne, and then, light seared away the image. To say it hurt like crazy wouldn't come close to describing the actual feeling of burning eyeballs.

A cold hand clutched my arm.

"Keep still," Luka said. "Let your eyes adjust."

"What did you do?" I blinked to clear the spots. "I can't see!"

"Steady, little cat." The coolness of Luka's hand seeped into my bones. "Easy does it."

"Where's the light coming from?" I massaged my eyelids.

"You have to open your eyes to find out."

The humor in his tone, like he had played some cruel joke on me, raised my hackles, but curiosity won over annoyance. I tentatively opened my eyes. Vision still blurred, I blinked to focus. First shadows, then outlines, then buildings. I inhaled sharply.

We stood on a magnificent balcony, overlooking a medieval city. The buildings ranged from two to four stories tall. Nearest to where we stood were a group of elegant mansions of gray stone, shingled roofs, and sprawling gardens, all arranged in a semicircle. The next ripple consisted of a bustling marketplace with stalls and colorful flags flapping in the breeze. There, Zhamvy dressed in a mix of modern and medieval garments were gathered; some were buying stuff while others wandered from vendor to vendor. The last two layers had homes that decreased in grandeur. At the edges sat small huts built of straw. Their plots of land were divided into perfect squares, growing turquoise-colored crops. Definitely not corn or wheat.

~ ☾ ~

Speechless, I turned around and looked up. The palace stretched before me in white marble, the center of the ripples. Four tubular towers with blue spires completed its four corners. On top each spire hung blue and white flags of the Barinkoff coat of arms. A curtain wall connected each tower where armored Zhamvy patrolled. Another tall tower jutted upward from the center of the castle. On top of it, a pedestal supported a sphere of radiant white light. But where was the sky? All I saw was a weird, gray, close hanging cloud. It was almost oppressive the way it loomed high above us. I returned my gaze to Luka, who stared up at the sphere, his angelic features twisted into a grimace.

"What's wrong?" I asked.

"It's unnatural. But we need the light to see and survive," he said.

"Like a big lamppost."

"Something *like* that."

Then what he said clicked.

"We're underground!"

"We're within the Caucasus Mountains. The whole range is hollowed out."

I gaped. They lived inside a freaking mountain range! But how could they remain hidden from the world? What about radar? Satellite imagery? Surely, the sophisticated Russian government would have discovered this kingdom of Zhamvy long ago. But another thought overpowered the more practical ones.

"That's why I can't get any service." I fished out my phone from my skirt pocket and held it up. No bars. Not with the thick walls of a mountain blocking the satellite's feed. I looked to the sky—well, the *ceiling*—again and a shiver ran up my spine. "Aren't you afraid of it crumbling down?"

Luka laughed at me again. It became a budding routine between us. He'd say something intelligent, I'd ask something stupid, he'd snicker, and I'd want to punch him. His handsome face wasn't enough to distract me from his condescension.

"You know," I said, pocketing my phone, "I'm getting tired of you laughing at me all the time."

~ ☾ ~

"You're too adorable. The others"—he gestured at the buildings below—"are so boring. You're the first one to catch my interest in years."

"I don't think that's a good thing. I really, *really* don't."

"Of course it is, Phoenix."

I felt a slight blush warm my neck and creep into my cheeks. Luka had a certain magnetism to him I couldn't quite resist despite the attitude problem. He pulled me in like gravity, and I wasn't quite sure if I wanted to pull away. Then Demitri's confession to his father that he wanted to see the world anchored me. I glanced at the underground city again. If this were all I saw day in and day out, I would want to run away too.

"Is something the matter?" He touched my forehead. "You look flushed."

I stumbled away from him. The edge of the balcony bumped into my lower back, and I hissed from the sudden pain. I'd let my guard down too long.

"Careful." Luka gathered me close. "I wouldn't want you to fall over."

"I—I've got to go."

"You are not seriously considering following Demitri around all day, are you?"

I was seriously considering getting away from Luka. That was what I was considering.

"Then bring me to Dray's lab. I'm sure you know where *that* is," I said.

"I can take you there. But don't you want to know more about us and how we live?"

His question made me think. My curiosity sparked. Of course I wanted to know more. When did I ever not want to know more? I made a quick list of the pros and cons.

Pro: More answers awaited me if I said yes.

Con: I risked exposing myself.

Pro: I would learn more about the Zhamvy than Demitri would ever let me know.

Con: I'd be with Luka.

Pro: I'd be with Luka.

Chapter 11

Empty

Luka led me out of the palace through a back entrance. I had to widen my steps to keep up with his ground-eating strides. Not once did we run into anyone as we made our way through a long tunnel lit by lanterns on the walls. Without them, the tunnel would be pitch black and difficult to navigate, even with my newly enhanced Zhamvy vision. The musty smell of the damp walls caused me to wrinkle my nose. I paused.

"Little cat?" Luka said, halting to study me.

"Don't you think it's odd that we haven't passed anyone since we'd left the balcony? Where is everyone?" I asked.

"The market, probably. And Parliament has started. There's not that many of us around. And many of the servants are busy preparing for the Festival."

I hated the dismissive way he spoke.

"Then where are you taking me?"

"Barinkoff."

"What?" My brows rose in shock. "But I'm not supposed to go there."

Images of my classmates walking around and my potential reaction to the way they smelled pinged in my head. Was it really like being in front of an all-you-can-eat buffet? I swallowed. The last thing I wanted was to think of Preya as a double cheeseburger.

"That's what makes it fun." He inched closer, fire behind his clear eyes.

~ ☾ ~

"No, Luka, you don't understand. I can't be among the Day Students right now." The thought of human flesh actually made me salivate a little. I grimaced and pushed down the primal instincts that crawled up from deep inside me.

"It's night up top. No Day Students will be on campus. I have a class to attend, which I'm already late for." Luka frowned. He ran his fingers through his curls, a worried expression marring his face. "After it's over, I'll take you to the market."

Unimaginable relief flooded my insides, followed by a brand new kind of eagerness—one that made my fingers tingle. He was taking me to a class. I would get to sit in a classroom filled with Night Students. Considering how Demitri wanted to keep me locked up in my room, I couldn't help feeling giddy at Luka giving me a chance to attend class with him. Were the Night Students so different from those who came to school during the day? I gave him a mischievous smile.

"Lead on," I said.

"That's more like it." He returned my smile with a devastating one. I had to blink several times to break its spell.

In minutes, we reached the end of the tunnel. A wall lamp illuminated closed elevator doors. Luka fished out a key card from his jacket and slipped it into a slot. Then he quickly punched in a code on a number pad and the doors parted.

With a bow and a flourish, Luka motioned for me to enter the elevator car. I gave him a small curtsey before stepping in. He joined me and pressed the only button, which I assumed led up to the surface. A swift tug and the cab rose at a speed that made my stomach flip.

"How deep underground are we?" I asked, staring at my reflection on the stainless steel paneling. I still felt disconnected from the girl I was seeing, like I was seeing someone else. She looked too pretty, too perfect...

"A hundred stories, give or take." He leaned his back on one side of the elevator and crossed his arms in front of his chest.

He stared at a point beyond where I stood in silent contemplation. Such a faraway look for such a small space. I couldn't stand it. Warmth blossomed in my chest. It begged me to peel away the layers Luka had until I met the real Zhamvy underneath. He may smile, he may joke, but deep down, he drowned in a sorrow I understood on some level. A level I hardly visited in fear of breaking down and being unable to function on a daily basis. What could have caused Luka to be so unhappy? What could have happened in his life that pushed him to shut himself away? Demitri played the emotionless robot, but something told me Luka held more behind his smile than Demitri ever did beneath his expressionless mask.

"What are you thinking about?"

"Was I thinking?" He seemed to have forgotten that he had company. He blinked several times before his eyes focused on me.

"Well, you were *something*," I said.

Smooth as a limo, the elevator slowed to a stop. My ears popped at the sudden pressure change. With a ding, the doors opened into a clearing powdered by fresh snow. The waning moon cast the pine trees and benches in a silvery light—a barren winter paradise waiting for spring. Haunting, and yet, so familiar.

I stepped out of the cab.

"Are we in the Solar—?" The question died on my lips as I spun around and looked up. We'd exited the bell tower. Luka came to my side as the elevator doors shut.

"Come," he said, taking my hand. I was too dumbfounded to blush at the contact. "I'm late enough as it is."

I let him pull me away; my gaze still locked on the tower that I had thought held nothing but the bell. The genius of it blew my mind. Nobody ever visited this section of Barinkoff. Campus had far more interesting places for students to hang out in. To think the entrance to the Zhamvy kingdom had been hidden in plain sight. No one would ever suspect the marble structure with its pointed steeple and plain-faced clock as anything other than a tower.

After my surprise wore off, I focused on where we were headed. It felt strange to be following someone along halls I knew by heart. Barinkoff wore a darker dress at night.

~ ☾ ~

Shadows danced around the flickering sconces. I squeezed Luka's hand to get his attention.

"What class are we attending tonight?"

"Sociology 102," Luka answered over his shoulder. I choked down a laugh.

"Learning about humans, I suppose?"

He stopped and stared at me. The orange light gave his hair copper highlights. As seconds ticked by, his silence grew too loud for comfort. My jaw dropped.

"You're serious?"

"Don't sound so surprised."

He winced, so I tried for a more curious tone. "You're serious?"

"Okay, now you're just mocking me."

"I'm not." I disguised a giggle as a cough.

"Right." He smiled, all teeth. Totally predatory. "Oh, a small request?"

"Name it."

"We're sneaking into this class, so if you can just observe and not say anything, that would be great."

"I can't make any promises."

I entered the classroom we stood outside of and heard him curse. I tried not to smile as I chose a seat at the top row of the amphitheater. Luka settled in beside me, slouching and entwining his fingers over his torso.

"What sets us apart from humans?" A wizen yet still handsome Zhamvy wearing barrister's robes asked as he stood on the teacher's platform, his voice like gravel rubbing together. "This is the question on our minds this semester. We ponder its truths and its falsehoods to better understand ourselves." He paused to scan the room.

My gaze surfed through the sea of twenty or so students. Disappointment clawed at my ribcage. Nothing about the class seemed any different from those held during the day. Were Zhamvy just like humans? Did they live their lives the way we did?

Black-haired students composed a majority of the class. A small group had brown hair like mine. They sat together to the side. Luka was the only blonde. Interesting. I had trouble identifying who smelled like what since they sat too far away. Then my eyes landed on Demitri's unmistakable blue-black hair held by a ribbon.

My heart revved up, sending scalding blood to my cheeks.

To his left sat a petite Zhamvy with a cascade of midnight locks held in place by a silver circlet. Calixta.

A pinch of annoyance came out of nowhere at the sight of them sitting together. I focused on Demitri. The room's dim lighting had shadows playing over his coat. Beneath all the layers of fabric of his uniform was the bite mark that connected us. If I held my breath, I could almost distinguish his heartbeat from the rest of those in the room.

A student raised his hand and recited the differences between the Zhamvy and humans. It was Eli. I was sure of it now. I recognized his voice as he listed what I already knew about them. They healed. They had preternatural speed. Blah, blah, blah. I had a feeling the professor wanted a more philosophical answer. I wasn't worried about him recognizing me. If he were under the Silence, he wouldn't be able to talk to anyone about me.

I leaned toward Luka and whispered, "I thought Demitri was at Parliament."

"Sociology 102 is a required subject." Luka followed my gaze down the rows of seats. "You can't miss it, or else you fail. And for a subject that's only a pass or fail, being absent is a big mistake. Why do you think we're here instead of exploring the marketplace?"

I couldn't take my eyes off of Demitri's broad shoulders. Calixta reached out and rubbed his arm. He stiffened slightly, as did I, but made no attempt to move away. She leaned in and he bent down as she whispered something into his ear. From her profile, I saw half her flirtatious smile. So different from the murderous intent she'd shown me the first time we'd met. Demitri shrugged without looking her way.

A low growl vibrated inside my chest. My fingers curled, scratching grooves on the desk's wooden surface as I made a fist. Tremors reverberated all over my body, so strong I thought my chair would collapse underneath me. I couldn't understand why I felt a sudden urge to rip off the hand

~ ☾ ~

resting on Demitri's arm. It was an irrational rage. Demitri could sit with anyone he wanted. Who was I to stop him?

A cold hand wrapped around my fist.

"Phoenix," Luka whispered. "You look like you're about to pounce. Calm down."

"Huh?" I turned to him to discover only a few inches separated our lips. I leaned back.

"It's okay." He squeezed my fist. "Relax."

I blinked several times before coherent thoughts formed in my head. Luka regarded me through heavy lidded eyes.

"Why's Calixta sitting beside Demitri?" I finally had enough sense to ask calmly.

"She's his fiancée."

The news sunk like a concrete block in my stomach.

"He's engaged?"

"More like arranged, but yes."

Somehow, knowing his engagement had been arranged didn't make me feel better. That was why he'd wanted me to control my urges around him. He was already taken. It certainly explained Calixta's reaction when Dray let it slip that Demitri had driven me back to the dorms that first night. I'd be up in arms if someone threatened my relationship too.

Calixta raised her hand and said, "Professor, may I interject?"

Her voice sounded pleasant; far from the heat she'd shown when she threatened to end my life. The teacher nodded at her.

"You may, Ms. Oslov."

"Eli has a point when listing our differences from humans," she began, straightening in her seat. "We are stronger, faster, and we live longer, which only befits the hunter of prey as smart and as formidable as the humans. But those are only superficial differences."

"Continue," the professor urged.

I sat on the edge of my seat, intrigued.

"I believe we are not that different from humans," Calixta continued. "We gossip. We are social. We like material things. We make connections, friendships. We have families. We love."

~ ☾ ~

She glanced at Demitri as she said the last item on the list. My vision narrowed. I saw nothing but red. What little control I had crashed and burned. My lips moved of their own volition before I could think of stopping myself.

"I disagree," I said, not missing a beat as all heads swiveled to face me. I didn't even care that Eli looked as if his eyes would roll out of his head the moment he recognized me. "Even if feeding on flesh is forbidden, it doesn't remove the fact that we are natural predators." We? What did I mean by "we"? Still, I went with it. "We prey on sentient beings with—as you said—feelings and personal connections. Doesn't that make us beneath them?"

Calixta's expression was priceless. Her left eyebrow lifted so far up that her circlet shifted. Her pouty lips parted in shock. The look on Demitri's face came in at a high second. His stunned disbelief at my presence in his class broke his impeccable emotionless façade. His gaze flicked toward Luka, and in that second, I knew the face of someone truly wishing someone bodily harm.

"And who are you?" the professor asked, breaking the tension mounting between the empty rows separating Luka and myself from Demitri and Calixta.

Before I could speak, Luka said, "She's new."

"May I address her claims?" Calixta turned to the professor.

The old Zhamvy gestured his assent by flicking his hand at her.

"I understand where our new *classmate* is coming from." She shot a pointed stare my way. "But, like she said, we are forbidden to consume flesh. Humans must consider themselves lucky. They have their freedom. That is the fundamental difference between humans and Zhamvy. We must deprive ourselves of human flesh because we have been forbidden, while they are free to live their lives without any restrictions other than the laws that govern them. Imagine what would happen if we were allowed to consume their flesh? Humans would be nothing more than cattle to us."

A murmur of agreement came from the other students.

Some nodded while others whispered to one another. The hunger that entered Eli's eyes was unmistakable, but I refused to show fear. I shot up from my seat and pointed at Calixta.

"So you're saying you want to eat human flesh again, is that it? You want to hunt, to consume flesh." My voice quavered. "That's unforgivable!"

With a gotcha smile, Calixta said, "Don't you?"

Demitri shot me a keep-quiet-if-you-know-what's-good-for-you look.

"Not the point," I continued, ignoring his warning.

"Then what point are you trying to make?" Calixta waited, and so did the rest of the class.

Demitri scowled and faced forward.

"Phoenix!" Luka warned.

"You're saying humans are lucky?" I scrambled for my next words, totally losing my cool. "What's so lucky about getting sick and having none of the doctors know how to make you better? What's so lucky about wasting away day after day, month after month, and only finding relief in death?"

Luka had his hand wrapped around my arm before I could say anything else. In one tug, he steered me out of the classroom.

"What happened to just observing?" He growled at me.

"I couldn't help myself," I said lamely, allowing Luka to sweep me onwards. To struggle seemed futile. Now that I was outside the classroom, the fight left me. "Calixta started speaking and something in me snapped. I can't stand her! I swear I can't."

"And what was with that speech?"

"I got carried away." I shrugged.

"And then some."

"I was just citing an example."

"Why am I finding that hard to believe?"

My eyes stayed glued to the floor, as we kept moving toward the Solar Garden. I wasn't about to spill my guts to someone I barely knew, especially when it involved my mother. I really didn't know where my tirade came from. My

~ ☾ ~

rebuttal to Calixta's argument spilled out and it was too late to rein it in.

"You can believe whatever you want," I whispered.

"We're going back to the palace," he said.

"What about your class?" Guilt punched my gut, but I couldn't face Demitri right now. Remembering the way he scowled at me after I ignored his warning broke my heart a little. He was just trying to save me from myself, like he always did, and I spat at the face of it.

"I've made my appearance." Luka forced a grin. "That's more than enough for today."

"Well, look at you, Mr. Model Student." Something vibrated in my pocket. "Luka, one sec." I fished out my phone. Preya's number flashed on the screen. Urgh! What now?

"Who is it?" Luka peered at the glowing screen in the dim light of the hallway.

"My roommate." I groaned. I tapped the screen and held the receiver close to my ear. "This isn't a very good time."

"Where are you?" Preya's stern voice came clearly from the other end, as if she stood right in front of me. "When I went back to the clinic to get you, you weren't there. And then you didn't come back to the dorms that night. I was worried sick, so I went to Headmaster Kiev for answers. He said you're on some sort of retreat?"

From the way she spoke, I could hear her disbelief. I scrambled for the appropriate lie. A retreat? That was what Demitri thought was "handling it"? I wanted to smack him.

"Yeah, something *like* that," I said.

"Why?"

"Headmaster Kiev thought it would do me some good to get away."

"I don't understand."

My heart skipped in panic. Preya wasn't buying my story. Luka's brows came together as he watched me.

"Like I said, now's not a good time. If they catch me on my phone, they'll take it away." I ended the call and tapped the off switch. Guilt immediately replaced my panic. I hated lying to Preya, but it was for her own good. She didn't need to start

~ ☾ ~

investigating where I really was. And if I knew her, her experiments would hold her attention long enough that she'll forget about me for a while.

"You're not going to say 'it's complicated' are you?" asked Luka.

"Ha!" I laughed bitterly. "I wish."

Chapter 12

Status

Running along endless white walls and tons of navy curtains didn't strike me as fun. It sucked the adventurous mood out of me faster than a Sex Ed lecture on STDs. I had no idea sneaking into the palace could be so tedious. At my impulsive decision to follow Luka, I expected exotic locations, a bounty of information, secrets revealed. Instead, I made a fool of myself in his class and ended up playing hide and seek with palace guards afterwards. Well, the guards didn't exactly know we hid from them. Every time we ran into someone, Luka would drag me behind a curtain into a secret alcove, pressing me back until I had my spine pressed against a wall. Luka would face me with his hands splayed on either side of my head. Was he thinking he was "protecting me" from the guards? Yeah, right.

I wanted to scream my annoyance at him for constantly invading my personal space, but being sandwiched between a wall and Luka's long, sinewy body turned into a practice of ultimate patience. I was bathed in the scent of honeysuckle clinging to his skin—the scent of the cusp of spring and summer.

Easy on the eyes, Luka's handsomeness crumbled the logical side of my brain. Michelangelo's David couldn't compete with Luka. With Dray's formula still flowing through my veins, let's just say I wasn't thinking with my head. And even if I could behave myself because of the Pill, it didn't mean I didn't feel hot and bothered by standing so close to him. Just a little tilt of my head and a shift of weight to my toes was all I needed to claim those slightly parted lips. Tempted. Sorely tempted. God, too tempted. Was this what Demitri meant about the urges zooming through my body? But, if I bit Demitri and we had this strange physical connection, why was I feeling attraction for Luka as well? Demitri and I didn't have a set definition for our relationship (or lack thereof), but it didn't seem right to feel all flushed so close to Luka either.

I licked my lips.

"What is it, little cat?" Luka asked, curiosity in his enticing eyes.

I cringed. The answer to his question had potentially dangerous and totally delicious consequences. Why did he have to notice me now?

"Are you in pain?" he asked, pressing me. A blond curl fell across his forehead.

Without thinking, I reached out. My index and middle finger curled around the spiral of sunshine—soft as mink fur and smooth as baby oil. I shuddered. Instantly embarrassed by the sudden heat pooling in my gut, I dropped my hand.

"You're dangerous," he said.

"In more ways than one," I said. "Why are there so many of these anyway?" I glanced up and to the side to indicate the enclosure we hid in.

He brought his lips closer to mine and whispered, "Let's just say spying and gossip are a big part of what entertains us here."

I needed…no, *wanted* fresh air. Like yesterday.

"It figures."

"And you're not afraid?" He raised an eyebrow that I suddenly wanted to trace with the tip of my tongue.

Oh, for the love of— "Should I be?"

For an answer, Luka leaned against his right hand while the forefinger of his left drew a line from my temple to my cheek, down my neck, and stopped at the hollow of my collarbone. I gasped. Delicious shivers washed over my body. Any lower and he'd touch—

~ ☾ ~

"I think ..." I licked my lips and tasted salt. "Yes. Umm, yes. I should be afraid. Very, very afraid."

With all my might, I suppressed the urge to push him and stumble out of the alcove. His close proximity tortured my heightened senses. Too much to take in all at once. The heat in the tiny space between us—even with his cooler touch—threatened to cause spontaneous combustion if he continued to touch me the way he did.

Just when I'd reached my limit, Luka pulled me out of our hiding spot and away from the palace. I forgot my wobbly legs when we stepped outside, wonder replacing my frustration. The outer courtyard stretched two soccer fields wide and overflowed with mayhem. Women in French maid uniforms and men in butler's suits—all with gray hair and eyes—scurried about. Some carried linens. Others were constructing a platform. And a group pulled long tables together. Guards in black breastplates helped out, too. Lev wasn't kidding when he said the queen had everyone running around like mad. All the movement made me dizzy.

"Luka?" I said.

He pulled me away from the courtyard without responding, so I yanked back, not giving him time to brace himself. The momentum of my pull caused his footing to fail. He hovered in the air a second before landing on the gravel with a loud *crunch*.

No matter how handsome he was, even he couldn't pull off the fallen-and-startled expression on his face. He gaped like a five-year-old. His pants were gray with gravel dust, his jacket had slipped off one shoulder, and his curls were now a wild halo. Laughter tickled my stomach and quickly bubbled up my throat. I couldn't help myself. The stitch on my side caused me to hug myself. He frowned and let go of my wrist.

"I didn't mean to pull so hard. You just wouldn't listen to me." Shame blossomed in my chest when I reached out to him.

He took my hand, but ended up wrenching me down instead of me pulling him up. I crashed to my knees. Hard. The gravel *crunched*. Every stone cut into my skin like razorblades despite my thick skirt and stockings. My giggles died. I rolled to my side and curled into a fetal position,

squeezing my eyes shut tightly. Pain pulsed as if a mad drummer used baseball bats to play a beat on my knees. Clamping down on my teeth to keep from crying out, I waited for Luka's laughter or insult. I certainly deserved it. But to my surprise, nothing came.

I peeked out of one eye. Luka leaned on his hands, his expression guarded. I opened both my eyes and stared at him in wonder. In a swift move, he shifted to his hands and knees and came closer like a big cat on the prowl. In my attempt to stretch my legs, I winced. Instant pain sent electric currents up my thighs. Luka stopped his advance for a second. Then he touched my ankle and slowly ran his hand up my leg, taking the edge of my skirt with him. As I pulled my leg away, he grabbed my calf and kept me still. The untamed spark in his eyes froze me in place more than his cold, restraining hand did. Sensing no further resistance from me, his hand continued its ascent up my leg until the edge of my skirt crested the hill of my knees. I groaned.

"Pain?" Luka asked.

"My stockings are ripped," I said.

He returned his gaze to my exposed knees. A trickle of blood ran down my right leg. He bent his head, took a whiff, and wrinkled his nose. He pulled out a handkerchief from his jacket pocket and pressed it on my wound. I flinched.

"You're stronger," he said.

I avoided his stare.

"What happened to you, Phoenix?" He removed the cloth and studied my now healed knee.

"Nothing."

Not asking for further explanation, Luka stood up and dusted off his pants. He straightened his jacket and ran his hands through his hair—the curls bounced into place as if nothing had ruffled them.

He stretched his hand out to me and warned, "Don't pull me down again or you'll get more than a bleeding knee."

"Wasn't planning on it," I said.

In one heave, Luka pulled me up and managed to wrap his arms around me. I gasped at the shock of suddenly being in his cool embrace.

~ ☾ ~

"I apologize for hurting you," he whispered into my ear.

"Luka?" I asked after a shudder ran through me.

"Yes?"

"Do Zhamvy have no respect for personal space?"

"Only in the presence of a beautiful woman."

"Ugh!" I gathered the pieces of myself that had fallen apart the moment our bodies touched. "That's so cheesy. If you don't let me go this instant—"

"Prince!" someone behind us called.

My whole body went rigid. My first thought went to Demitri, that he'd followed us. But the familiar rush I felt every time he was near didn't manifest itself. I was just about to breathe a sigh of relief when Luka took my hand and led me the rest of the way through the courtyard.

"Come on," he said.

After we'd left the courtyard, and with no sign of pursuit, Luka slowed down and finally gave in to giving me a quick lesson on the Zhamvy caste system. I'd like to think my personal charm had a hand in the lesson, but judging from the knot on his brow, he just wanted to shut me up. Sometimes, whining is more effective than torture. So, after my first dozen questions, Luka sighed and began the lecture.

When he paused for breath, I interrupted. "Let me see if I've got it so far. The Royals are at the top. They have black hair and eyes like Demitri. The Merks—or merchants—are the next level with varying shades of brown hair and eyes. And both castes can interact without extreme prejudice, hence the mix of students in your class. But what about you?"

He shook his head. A shadow of the sadness he'd shown in the elevator flitted across his features before he smiled it away.

"I'm different," he said.

I didn't want to leave it at that, but he had already launched into the next half of his explanation.

"Now, the Bogatyr, the guards in black armor," Luka said, gesturing to a group of them passing us, "come from a special class of Merks bred for the job of security."

"Like Spartans."

"The Spartans got the idea from us." He winked. "The

Bogatyr train under the harshest conditions to weed out the weak from the strong. Once you are born a Bogatyr, you are a soldier, no questions, no exceptions."

"What happens if you don't want to be a Bogatyr?"

"You are killed. Having no use in this society isn't tolerated."

"That's harsh."

"You don't know half of it."

I glanced at him and caught the tail end of a bitter smile. I wondered what the expression meant. The guy had issues. I kicked a pebble and watched it bounce away, continuing to listen to the calm cadence of his voice.

"So, if having no use isn't tolerated, what do you do?" I gave Luka a sidelong glance and caught the stiffening of his shoulders. "I get that you're a student, but Demitri is a student and a prince as well. That he needs to attend Parliament. Not that I don't like hanging out with you, but don't you have something else you need to do besides escort me?"

"At the lowest level are the Serfs—the farmers and The Silent, characterized by their gray hair and eyes," he said.

"Oh, so that's how it's going to be, huh?" I stopped and faced him. "You get to pick which questions to answer, is that it?"

Luka paused, searched the dark ceiling for something before his gaze landed back on me. "Phoenix, some questions have more interesting answers than others."

"Don't think you're getting away that easily."

He smiled and continued walking. "I would be disappointed if I did."

Before I could ask my next question when I'd caught up with him, Luka answered it as if he'd read my mind. "The Silent are Serfs who want to serve the Royals. With the privilege of serving comes the vow of silence. Whatever they hear or see, they can't share with anyone."

My eyebrows rose. "What if—"

"They're put to death along with their family and their family's family."

I let out a low whistle. "Lots of killing happening around here."

~ ☾ ~

"The vow was only broken once," he said, ignoring my quip. A twinge of sorrow colored his tone. "Six centuries ago. It was with good intensions, but because of the law, the one who broke the Silence sacrificed his entire family. We lost fifty that day."

The misery contorting his face broke my heart. In a society so small and isolated, fifty was too many. I'd only read about that kind of cruelty. Sure, wars still raged around the world. Men still killed each other because of their misguided beliefs, but to sacrifice an entire family because of a broken rule bordered on tyrannical. I understood the need to set an example, to punish a wrong doing, but the Zhamvy took things to a level the Geneva Convention wouldn't approve off.

Luka stopped walking and looked up again. He seemed to like doing that a lot, so I followed his line of sight, but saw only the gloom of the ceiling of a hollowed out mountain. My gaze landed on his face instead, pain apparent in its hard lines. We stood silent, until I impulsively touched his arm. Those eyes—the color of the sky—met mine. They glistened with unshed tears. If I'd ever felt like comforting someone, Luka certainly deserved it in that moment. His stillness, the secrets he kept inside, called to something inside me I thought I'd lost when my mother had died. Compassion coursed through me, so strong, so encompassing, that I wanted to wrap him up in it until his carefree smile returned. On the other hand, Demitri, that cold icebox of a guy, had never done anything to deserve compassion. Bossy, that was what he was.

"You shouldn't feel any pity for me," Luka said.

"I don't pity you," I explained. "I *feel* for you."

"Me?"

"I know how it is to feel so sad that there's nothing left but echoing emptiness."

"Let's go," he said, leaving me bewildered and a little hurt.

I watched him weave through the crowded market.

"Come, little cat," Luka beckoned.

I beat my confusion into submission and hurried to his side. He pointed out several stalls. Some sold jewelry—silver bangles and hoop earrings and rings—while others sold

~ ☾ ~

clothes and household items. And a multitude of produce stands offered fruits and vegetables. Within minutes, he held a basket with a few odd mushrooms inside: electric blue with ivory spots, a brown variety the size of my fist, and orange ones so flat I needed to look twice to make sure I stared at mushrooms.

"Those can't be mushrooms, can they?" I asked.

Luka paid the woman selling the funky-colored vegetables with a coin then said, "Genetically engineered. They mimic many of the nutrients found in human flesh. Plus, they contain more protein than average mushrooms."

"Did you just use gold to pay her?"

He fished out a few more from his pocket and showed them to me. They had the Barinkoff crest stamped on one side and the motto on the other.

"We still use gold and the barter system here," he explained. "Simpler that way. But we do have human currency on hand for transactions made outside the kingdom, which we use trusted individuals to conduct."

"Like the headmaster," I said.

Luka nodded. "Among many."

I followed him as he moved away from the stall. "So, where next?"

"I want you to taste kikaron."

Luka's excitement infected every part of me like a fast acting virus. He managed to bring down my guard, crumbling my walls to dust. Hanging out with him was as easy as breathing. No complications, no expectations, just wholesome fun. He didn't hesitate to show me the world he lived in, unlike Demitri, who seemed hell-bent on keeping secrets.

The smells intermingled to the point where I couldn't distinguish between the Zhamvy and the environment I was in. Just as I'd identified roses, jasmine would wipe them away. Soil overpowered wood. Honey mixed with cotton. Pumpkin and dirt. Lemons and leather. My nose went on overdrive. So this was what being a dog must feel like. Ugh!

"Hey, Luka," I called out to him.

He stopped, and we became the only two standing still as a

stream of Zhamvy glided past us. His eyes met mine and held.

Up close in such a casual environment, the Zhamvy seemed so human. They wore different styles of clothing. Several men wore tunics and breeches. Many women wore skirts and blouses. Others preferred jeans and T-shirts like they'd stepped out of any mall in the US. I'd never seen so many beautiful people in one place. Zhamvy City, Luka had told me, had more attractive people per square feet than Brazil. How was it possible for all of them to look photo-shoot stunning? Gah! Too much beauty. Too much pretty. And Luka was the worst of them.

I felt a blush creep across my face. "Uh, I was just wondering…I haven't seen any children around. Are they in school, too?"

Luka looked away, a tic beginning along his jaw line. "We've had a slew of miscarriages lately."

First shock, then sadness. "I'm sorry. I shouldn't have asked."

"Don't worry about it."

I dropped the topic and moved on. "It's like the past and the present commingling here."

Luka smiled. The corners of his eyes bore the ghosts of laugh lines. "The older Zhamvy prefer to wear clothing from the era in which they were born, while the younger ones like to play dress up more. I honestly don't understand the need to wear what you call *jeans*, but there are those among the Merks and Serfs that enjoy them. Adopting the English language came as a fluke, though."

"What do you mean?"

"The queen—bless her beauty—loves Shakespeare's plays. She had many of the Royals perform them, sparking a trend that changed the way we speak. The old tongue is still part of who we are, but I must admit, English is easier."

"So what's your rank?" I asked out of left field. "If you managed to make Demitri—the crown prince—kneel before you, what does that make you? What's higher than a prince?"

"Has anyone told you you're too smart for your own good?"

"None that lived long enough to blab about it."

~ ☾ ~

The window display of the deli Luka had led me to caught my attention. Large squares of flesh hung from hooks. I swallowed a gag.

"I thought you can't eat flesh."

"Human flesh is forbidden." He pointed at the hanging squares. "That's pig flesh, a close substitute. The Royals touch none of it because they believe it's beneath them. They settle for *yusha*—"

"Which is synthetic."

"You know more than you let on."

I snorted. "Believe me, not as much as I'd want to."

Luka gestured for me to enter the shop and followed me in. The smell of something fried wafted at me as we crossed the threshold. Reminded of fast food, I faced the glass counter. Curly, puffed, and fleshy things were piled into high mounds on several trays.

Luka asked for a sample from the elderly woman with a red bandana covering her brown hair. She smiled graciously and handed him a plate with several pieces of the puffy things. She said something in their language to Luka, and he glanced at me. His reply made her giggle like a schoolgirl.

"What did you tell her?" I narrowed my eyes at him as the woman went to help another customer.

"That you're beautiful."

I smacked his arm, unable to hide the blush that burned my cheeks.

"Here, taste this." He picked up one of the puffs.

Unafraid, I opened my mouth and allowed him to drop the piece inside. A dry, rough texture tickled my tongue. I chewed experimentally and fell in love with its crispness. It tasted like air and salt and something I couldn't quite place. Potato chips? I chewed some more. Close, but no dice. Definitely different, but not bad.

I covered my mouth and asked, "What is it?"

"Kikaron. It's what happens to pig's flesh when you dry it and fry it." He popped one into his mouth and chewed merrily. "It tastes the best plain with a little vinegar, but you can get it in other flavors, too."

I shared Luka's smile; however, before I could swallow, the

~ ☾ ~

deli around me skewed and swirled. I grabbed the counter to stay upright as the sudden wave of nausea threatened to topple me. I pressed my other hand tightly over my lips, trying not to spit out the kikaron. My stomach twisted sharply. Bile came up my throat. Gagging and coughing, I doubled over, eyes closed. A hand on my back attempted to ease my wracking convulses, but the contents of my stomach kept coming up.

"Phoenix!"

Luka's panic-stricken voice had me opening my eyes. A pool of blood spread across the tiled floor. Its spatter covered part of the glass counter I held on to. My corset and skirt was damp with it, too.

Everything seemed to be in motion at once. The woman behind the counter screamed. Customers ran out of the deli. Zhamvy on the streets gathered and pointed, whispering to each other with horror stricken expressions.

"Phoenix! Are you okay?" Luka had one hand on my back and the other hovered nearby, ready for anything. The basket he had brought with us lay on the floor, discarded and soaked with blood.

My world titled to a sickening angle again. I shut my eyes as another stream of blood rushed up my throat and out my mouth.

"Dray—"

"What?" Luka bent over me.

"Dray's lab." Cold sweat dotted my forehead. I grabbed his arm. "Take me there."

Chapter 13

Answers

Cold.

I lay in a shadowy place, on my back, unable to move. The chill seeped into my bones. Heavy arms, numb legs. In the distance, someone called my name. Mom? Every breath rattled my lungs. My chest labored to rise. It would be simple to stop breathing all together. Fatigue clung to me like a second skin. My insides had turned to ice. Only a matter of time, and I'd see her again. I'd listen to her laugh again.

Smell.

The sweetness of honeysuckle filled my lungs. My nostrils flared a little, greedily inhaling more. The icy air faded except for a spot on my right hand. Someone called my name—soft, melodic, but not deep enough for the one I wanted to hear. Nevertheless, I let the sound take me away from the frozen, dark numbness.

"Luka," I said and breathed more of his honeysuckle scent.

"How did you know, little cat?" he asked.

"We were supposed to have a picnic, right? Well, that's not happening now."

The breath of a gentle, hitching laugh touched my cheek. I turned to face its source and opened my eyes. Luka sat by my bed with his face close to mine, lips quirked into a grin. Dark shadows under his eyes made their blue so startling.

I couldn't lift my arms. I couldn't even wiggle my toes, but I still felt them attached to my body. And Luka gripped my

~ ☾ ~

fingers like a lifeline. At least that meant I hadn't ended up paralyzed. Where had my super strength gone? And all that blood? I shuddered as the memory of the deli came back to me.

"How do you feel?" someone behind Luka asked.

"Like hell froze over." I tore my gaze from Luka and settled it on Dray. He held a silver clipboard.

"What've you done to me, Dray?" I aimed for menacing tiger, but only managed irritated kitty. Dray smiled compassionately at my attempt, which aggravated me further.

"As much as I hate to ask this question again, I really have to know: how are you *fee—ling*?" He mimed sign language by rubbing his belly.

"I'm tired and weak, not deaf, you jerk. I'm the complete opposite of a few hours ago." I closed my eyes and took another whiff of Luka's scent. "It's just a few hours ago, right?"

"A day, actually," Dray said as he scribbled on his clipboard.

"I've been out a whole day!"

"Yes."

"Where am I? Are we still in the palace?"

"The Medical Wing. Beside my lab."

I grimaced. "How bad is it?"

Luka's grip on my hand tightened.

I knew it. No one could puke that much blood and live. "I'm dying aren't I?"

Dray's curious smile and the hint of triumph in his eyes confused me. "Not today."

"But at the deli, all that blood ..." I couldn't finish. Remembering mortified me. "What about the Zhamvy who saw?" I glanced at Luka.

"I took care of it," he said.

Again, someone "took care of it." I began to think I had no control over anything in Zhamvy City. Quite humbling and doubly annoying, actually. These Zhamvy got under my skin faster than anyone in my life ever had. The million-dollar question: how far would I be willing to let them in? The door had already been left ajar. Could I let them slip through? Who could it hurt? Unfortunately, the answer to my last question was me.

"Thank goodness Luka was with you," Dray practically rejoiced.

I wanted to get up and smack him silly. Whose fault was it that I was on my back, weaker than a newly hatched duckling? I swear. The boy needed to be taken down a notch.

"What you did to her is unforgivable, Barinkoff!" Luka snarled.

Dray rolled his shoulders and stood his ground. "What's done is done. She's alive and my research is moving forward. You're one to talk, Visraya. You shouldn't even be with her. The only reason you're being tolerated is because—"

"Know your place!" Luka said through his teeth.

"Fine." Dray sighed and he leveled his gaze at me. "I'm sorry for what happened, Phoenix. It—"

"You're not," I interrupted.

"It was unexpected," he continued. "But we were able to contain the damage the formula had done to your body. Nothing permanent. The healing helped, too. You'll be weak for a while, but I don't expect it to last long—"

I tuned Dray out and studied my surroundings—white walls, flat adjustable bed, and a nightstand with a vase. Its crystal held the most wonderfully blue carnations I'd ever seen. They matched Luka's eyes. The window to my left had its blinds closed. Was there a universal code for hospitals rooms? Bland, bare, and sterile. And no TV. Great. No source of entertainment.

The IV stuck to my left arm chafed, and the beeping machine attached to my chest annoyed the patience out of me. I hated hospitals. Memories of my mother punctuated the feeling. I couldn't recall how long she'd lain in a hospital bed wasting away after the day she'd complained of being dizzy. After that day she'd lived with countless tubes snaking out of her and a respirator to keep her alive. Not once had my father visited her. The butler had taken me to see her after school every day, until one day, I'd arrived to find nothing in her room except for an empty bed. No one had told me she'd

~ ☾ ~

passed away until a nurse saw me standing outside my mother's room—staring, unmoving.

A crash brought my attention back to the present. I'd lost myself for a while, so I couldn't pinpoint the exact moment everything spiraled into chaos, but I certainly enjoyed what I now saw. Luka had a self-satisfied grin on his face. Dray picked himself up from a corner of the room, his silver clipboard forgotten on the floor. And the cause of Dray's current dishevelment stood by the door, a raging bull ready to charge. My breath caught and my skin tingled at the sight of him, a rush of desire had my body aching.

Demitri stood tall, fists clenched and trembling. Every inch of him corded muscle. His blue-black hair—no longer tied—cascaded over his broad shoulders. Everything he wore—shirt, pants, and boots—were midnight black. He looked like a dark pirate ready to swing onto the deck of a ship. I wanted to touch him, to trace my finger over his skin. I hadn't seen him in a while and a part of me missed him terribly. My gaze climbed to his face. His expression held the type of calm before a storm—eyes alert and intense, lips in a half grin, chin jutting out in challenge. My lungs burned. I exhaled the breath I hadn't realized I'd held in.

"Dray, why did I have to learn from Lev of what happened to Phoenix," he said in a solid voice that caused delicious tremors to dance all over me.

Dray simply shrugged. "You were attending Parliament at the time. I thought I'd wait until she was better to tell you."

Some of Demitri's calm chipped away. "Brother, never have I come so close to killing you as I am right now."

"Go ahead," Dray countered. "I'll say it again. I don't regret what I did and what I will continue to do."

Demitri let out an uncharacteristic growl and lunged. But before I could process what was about to happen, Luka had already wrestled Demitri back while Dray watched. The emotion Demitri showed and his actions surprised me. He let go of his robotic mask in a primal need to protect me. His actions touched me deeply. No one had ever wanted to keep me safe as determinedly as Demitri did. Not only did I feel anger radiating from him, I felt fear there too.

~ ☾ ~

"Release me," Demitri barked.

"No," Luka said as he struggled to keep Demitri at bay. "I won't allow you to hurt your brother."

"Then take his place," he said. "You should have told me about this too, yet you neglect what little responsibility you—"

Luka heaved Demitri out of the room, cutting the rest of his words off. They both moved so fast that I didn't have time to protest. I looked to Dray for an explanation. He came to my bed and fished out a syringe from the pocket of his lab coat. The machine by my bed beeped wildly.

"What're you doing?" I asked.

"You need to rest," he said as if his brother hadn't threatened to kill him a second ago. "This is a synthesized version of our blood. It will help you heal faster. I've mixed a sedative with it to help you sleep."

"Bu...ugh." My eyes lost their focus.

Dray pocketed the syringe he'd emptied in my IV. "You need to get well for what I have planned for you."

Unable to protest, I let out a single breath and closed my eyes.

Hours later, I woke up alone to dim lighting. It took me a while to remember I still lay on a hospital bed in the Medical Wing. Each beep from the machine grated on my nerves. I wished the wall across from my bed had a painting or something. The fragrance of honeysuckle comingled with morning dew in the air. It was useless to wonder about what had happened to Luka and Demitri. They were both Zhamvy. Chances were they'd be healed by now from whatever injuries they'd inflicted on each other. Boys and their need to fight things out.

I sighed and tested my fingers. They moved effortlessly, no longer weighing like an elephant. Whatever Dray had given me had worked. I lifted my right hand and stared at the lines on my knuckles. How long should I continue helping Dray? How far would his experiment go? Thoughts of experimentation had me turning my attention to Preya and how worried she must be that I'd suddenly cut our phone call off. Hopefully, her own curiosity wouldn't get her in trouble.

Out of the corner of my eye, I saw a shadow shift. The

scent of morning dew that only a moment ago was faint now bathed every part of me. I closed my eyes and let the smell of him send delicious tingles to shoot through my system. Again, I felt safe, secure in the fact that he was with me in the room. Nothing could harm me anymore because he was here. I opened my eyes and smiled.

I rested my cheek on the pillow and asked, "How long have you been sitting there?"

Demitri sat with his elbows on his knees, brooding. His lips were hidden by his entwined fingers. His brow was puckered.

"A couple of hours," he said.

I gave him a half smile. "Standing guard?"

"More like trying to make sure you never slip into a coma again," he mumbled.

"Well, what can I say?"

Letting out a long and weighty breath, he unclasped his hands, then reached up to trace a line from my temple to my chin with his finger.

My throat dried instantly.

"Stop that," I said. My face burned a thousand degrees.

Demitri stared at me. "Admit it. You like it when I touch you."

I took several long, calming breaths. "Give me a break. You have more self-control than that. At least, I'm hoping you do."

"What Dray did to you..."

"As much as I like this less uptight version of you, quit it." I closed my eyes, willing the butterflies in my stomach to behave. Staring at him made me want to pull him on top of me. "Unlike you, I want to continue behaving myself. Thank you very much."

"I remember telling you to stay away from Luka."

"A sudden non sequitur. Fine." I focused on the ceiling when I opened my eyes. "If I wasn't with him, no one would have been there when I started vomiting blood."

"He took you to our class."

I grimaced, remembering my less than stellar performance.

~ ☾ ~

"Stupid Calixta." I huffed. "How bad was it? Did I totally mess up?"

Demitri crossed his arms. "No. Calixta kept talking about how new students always got too excited for their own good, trying to impress the professor."

"Gee, I guess I owe her one." The thought made me itch. Remembering her hand on Demitri's arm made my blood boil. "Luka told me about your engagement. Congratulations, by the way."

For the first time, Demitri looked truly uncomfortable.

"Luka should really learn how to keep his mouth shut," he said.

"Well? What do you have to say for yourself?" I waited.

"Our engagement was arranged centuries ago," he explained.

My tongue stuck to the roof of my mouth. I swallowed the discomfort away and forced myself to speak. "Do you love her?"

He regarded me with those bottomless eyes. "It is my duty to my people."

"Do. You. Love. Her?" I enunciated each word. "That's an easy question to answer, right?"

"No," he said. "I have no feelings for her."

In an unprecedented move, I touched his cheek. Surprise etched itself on Demitri's face, but he didn't move away. He closed his eyes, leaned into the contact, and groaned. I snatched my fingers back. My own surprise finally caught up with me. I'd touched him of my own volition. Like, I had really reached out and touched him. This wasn't good. Not good at all.

The look of silent determination in his eyes caused heat to gather in my stomach. Something in me craved his presence. The relief that came with his admission of not loving Calixta unnerved me. The emotions were different than the pure lust the change Dray's formula created in me. The lust I could understand. This, I couldn't. It scared me to think I could find myself caring for this Zhamvy sitting by my bed despite the confusion our connection presented.

"Can you do something for me?" I asked.

~ ☾ ~

"Anything."

The twist in my gut told me he'd meant it. "Take me out of here? Just for some fresh air. I'm feeling a little closed in."

Demitri's gaze drifted to my IV.

Without waiting for him to move, I pulled the needle out, then took off the pads stuck to my chest. Thankfully, my hospital gown was the kind that wrapped around my body, secured by several ties. I may be headstrong, but I never thought of myself as an exhibitionist.

An endless *bleep* rang out, and I wondered if a computer monitored my heart rate in a nurse's station somewhere. Did the Zhamvy even have nurses? Demitri unplugged the device.

"I think that will buy us some time," he said. "And it *will* annoy Dray."

I grinned. "My thoughts exactly."

In one smooth move, Demitri had me in his arms the way a prince carries a princess. Granted, he really was a prince, but still. My embarrassment seemed endless.

"Hey!" I squawked. "Put me down. I can walk."

"If you want to leave this room, you will do it in my arms."

I stopped struggling and thought about his proposal. No one had ever carried me before. It felt weird. But when the smell of morning dew from his skin entered my lungs, all rational thought dissipated. I buried my face into the crook of his neck and inhaled. Demitri walked out of the room, a rumbling in his chest like a cat purring. I kept my eyes closed until he'd put me down and my feet touched stone.

"Seriously?" I asked while leaning on the banister. My hospital gown flapped against my legs. Someone had turned down the artificial sun and the lights from buildings and streetlamps created an imitation of stars in receding semicircles. "The balcony by the throne room?"

"I take it, Luka beat me to it?" Demitri said as he stood beside me.

"He did. Almost blinding me in the process."

"I cannot say I approve."

"Of course you wouldn't."

"Why were you with him, anyway?"

"Because I wanted to be."

~ ☾ ~

Demitri mimicked my pose by resting his elbows on the banister. His arm brushed against mine, sending electric sparks all over my skin. Even in his relaxed state, his strength still oozed out of him. Within the most secret place of my heart, I had to admit I liked the way he made me feel.

I tore my gaze from the sparkling city below us and focused on Demitri. In his silence, he looked so young, which made it hard for me to imagine him as the future king of the Zhamvy. The way he handled Eli and his group when they threatened to taste my flesh was certainly admirable. He commanded them like the crown prince he was brought up to be. But when I remembered how he told his father that he wanted to see the world, his expression changed. Beneath the uncertainty was real passion. Granted, I was too far away to be sure, but looking at him now, I had to try and find out a little more about the Demitri who was willing to remove the robotic mask to show the real face beneath.

"Demitri?" I asked.

He turned to face me, an eyebrow raised in question.

I dropped my gaze just as a hot blush crept into my cheeks. His gaze always unsettled me. I gathered up my courage and asked the question I really wanted to ask.

"How does it feel to be the crown prince?"

"You always ask the hardest questions to answer."

I looked up at his response. He'd returned his gaze on Zhamvy City. Something told me if I waited he would answer. To my surprise, my wait didn't last long.

"My father is the king, so by right of birth, I am the prince. Heir to the throne."

"That doesn't really answer my question though," I said.

"I have a duty to my people," he said.

I shook my head. "Still not an answer to my question." I paused. "Do you like being the crown prince, Demitri?"

He looked at me and blinked. "What makes you ask that?"

How to continue without exposing the fact that I overheard his conversation with his father? I shrugged and avoided his intense stare by counting the mansions that formed a semi-circle below us.

"Oh, I don't know," I hedged. "It just seems like you'd

rather be doing something else than be a prince. That time you drove me back to the dorms, you pointed at the travel stickers on my e-reader."

"So what if I noticed a few stickers?"

"I just thought maybe you'd like to travel someday—"

The heat in his eyes interrupted the rest of what I wanted to say. I gasped. If I'd known he'd get mad, I wouldn't have gone down that road.

Demitri closed the gap between us. A static current shot from my nape to my heels. He reached out and rested his hands on the banister, corralling me within the circle of his arms. The moment his lips touched my ear, I shuddered with such force that I thought the ground would crumble below me.

"Demitri, step away from me," I pleaded.

"No."

My mind screamed, yet my heart sang. The intimacy of his body pressed against mine had me wanting to slam my elbow into his gut. But a deeper part of me wanted more. I didn't know what to listen to: my mind or my heart.

"Did he touch you?" he whispered.

I swallowed, confused by his question. "Who?"

"Luka. Did he kiss you?"

His growl reminded me of rolling thunder. I hesitated, unsure of how to answer. My control died little by little. The sheer masculinity of him overwhelmed me. I could no longer piece together a reason why I had to stay away from his touch. In answer to his question, I shook my head.

"Good." His voice turned rough.

"Why?" I asked.

"Because," he paused, his breath hot on my neck, "you belong to me."

Our lips met, greeting each other with a fierce kiss of welcome, of wanting, of longing. With one hand, I gripped the arm he had around my waist while I lifted the other to his hair, snaking my fingers into the silky strands. His other hand lifted my chin, allowing him to deepen the kiss.

When Demitri broke free, I found myself gasping for every breath. My fingers on his arm hurt from holding on so tightly.

~ ☾ ~

My heart bounced around in my chest like a pinball. I couldn't quite focus.

"Did I make my point?" he asked.

Like a cold shower, clarity overrode the euphoria brought on by our connection. The will to stop came from somewhere deep. A place not even the primal instinct that came from my body mimicking that of a Zhamvy could reach. A human place. One of hurt and emptiness.

"Let me go."

"What?"

"It's simple: Let. Me. Go."

It must have been the heat in my voice more than the actual words I spoke that had Demitri backing away from me. I breathed in as much of the frigid night air as I could. It helped bring me back to myself.

"I can't do this..." My voice trailed away. I couldn't explain how empty I felt. How his presence couldn't fill that void carved out so many months ago. Not enough words came to mind to fully express how broken I felt, and no matter how hard he tried, he wouldn't be able to put Humpty Dumpy back together again.

The silence between us grew thick and murky.

"Phoenix?" He spoke my name like he was holding back the power from his voice, the command that came from being a born leader.

My stomach clenched. His face blurred. I blinked in a vain attempt to keep the tears at bay. He shook his head. Tears broke away, dripping from my chin to my aching chest. I stared at my bare feet and swiped at the streams with the heels of my palms.

Gathering my courage, I looked up and said, "I'm tired. Can you take me back to my room now?"

Demitri's expression returned to the cold mask he usually wore. He nodded once and walked away. My heart broke.

Chapter 14

Connection

From the balcony to my room, Demitri didn't check to see if I was following him. He didn't so much as glance back. Irritation squirmed inside my chest, but by some miracle, I'd managed to keep myself from throwing him against the wall like I had the last time he'd acted aloof. So I'd panicked. Big deal. I wasn't good when things got real.

Back in my hospital room, I suffered through Dray's fiery lecture. He yelled something about how my body wasn't well enough to be outside and that I should have waited until morning. *Blah, blah, blah, blah.* At one point, he sounded like a clucking chicken scolding an unruly chick. I sat on the bed, staring at the crisp sheets and pretended to listen. Secretly, I watched Demitri from my periphery. He leaned against the wall, arms crossed, watching his brother with disinterest. I expected him to leave. To my surprise, when Dray told him to leave my room, he said he would sit outside my door.

Finally alone, I studied the ceiling and tried not to think of Demitri. But my thoughts kept coming back to what happened at the balcony. I let him kiss me. *Me*. I let him touch me; let him do what he'd wanted. I wanted to blame the formula and the connection my bite had created, but if I had to be honest, I only had myself to blame. I'd lost control. I'd let my urges takeover. Whatever happened to behaving myself? So much for personal commitments.

I closed my eyes and attempted to sleep, but the idea of

~ ☾ ~

Demitri sitting yards away wouldn't let me. I pushed aside my blanket, got out of bed, and strode to the door. As I reached for the knob, I hesitated. I whirled around and leaned my back against the cold wood.

"Phoenix?" Demitri called from outside.

I slid down to the floor and hugged my knees to my chest.

"Phoenix, are you all right?"

I sighed. "How can you ask me that after the way I treated you?"

A long pause stretched between us before Demitri said, "I will not force you into anything. You have not grown up as Zhamvy, so you have no understanding of the feelings that come with the kind of connection we have with each other."

"You stayed anyway." I sniffed. "You don't have to. You can leave, you know."

"None of this is your fault."

"But *it is*." I thumped the back of my head on the door. "I'm the one who said I wanted to behave, and yet I couldn't. How pathetic is that?"

"Believe me, it is not all your fault. I pushed you into giving in. Unlike you, I understand the urges that course through my body. I apologize. I should have known better."

The conviction in his voice made me think. I searched the ceiling for reasons not to do what I thought about doing.

Seeing no other way out of my decision, I said, "There's something I want to tell you."

"Hmm?"

"First," I took a breath, "you have to promise not to interrupt until I'm done or else I might not be able to finish."

Another long silence.

"Do you promise?" I whispered.

"I promise," he said softly.

I closed my eyes and gathered my thoughts. A part of me rebelled against the idea, but another part—one that had changed the moment I'd agreed to help Dray—wanted to share a little of myself with the Zhamvy sitting outside my room.

"When I was little," I began, staring at the city lights slanting into my room through the closed blinds, "my mother woke me up early one morning and said she was going to teach me how to make snow angels. At first, I didn't want to go because it was too early and too cold. All I wanted was to go back to bed." A small smile crept onto my lips. "But Mom bundled me up, still half asleep and totally surly, and rushed me outside. We made snow angels all over the snow-covered ground. That was the last good memory I have of her."

"Why?" Demitri asked.

"What happened to not interrupting?"

"I apologize. Continue."

After swallowing the nasty lump in my throat, I said, "She got sick. For years, she wasted away in a hospital room and the doctors didn't know what was wrong with her. Every day, I watched her get sicker and sicker." I paused. "And then, one day, she was gone. That was eighteen months ago."

"Phoenix."

"The day she was buried, I didn't cry. I don't know why, but I didn't cry. I've cried since, but there was something about that day. Shock, maybe. And my dad? His heart just froze over. He became cold as ice. And I can't even begin to describe the kind of mess I am." I bit the inside of my cheek to keep from tearing up. "Basically, what I'm trying to say—and I don't even know why I'm telling you this—is that I'm too screwed up to be put back together by anyone." I barked a sad, little laugh.

"Is that why you agreed to help Dray with his experiment?"

His question hit me square on the chest. "A part of me still wonders if I could have done something to save my mother. But it's not just that. When I was growing up my dad taught me never to say no to someone who asked for my help. So, I guess Dray has him to thank for all this."

"Phoenix, can I interject?" Demitri asked.

Even muffled, his voice still held the confidence his royal position gave him. When he wanted to get his point across, he didn't hesitate. I shook my head, suppressing a smile. I had to give him props for trying hard not to interrupt.

"Phoenix?"

"Yeah?"

~ ☾ ~

"I may be overstepping my bounds, but ..." He stopped.

"You might as well spit it out." I hugged myself, forcing the need to have him hold me out of my mind.

"Could it be that the reason your father pushes you away is because he is afraid that if he lets you in he would lose the last thing he holds dear in his life?"

His words cut me deep. They sounded so true that every inch of me fought against believing him. Could it be that simple? Did my father really shut me out because he was afraid of losing me? Demitri's logic made sense. I wanted so badly for him to be right, but my own fears of getting hurt had me changing the subject before I lost myself completely to tears.

The scene from the throne room played over in my mind. I bit the tip of my thumb. "I'm about to tell you something but you have to promise not to get mad, okay?" I said.

A long pause followed. When I thought Demitri wasn't going to say anything, his voice came through the door.

"I will not get mad."

"You promise?"

"I promise."

"Well ..." I thought about it for a second, but there was no backing out now. "When Lev was supposed to escort me to my room, I managed to lose him and I snuck back to the throne room. I heard you and your father talking about needing to keep your family safe and that you should take the throne after Darius."

"I shall have words with that Royal Liaison," Demitri said, his tone clipped.

"Don't be mad at him. I'm the one who—"

"But you made me promise not to be mad at you, so—"

"Oh, just be mad at me then," I cut him off.

There was another long pause before Demitri asked, "What else did you hear?"

My heartbeats redoubled. I knew what he was referring to. "If you want to travel the world, I don't think it makes you less of a leader if you go. There's no use forcing yourself into something you aren't happy about. You're more than just the future king, Demitri. If you want to, you can do anything you want."

~ ☾ ~

Another stretch of silence spread between us. I waited and waited, but Demitri didn't say anything. My discomfort reached a point where I thought he was angry with me for suggesting he travel that I almost took back my words.

"Phoenix?"

"What?" I hated that my voice hitched.

"Can I open the door?"

I blinked in surprise. "Why do you want to do that?"

"Because I want to hold you."

I got up so quickly that I practically stumbled forward. "No!"

"Please let me hold you."

"I said no, and that's that. I swear, if you come in here ..." I climbed into bed and buried myself in its sheets. My feelings were still too raw. If he touched me now, who knew what would happen between us.

Chapter 15

Struggle

I sat in bed the next morning staring at the white sheet covering my legs. I closed my eyes and concentrated on Demitri's steady heartbeats. He really did stay with me all night. I blushed at the thought of what had happened between us. He knows more about me now than I ever thought of sharing with him, and I wasn't exactly sure how I felt about that.

Dray entered my room with a loud "Good morning!"

I jerked in surprise. "What's the matter with you, Dray? Are you really trying to kill me?"

Dray unceremoniously dumped a black tracksuit and rubber shoes on my bed.

"Put these on. We have a long day ahead of us," he said, then left.

I blinked at the velour pants and pouted in dismay. He was way too cheerful for comfort. I was almost too afraid to find out what my outfit change involved, but if I didn't dress I had a sinking suspicion he would return and force the clothes on me anyway.

After slipping into the tracksuit and shoes, I exited the room to find Dray and Demitri waiting for me outside. Dray smiled while Demitri remained tight-lipped. His eyes raked over my body like a caress. I shivered, avoiding his gaze.

"What now?" I asked.

The wicked enthusiasm in Dray's face made me nervous.

~ ☾ ~

His words from the other day bounced around in my head. He'd said something about needing me well for what he had planned. What did he want to do to me? What could he have in store? I tried not to dwell on it too much. I could easily say no to anything he wanted me to do. I could, couldn't I? I mentally shook my head. I had a bad feeling about this.

"The lab," Dray said. He smiled, showing all his teeth.

I couldn't be sure if the action constituted a smile. He never looked more like a mad scientist than right then. He led the way while Demitri followed behind me. The quiver running up my back told me he was staring, and I had a feeling he was tracing the lines of my body with his eyes. I squirmed.

In Dray's lab, watching his assistants run around like panicked chickens, I pretended to ignore Demitri while stealing glances at him, like some schoolgirl with a crush. I still felt drawn to him. The need to touch him or be close to him tugged at me every time I glanced in his direction.

"Phoenix." Dray pinched my arm.

"Ow!" I scowled at him. "What was that for?"

"Stop ogling my brother and pay attention."

I snorted and did as he'd asked. He took out another hypodermic needle from his pocket. Sweat dotted my upper lip.

"Another shot? Seriously?" I stared at the needle filled halfway with clear liquid. "How many of those do you have in there?"

"I need to give you another booster," Dray said.

"What's in it?"

He looked at the needle and then at me. "The same as yesterday's, but without the sedative."

"The synthesized version of your blood."

He nodded. "Our blood has really high amounts of antioxidants and strong regenerative properties. Our cell replication is a thousand times that of a human's."

"That's why you heal so fast."

"Yes. And a synthesized version of it quadruples the healing." He removed the cap and tapped the syringe. "I need you close to a hundred percent for the tests."

~ ☾ ~

"Why not a hundred?"

He blanched. "That's what I'm trying to find out. Now hold still."

I had no time to flinch by the time Dray had injected me. A small prick, a quick push of the plunger, and the job was done. In seconds, my heart pumped with renewed energy. A buzz zinged through my body like I'd downed a combination of espresso and energy drinks.

"Will you at least warn me next time?" I rubbed the spot where the needle had penetrated the skin with the alcohol swab he handed me. Then I shook my hands and shifted my body weight from foot to foot to dissipate some of the energy rocketing through me.

Dray pocketed the spent needle and said, "It's easier to ask for forgiveness than for permission. Now, this way, please." He indicated a row of dumbbells. "What can you usually lift as a human?"

Lower lip jutting out, I moved to the beginning of the line. "I don't really know. Ten pounds, maybe? Been a while since I hit the gym."

I lifted the dumbbells. They weighed less than toothpicks, so I moved to the twenty. No real difference. Up the scale I went until I'd reached a one-ton block.

"Is that it?" I looked to Dray for confirmation before putting the block down.

Dray waved at me to follow him to another room. My brows shot up. More weights lined up against the wall from three tons to ten tons.

"You expect me to carry three tons? You've got to be kidding."

He gave me a cheeky grin. "Just until you reach your limit. We need to determine what you can lift comfortably."

"You mean someone can lift *ten tons*?"

Without losing his grin, Dray pointed at the three-ton weight.

Shoulders slumping in defeat, I stomped over to the 3D trapezoid and slipped my fingers into the holes on its sides like picking up a bowling ball. Gritted teeth and all, I lifted with my knees. My limit? Five tons, which I'd managed to lift about an inch off the floor for a second. Super strength rocked! I could lift a car if I wanted to, maybe even two.

I put the weight down. "What?"

Dray rubbed his forehead. "To be honest, I didn't expect you to be able to lift that much."

"Why can't you look me in the eye?"

He relented a few seconds into my glare. "I lost a bet, okay!"

I raised an eyebrow. "With whom?"

"Luka."

A small jolt of panic went through me at the mention of his name. When did he speak to Dray? How much did he know about my involvement with the experiment? The fact that they had taken bets in connection to how well I'd do annoyed me the most.

Dray dropped his hand and continued, "He said you'd do superb during the tests."

"What did *you* say?"

"I said you wouldn't."

I wanted to clobber him, but my competitive nature pushed me to say: "What's next?"

For the next couple of hours, I concentrated so hard on what Dray asked me to do—holding my breath, pull-ups, pushups, throwing a ball—that when Dray called for a break I realized I hadn't noticed Demitri had left.

"Where'd Demitri go?" I let the feelings of missing him rush inside my veins to my heart. What did I expect? He'd already stayed with me all night. Surely he had other better things to do.

"Lev took him," Dray said as he handed me a bowl of *yusha* and a goblet of water while we sat at a small table in a corner of his lab. "And thank goodness for it. His presence was disturbing my mojo."

I grinned, remembering what I did to Lev. "Where'd the glorified assistant take him?"

"Parliament. And don't let Lev catch you calling him that. He's scary when pissed." Dray popped *yusha* into his mouth like candy. "Luka must have missed Silencing someone who'd been at the market because there's talk of a human in the kingdom."

~ ☾ ~

Concern pricked my insides. "Is everything okay?"

"There are always rumors of humans in the kingdom," he replied dismissively. "Nothing to worry about."

My gaze settled on the goblet I clutched with both hands. Last night with Demitri played through my mind again. We had this connection because I bit him and yet when Dray asked if I'd bitten him, Demitri wanted me to keep it a secret.

"Dray? I'm curious," I said.

"You always are."

"Ha, ha." I squinted at him. "You promised me answers, remember?"

He nodded reluctantly.

I paused. I knew I had to ask the right questions if I wanted real answers. "Why did you find it odd when I said I didn't want to bite Demitri?"

His brows rose. A wave of panic hit me. Maybe I made a mistake in asking him. He might wonder why I'd asked that particular question. I prayed he didn't ask why.

He replied slowly. "Zhamvy are driven by the hunger that we feel inside. The young need to learn to control this urge to feed or else we end up gorging ourselves. Slaves to the hunger even when sated. It's easier to think of it in the Freudian sense."

Relief washed over me. "You mean the id, ego, superego?"

"Exactly. Only much, much worse. The id acts according to the pleasure principle, hence our need to sate the hunger we feel inside. The ego looks for realistic ways to satisfy the id. This means avoiding the mass slaughter of humans. It takes a lot of guidance from the adults to get the younger ones to transition from their id to their ego state. But we Zhamvy aim for the state of the superego, which allows us to set aside our baser instincts in order to achieve perfection. Some take longer than others to transition, while others don't. The Pill has made things easier in terms of dealing with one or two humans. We end up slipping into the id when there are too many of you around."

"Luka mentioned something about that." I considered our conversation in the library. "Is that why you still go to school?"

~ ☾ ~

"That's part of the reason. We like to learn." Dray shrugged. "You should have seen Luka and Demitri when they were younger."

I sat up straighter. "Oh yeah?"

Dray launched into a narrative of a time when Luka and Demitri were children. Luka had loved being in the state of id, loved to hunt, enjoying the act of stalking his prey and relishing the satisfaction of the feed. I cringed at this, but Dray was quick to say that all young Zhamvy were this way. While Demitri—as Darius used to tease—had been born in the state of the superego. Demitri had quickly learned, even at a young age, that he needed to serve his people. Luka had found this attitude tedious, always daring Demitri to do something reckless for the sake of having fun.

"Once," Dray continued, "Luka managed to convince Demitri to hide the king's ceremonial robes. And one thing you should know about Zhamvy culture is that the king cannot sit on the throne without wearing his robes."

The urge to giggle tickled my throat. "What happened?"

Dray grinned. "About halfway through the prank, Demitri got so guilty that he confessed to hiding the robes. Unfortunately, in his need to please the king, Demitri managed to drag Luka down with him. In the end, after much bickering between Demitri and Luka, the king sent them to train with the Bogatyr for a year. That's equivalent to hard labor in human terms."

I could just imagine Luka trying to coerce Demitri into stealing the king's robes—two young boys up to no good. I laughed. They must have looked so cute. Luka still had that sense of mischief in him, but I sobered when I recalled the sadness he held on to. What could have happened to cause him moments of quiet melancholy?

It pinched my heart just thinking about how heartbreaking he looked sometimes, so I moved on to a different question.

"You said you're forbidden to taste flesh, right?"

Again, Dray nodded, staring at the bowl of *yusha* between us.

"What happened more than six hundred years ago that led you to forbid it?"

~ ☾ ~

"Correction." He raised a finger. "*I* didn't forbid the tasting of flesh."

"You know what I mean," I said, totally vexed.

He gave me a smile that disappeared so fast, I had to convince myself it actually happened.

"Around the fourteenth century, the Black Death decimated the human population in Europe," he said. "This was before we lived underground. Human flesh had been difficult to come by. The plague caused oozing boils filled with pus and blood on the skin. None of the Zhamvy wanted anything to do with human flesh back then." He grimaced. "With our food supply dwindling, we starved to death. Those who were hungry enough to try the diseased skin contracted the plague and died a painful death. They withered away, flesh rotting until nothing was left. Even now, no one is sure why our bodies can't heal from an infection of the Black Death."

The idea of eating pus riddled flesh caused bile to rise up my throat. I swallowed. That was just beyond gross.

"In an unprecedented move, the Traditionalists and Reformists gathered to find a solution," he continued. "Some suggested rounding up as many healthy humans as possible and breeding them like livestock. A solution that was considered for a while, but it meant feeding the humans, and that was difficult to do when our own people were starving. And to wait for humans to breed before tasting their flesh was unbearable."

I urged him to keep going, "Then what?"

"Bickering began." A muscle on his cheek twitched. "Soon, reports of Zhamvy turning into cannibals reached the palace. These were the Serfs living at the edge of the city who received flesh rations last."

"That's horrible."

"Hunger brings out the animal in anyone."

I shuddered.

"The king at the time—"

"Why don't you say hail the king?" I interrupted.

"We don't acknowledge exiled kings."

"Why was he exiled?"

~ ☾ ~

"That's unimportant." He took a sip from his own goblet, his skin looking paler than usual. "You have to understand that because of the bubonic plague, flesh was forbidden. And we worked tirelessly to find a substitute."

I popped a cube into my mouth. "*Yusha*."

"Correct." He regarded the cubes with a certain wretchedness I couldn't quite understand.

"This experiment...where does it all fit in?" I asked. "Your family's in danger because you did this to me, right?"

"How'd you know about that?"

"The afternoon I was supposed to stay in my room, I went back to the throne room. Darius and Demitri were talking about the Traditionalists getting their way, and that your experiment endangers everyone. What is this all about, Dray? Why did you need me?"

Dray sighed. "Have you ever tried being a vegetarian, Phoenix?"

"How does that—"

"Just answer the question."

I shook my head.

"Ever deprived yourself of anything?"

"You mean you want to eat flesh again?"

Dray pinched a cube of *yusha* between his thumb and index finger and examined it like a precious stone. "Our society is dying, Phoenix."

"Dying? How can a long lived creature be dying?"

"The average lifespan of Zhamvy is three thousand years. That's sixty in human years. One human year is fifty in Zhamvy. Now, I know that this is a long time to live, and why would I be worried about our race dying?" His brows knotted. "We are sick." He handed the cube he held to me. "And this is what's making us sick."

Frowning, I considered what Dray had said. "The *yusha*?"

"We try to mimic the nutrients found in human tissue. Apparently, the chemicals we ingest are killing us. It took me five hundred years to notice. But now I have. There is a rapid degeneration that is caused by the *yusha* and the other genetically engineered fruits and vegetables. And pig's flesh is more like junk food to us, which isn't healthy either. We're becoming the textbook definition of what humans call a zombie. A rotting corpse. The walking dead."

"Your father ..." I suddenly found myself unable to swallow. "Darius...I saw him," I whispered. "In the throne room."

"What?" Dray squeezed my hand. "What did you see, Phoenix?"

"When I snuck back to the throne room, I thought my eyes were playing tricks on me because when I'd left him, he looked so healthy. Not ten minutes later, he looked desiccated. His skin was all wrinkly and dry." I shook my head in disbelief. "Then he took a deep breath and was normal again."

Dray let go of my hand. "What you saw is the middle stages of the disease." He rolled up his sleeve and showed me his arm.

I stared at the smooth skin slowly dry out and then wrinkle. "Dray?"

He took a deep breath and the skin became smooth again. He rolled down his sleeve. "Since my father is older, it takes him a while to heal from the ravages of the disease."

"Why don't you stop eating the *yusha* then?" Panic entered my voice.

"That would mean we'd have to ..." His words trailed away.

"Eat flesh," I finished for him. "Who knows about this? Demitri? Luka?"

"I haven't told anyone. Nobody even knows what this experiment is really about, and I'm running out of time. I can't contain the disease with the booster shots anymore."

I felt my eyes grow wide. "You mean to tell me you've been trying to cure what the *yusha* is doing with synthesized blood?"

"Not cure. Slow down."

"Then why am I here? Why did you turn me into one of you?" I looked at the half empty bowl. My stomach twisted. "God, you fed me those!"

"Calm down." Dray raised his hands. "It takes years of consuming *yusha* to feel its effects. What I'm trying to do is to find a away to—"

~ ☾ ~

"Turn humans into Zhamvy," I interjected.

"The opposite."

"*You* want to turn into humans?"

Dray tossed another cube into his mouth as if he hadn't just told me it was killing him. "I figured if I can turn our population into humans then we wouldn't need to consume human flesh anymore. It's a win win for everyone."

I sipped from the goblet and let the water cool my dry throat. "Why experiment on a human first? Can't you use a Zhamvy?"

"It's easier to manipulate a human's physiology than that of a Zhamvy. There's the healing to consider. A high metabolic rate is another. I need a formula that's already perfectly calibrated to Zhamvy physiology for it to work."

"How do you know when you're there?"

"I'm not there yet." He gave me a pointed look.

"Then how are you keeping all of this a secret? I'm sure there have been deaths already. How do you explain the bodies?" I asked, not knowing whether I should be impressed or disturbed by what I'd learned.

He shrugged. "I infected some Serfs with a new strain of the bubonic plague that mimics the degeneration caused by the *yusha*. It's less lethal and one that a booster shot of our blood could easily eradicate. I'd been experimenting with it since the 1940s."

"You *what*?"

"I infected—"

I waved away his words. "You already said that. But *why*?"

"Oh." His brows rose. "That's so I could issue a public warning and periodically inject everyone with the synthesized blood. This way no one questions the bi-yearly inoculation."

I had to admit, Dray's plan was ingenious. Create a diversion by releasing a disease that Zhamvy were afraid of to distract them from the real disease killing them, then give them a shot that would not only kill the distraction, but also keep them alive long enough for Dray to find a real solution. Huh. And I thought I'd been kidding with the whole mad scientist label.

~ ☾ ~

Then what Luka said in passing while at the market jogged my memory. "What about the miscarriages, Dray? How are you explaining those away?"

"Phoenix, I'm sorry," he said. "If I don't conduct these tests on you, I wouldn't be able to calibrate the formula. And if I don't calibrate the formula in time …"

"You all die," I answered in a daze.

"Or the Traditionalists get their way and we'll start consuming flesh again. It's the death of our race versus yours. That, and it might take a month or even another five hundred years for the effects of the *yusha* to reverse. I have no way of knowing."

Suddenly, the responsibility on my shoulders seemed more real than ever. I didn't know what I'd signed up for when I'd agreed to help Dray. But now that I saw the bigger picture, I couldn't quite wrap my head around the enormity of the task ahead of us. If I didn't help Dray, I'd signed all of their death sentences. And I certainly didn't want to condemn the human race to a life of being livestock to the Zhamvy.

I inhaled and a thought hit me. "Dray, why don't you smell?"

He let out a nervous laugh. "What do you mean?"

"Exactly what I asked." I looked him in the eye. "The Zhamvy I've met have a distinct scent." I moved closer and took a whiff. "You don't smell like anything."

"All Zhamvy have a unique scent signature." He paused, clasping his hands together to hide the shaking. "When we are dying, we slowly lose that scent."

"Oh, Dray." I leaned closer to him. "Can't you do anything? Stop eating the *yusha*?"

He shook his head. "I need to monitor the degeneration process."

The answers clicked in my head. "You're not taking the shots?"

"Phoenix," he said, then sighed.

"Dray!" I stood and towered over him. "Why are you doing this? What happens if you die? Who will save your people?"

"Phoenix!" He pulled me down. "Will you keep quiet? I'm fine."

~ ☾ ~

"You don't look fine," I said. "That's why you're paler than the others. This is insane, Dray!"

"I'm young, so my healing capabilities can still handle the disease." He tried to smile, but failed. "I would love to debate my health with you longer, but as I said, we don't have the luxury of time. Now, I think it's time to start the second round of tests. Shall we?"

Chapter 16

Confrontation

 For the rest of the day, I endured all of Dray's tests. His recent revelations about the disease ravaging the Zhamvy population forced thoughts of my mother to the forefront of my mind. I wished someone like Dray had worked hard enough to find out what her ailment had been. Dray's dedication strengthened my resolve to help him. Not once did I see the vulnerability he'd shown when I'd discovered he hadn't been taking the shots. He kept going, only taking a deep breath now and again, which told me he'd been healing himself. I didn't complain; however, I did have questions like: "Is this safe? I won't drown? I can walk through that? I won't get electrocuted? I won't fall?" Questions normal people asked when faced with potentially life threatening tasks.
 At the same time, I'd discovered the actual size of Dray's lab. Apparently, what had looked exactly like the Chemistry Lab at the academy only comprised a fraction of the actual space. Dray had a whole wing of the palace for his use: a Weight Room, a Genetics Lab, a Gym/Physical Experiments Lab, a Physics Lab, and the Medical Wing where I'd woken up after my deli incident. He even had a Water Lab. At first, I couldn't fathom what purpose it might serve until he dunked me over and over again into large vats of liquid concoctions with lovely odors ranging from vomit to skunk spray. That was to see how long my skin would last against various substances before melting off. Fun, fun, fun. Thankfully, he

~ ☾ ~

had special showers to clean myself of the wonderful aromas.

By the end of the day, I still had energy to spare. The booster shot he'd given me earlier kept me energized and strong. Dray's assistants, all bound by the Silence in the effort to keep his experiments confidential, gave me encouraging smiles. They sometimes cheered me on, which sounded totally fake to my ears. Results. They wanted results. And if they thought cheering kept me going, that was their misunderstanding. I said I'd help, and so I did.

"Can I go someplace where I can breathe? Please, Dray? I'm feeling closed in," I said when I'd finished the last of his tests.

His brows perked up, eyes shining with mischief. "I have a place. This way," he said.

After two left turns and a right, Dray opened doors to a garden bursting to the seams with color. Roses and lilies and orchids grew everywhere, alongside exotic plants I didn't recognize. A florescent green moss covered the roots of a willow with purple leaves, giving it a phosphorescent glow. On the bark of a maple clung electric azure orchids and climbing red ivy that had yellow thorns.

"You have a garden," I said in awe.

"Yup." He popped the "p".

I stepped out until the crisp blades of grass crunched beneath my shoes and moved to the small pond. Dray mumbled something about having results to correlate and that he'd pick me up in a couple of hours before he left. I ignored him and turned in a tight circle. I'd done my part in his experiment. Unless he needed something else, I saw myself as officially off the clock for the day.

I spotted a bright pink lily floating on an orange pad near the edge of the pond. I dropped to my knees and reached for the lily. My fingers touched a petal, its texture like a cat's tongue. Sitting on my haunches, I took my first deep breath of the day. Tension knotted my shoulders and every other muscle ached. A part of me was happy I'd helped the Zhamvy in some way. I felt a sense of purpose and even a remote sense of happiness playing a role in what might be a cure for the Zhamvy. To lose such a magnificent race to this wasting

disease would be a tragedy. To lose Demitri... I shuddered at the thought.

I quickly switched my train of thought to something less emotional. For example, where in the world was my phone? I knew it had been in my pocket when Luka had taken me to the market. Not that I could use it since they had no cell service underground. Even so, that gadget served as a reminder of the life that waited above ground.

Then my thoughts wandered to Preya. I missed her. No matter how scary she was sometimes, I still considered her a good friend. Had she tried to call again after I'd hung up?

The sound of light steps, clinking chains, and a rustling skirt sounded behind me and interrupted my thoughts. I stood up and dusted off my tracksuit pants.

"You," a soft feminine voice I recognized said.

"Hello, Calixta," I said and turned to face her, tossing my hair over one shoulder. I kept my muscles tense and my stance wide in case she decided to pounce. With Calixta, a fight didn't seem like such a farfetched thing.

She raised a hand to her mouth, covering an attempt to look shocked. "You're really here."

My lips twisted into a scowl. "Don't even try faking it. I know you recognized me when I came into your class."

"Well, I hadn't seen you since, so how could I be sure?"

I was surprised by her calm, almost friendly tone. And I'd thought she'd hunt me down just to make good on her threat to kill me. Embarrassment puffed my cheeks. "About what I said in class—"

"Oh, don't worry about it. No one pays attention to a hysterical outburst from a new student. It did fuel some rumors though."

Dread chilled my skin like a gust of winter wind. "What rumors?"

"Oh, it's not uncommon for those of the upper classes to make pets of those coming from lesser stations. Demitri mentioned something about you being a silk merchant's daughter from the north." She tsked. "I know the truth, of course. Just can't say anything about it."

I suppressed the need to exhale in relief. I didn't know

whether to be glad or insulted. Glad because the rumors of a human in the kingdom hadn't resulted from my inability to keep my mouth shut. Insulted because the Night Students thought I was Luka's pet. It did confirm my suspicions of him being of a higher caste, but to be called a pet? It just didn't work for me.

"Wait," Calixta said, pulling me back into the conversation. She sniffed the air and her eyes grew wide. "You're different."

I scratched my eyebrow with my thumb. "I'm getting that a lot lately."

She neared where I stood and circled me. "You look different." She touched a strand of my hair. "You smell different."

"Like what?" I stifled the urge to recoil from her touch.

"Vanilla." She stopped in front of me. "What do I smell like to you?"

I inhaled. "Lilac."

She clapped her hands. "Very good. What happened to you? You don't seem human anymore. At least, you don't smell like one, that's for sure."

Her smile shocked me. It looked genuine and actually warm. "Where did that girl who'd threatened to kill me go?"

She laughed—a tinkling sound that reminded me of sleigh bells.

"Did I say something funny?"

"I'm sorry about that," she said after she regained her composure.

"You're ..." I couldn't form the rest of the sentence, too dumbfounded to think.

"I'm sorry," she finished for me.

I thought about the night we'd first met and something occurred to me. "If Zhamvy are fast, why did you slow your pace when you were running after me? You could have caught me without a second thought."

She blushed, more from embarrassment than anything else. "Oh, I wanted you to feel hunted, that's all. I thought you were out to get Demitri. I'm his fiancé, you see. And I feel a little protective about my claim to him."

"Luka told me." I paused. "About the engagement, I mean."

She wrinkled her nose. "What are you doing hanging out with that disgrace anyway? Nothing good will come of it."

"Right." My gaze fell to the grass and I kicked at an imaginary pebble. "You seem like you're in a good mood—"

"You see it?" She twirled in a circle with a beaming smile on her face. "I thought Demitri had been ignoring me of late, but I was wrong. He spoke to me before he entered Parliament today. We'd made plans for this evening. I was so wrong to doubt his loyalty to me. When I asked him about you, he merely shrugged."

Ugly jealousy replaced my earlier unease. Several nasty words began to form in my head in response to what Calixta had said.

Calixta giggled. "Can you imagine? He wants to spend his free time with me now. I should have known he wouldn't want anything to do with someone like you."

Unfortunately, the question came out before I could censor it. "Have you bitten him?"

She stopped mid-twirl and regarded me with suspicion. "How do you know about that?"

"Since you said you're his fiancée, I just wondered if you'd already forged a connection with him."

"I'm going to repeat myself one more time." Heat entered her words. "How do you know about that?"

Casually, I said, "Oh, maybe because I *bit* him."

Calixta's features contorted into pure rage. She let out a blood-curdling snarl and charged me. I matched her snarl and lunged. I grabbed her wrists and pulled her into a head-butt. She staggered backward. She rubbed her forehead and stared at the grass as if puzzling over what had happened.

"How dare you bite him!" she said.

"Jealous?" I taunted.

She cartwheeled and landed a solid blow with her heel on my shoulder. My bones rattled. I seized her arm and took her with me as I whirled in a circle several times. I let go and Calixta collided with the willow tree.

Adrenaline coursed through my veins like wildfire. "Is that all you've got?"

No sooner had my words left my mouth than Calixta's fist

buried itself into my gut. I doubled over and groaned. She clutched the sides of my head and rammed her knee into my face, breaking my nose in the process. I grunted and spat out the blood that flooded my mouth. I lifted my fists to defend against any more blows.

Calixta admired her handiwork. "How does *that* feel?"

"Come on!" I wiped away the rest of the blood on my lips and chin with the back of my hand, nose already healed. "We can be at this all night."

Calixta took hold of my hair and yanked hard, throwing me over her shoulder like a Judo master flipping an opponent. All the air exploded out of my lungs when I landed. Uncontrollable coughs rocked my body. Every breath burned. Tears blurred my vision.

I rolled onto all fours and wobbled to my feet. Somewhere, Calixta laughed. But before I could orient myself, she came at me and shoved forward until I slammed into the maple tree. Hand-shaped leaves rained around us. What little air I had in my lungs puffed out again. She sneered with satisfaction, which made her face look like a cat's when it hissed—all teeth and wrinkled nose.

"I think I really will have to kill you," she said.

I froze. "I'd like to see you try."

Calixta slammed her knee into my gut. "Demitri's mine!"

Something in me snapped. I reached for her shoulders and pushed away from the tree with my foot as hard as I could. The momentum brought Calixta down, with me on top of her. I pinned her arms with my knees and held her head in my hands. She glared at me with pure hate. I bent my head until my lips touched her ear.

"You may be engaged to Demitri, but he let me bite him," I said.

Calixta let out a piercing scream. I straightened and let go of her to cover my ears. I noticed a shadow come at us from my periphery, but before I could react pain shot through the back of my head and I sank into darkness.

~ ☾ ~

Chapter 17

Disgrace

    I came to with a start. Ropes secured my wrists to armrests. Another rope wrapped my legs together from the knees down. Calixta and whoever had knocked me out had gagged me as well. Impressive, but excessive. Who knew where they'd gotten the filthy rag from?

    I tried my best to figure out the details of the room they'd dumped me in, but the only light came from a small slit under the door. I groaned and stared around the room, making out the outlines of a table, a bookshelf, and something oval-shaped on the wall. A mirror, maybe. Nothing gave away my current location. A lot of good it would do me anyway, since I didn't know enough about the palace to actually pinpoint which part the room could be in.

    Screaming didn't help either. No one came. And because of my attempts at catching someone's attention by shrieking, thirst plagued me. What I would give for a tall glass of water right about now. My muscles ached from struggling with my ties. I'd lost sensation in my fingers and toes.

    I squirmed against the ropes to try and loosen them, chafing my skin in the process. Without thinking, I put all my weight to one side. The chair tilted and fell with a *bang*, followed by my muffled whimper. Pain shot up my shoulder. I squeezed my eyes shut and channeled all my frustration into one cold-sweat inducing snarl.

    I shouldn't have taunted Calixta the way I had. But, at the

~ ☾ ~

time, I couldn't help myself. That dopey look on her face when she'd told me Demitri had spoken to her before Parliament disengaged all the rational parts of my brain. I chalked it up to the connection Demitri and I had. I had wanted to piss off Calixta, and revealing that I'd bitten him certainly did that. Of course, the Zhamvy who'd given me a good conk in the head had fought dirty. He or she needed to pay.

Lying on my side, in the dark, tied to a chair, I wondered how many times I'd faced death since encountering the Zhamvy. More than I'd cared to count. The pain on my shoulder throbbed. I couldn't understand why it continued to ache. I should have healed by now. And for that matter, where had my strength gone? I couldn't even get out of the chair Calixta and her accomplice had tied me to.

I'd started to plan my next move when the door opened. My attention focused on whoever had decided to join me in the quaint abandoned room I called my holding cell. My muscles tensed. I thought of all the nasty things I wanted to say when he or she removed the rancid gag.

A ray of light from the opening door hit my face. I squinted, my clearer vision sensitive to direct exposure to light. I could only make out the outline of someone tall. No skirts. No Calixta. Well, it could be Calixta in pants. But, then again, she wasn't very tall.

The figure charged at me. I whimpered in panic and closed my eyes, waiting for the deathblow I was sure was coming. Instead, the ropes binding my wrists and legs were torn away, sending me falling. Strong, capable hands kept me from hitting the floor. I opened my eyes as my whole body vibrated in response to his presence. I yanked away the disgusting gag and coughed.

"Demitri," I croaked out.

He pulled me deeper into his embrace. "When you were not where you were supposed to be, I immediately came looking," he said.

I forced myself to swallow despite the nasty aftertaste of the gag. "How did you find me?"

"I followed your scent from Dray's garden to here. What

happened between you and Calixta?"

Heat prickled my cheeks. "How'd you know about that?"

"I can smell her all over you." He sniffed as if to emphasize his point.

"Let's just say we had a little...*disagreement*."

Demitri held me at arm's length and searched my body with his gaze. "Are you hurt anywhere? Anything broken?"

I'd never heard him so agitated before. I took inventory of my sore muscles and shook my head. "My shoulder hurts a little, but I can finally feel it healing. And my headache from whoever hit me is starting to fade too. Besides a serious case of pins and needles on my arms and legs, I think I'm okay."

"This has gone too far." Demitri let go of me and took a step back. He turned his back on me. "This reeks of Vladimir."

"You know this for sure because …" I rubbed my arms and shifted my weight on my legs to get the blood flowing properly again.

"Calixta would never have left you tied up. If she wanted to kill you, you would be dead. You said someone hit you in the back of the head?" I nodded and he continued, "This could mean someone stopped the fight before it got out of hand and brought you here. Vladimir has been sniffing around. I believe he suspects something the moment he ordered an inquest into Dray's experiments."

A pang of loneliness hit me so hard at his attempt to distance himself that I almost fell to my knees. I reached out for him, but stopped myself and clutched my hand to my chest instead. I trembled. I couldn't find the words to answer what he'd said. What did it mean to Dray's experiments if Vladimir went sniffing? What could he do to Dray? Demitri's words planted a seed of foreboding in a corner of my heart. Could he know about the disease? Worse, could he know about my involvement in Dray's experiments?

"Demitri, what's going on?"

He whirled around so fast that I gasped. Barely leashed anger burned in his eyes.

"I thought I could handle the connection between us, but I was wrong," he said.

~ ☾ ~

My heart beat so hard in my chest that it hurt. "What are you saying?"

"The last thing I need right now is a distraction."

"I'm ..." I swallowed again, my throat closing on me. "You think I'm a distraction."

"Phoenix, my people need me." Demitri curled his fingers into tight fists. "I must fulfill my duty. Keep this kingdom safe."

"I don't believe you," I said, rising anger became my ally. "You're more than just a future king, Demitri. God, you have to at least see that, right?"

"You have no idea what you are saying. I have a responsibility to my people." He unclenched his fists. "I think it would be for the best if we stayed away from each other until the formula leaves your system."

I couldn't breathe. Was he seriously breaking up with me? After saying I was his? The nerve. We weren't even together, *together*.

"Demitri, don't do this. Stop lying to yourself."

"Sir, we have to hurry," someone said from outside the room.

Demitri moved toward the door and spoke to whoever was outside.

I pushed away the pain Demitri's words injected into my heart. No matter how much he insisted on being king, I could see his heart wasn't totally in it. Yes, he had a responsibility to his people, but there were many ways to be a leader. I would find a way to make him see that, connection or no connection. Demitri didn't have to be a martyr. He practically begged his father to let him travel when they were speaking in the throne room. I wasn't about to let him sacrifice himself for something he didn't totally believe in.

I looked up to see who had entered the room and my eyebrows shoot up my forehead.

"Lev?" I said, giving the impeccably dressed Royal Liaison an assessing glance.

"Expecting someone else?" he asked, condescension in his tone.

Demitri interrupted what I was about to say with: "Lev, please escort Phoenix to Luka's home."

~ ☾ ~

I frowned. "Why Luka's place?"

He kept his gaze on his father's assistant. "The palace is no longer a safe place. Lev, please make sure not to lose her this time," he said before he left.

When Demitri said we needed to stay away from each other, I didn't think he'd meant right this moment. The jerk wasn't getting rid of me that easily. He couldn't stay away before, so who was to say he could stay away now? He'd be back.

I held on to that thought and gave Lev a sheepish smile, which he tsked at. He turned around and began walking away. I moved to follow, giving the room one last glance at the door.

"Will you hurry up," Lev called from the end of a long hallway.

It was freaky how fast the Zhamvy could move.

I sprinted until I caught up to him. "I'm sorry," I said sincerely.

"You should be." Lev walked by my side, close enough that I felt his warmth but not enough for our arms to touch. "I almost had a heart attack when I looked behind me and you weren't there. If it hadn't been for Luka, I would have lost my mind looking for you. So, you should be sorry."

I bit the tip of my tongue. That was why I'd gotten away from Lev so easily on that first day. Luka had stopped him from finding me. This had to have been before he joined me between the curtains at the throne room.

We turned a corner and a bunch of the Silent parted to let us through. Many of them gave me curious glances.

The path Lev chose opened to the other half of the city behind the palace. He made a beeline for a massive house to the left. Once inside, I realized that what looked like a Victorian manor with ivy climbing its walls actually housed cabin-like features, with wooden beams and paneling. The only metal came in the form of light fixtures and the banister lining the curved staircase that led to the second floor. The mix reminded me so much of Luka. He'd dress in the Barinkoff Night Student uniform but would leave it undone in a relaxed sort of way as if by accident.

~ ☾ ~

"I'm sure you'd like to change," Lev said as he escorted me into one of the upstairs bedrooms. "I'll have someone help you."

He'd left in such a hurry that I hadn't even taken a breath to speak when the door slammed shut behind him. He was still angry, I got that, but he didn't have to be rude. Drama queen. I shook my head and surveyed the room. The sheer amount of girly pink frills blinded me. The sleigh bed duvet cover, the pillowcases, the cover on the loveseat, even the French curtains had frills. They seemed to have a life of their own, devouring every surface. And if I squinted, they seemed to move. A room, no matter what, shouldn't have so many frills. Creepy.

Before my brain exploded from a frill overdose, a light tap on wood startled me.

"Come in," I said, touching my chest to make sure my heart was still inside.

As the door opened, I expected a Silent in a French maid's uniform. Instead, one of the most beautiful girls I'd ever seen slid in, bringing with her the scent of sweet apples. Long curls so devastatingly flaxen that they mimicked golden sunshine bounced when she moved. Stunning sapphire eyes were made more dramatic by a fan of thick, long lashes that brushed against slightly flushed cheeks when she blinked. She wore a Gothic Lolita dress of white lace and navy blue ribbons, making her resemble a walking porcelain doll whose head barely reached my chin. I wanted to pick her up, brush her hair, and have a tea party.

"Oh, sorry." I moved my gaze to the beige carpet's chocolate embroidery.

"What for?" she asked.

"For staring." My eyes traced the vine pattern, cheeks flushed.

"Oh please, I'll have none of that."

I looked up at her. The brilliant smile on her face blew me away. I whirled around to face the curtains. "Give me a sec. I've never seen anyone as pretty as you. It's disconcerting. I thought Lev would send one of the Silent."

"Oh, he did. But when I heard about the special package, I insisted on seeing you for myself."

~ ☾ ~

I spun around. "So, you *know*," I hedged, not wanting any details to slip out unexpectedly.

She walked to the large armoire by the wall. "Not much, but Luka did mention Dray was working on something. Or should I say...*someone*? No wonder those crones who call themselves Traditionalists are suspicious. You're a walking breakthrough."

Who was this person? How could she know about me? And more importantly, what was her relationship with Luka?

She browsed through the clothing in the armoire. "Now, we should get you out of that tacky tracksuit. I can't abide them." She pulled out a Victorian inspired gown of emerald satin and showed it to me.

I dumbly shook my head.

"Would you prefer jeans and a shirt then?"

Jeans and a T-shirt. I longed for them. And my cell phone, which was still missing in action. But I had to keep up appearances.

I worried the edge of the tracksuit's hoodie with my fingers and asked, "You don't happen to have a Barinkoff uniform, do you?"

"Ah, yes. Simple is always good." She shoved away several articles of clothing and found what I'd requested.

The corset made me squirm. "And a shower?"

The girl pointed at the door next to the loveseat.

Sighing gratefully, I strode into the adjoining bathroom with a claw-foot tub and a shower closet. "What's your name anyway?"

Her radiant smile returned. "Yana Zulia Visraya. I'm Luka's younger sister. It's a pleasure meeting you, Phoenix."

"How did you know my name?"

"Why wouldn't I?"

Scary. She reminded me a little of Preya. I let the question drop. Why wouldn't she? Only Luka would have such a devastatingly beautiful sister. I committed her name to memory before answering the call of hot water and soap. Nothing surprised me about the Zhamvy at this point. Or so I thought.

All throughout my bath, Yana babbled on about some she-

Zhamvy or other. Then she switched to household matters like buying more vegetables from the market. Unlike her smooth operator of a brother, she turned out to be sweet and talkative. Normally, I'd avoid someone like her since yammering annoyed me, but listening to her singsong voice actually calmed me down. And I just couldn't bring myself to snap at her or to tell her to shut up. I wouldn't know what to do if she started crying because of something rude I said by accident. Someone that looked so delicate didn't deserve to be reduced to tears—albeit something told me she knew more than she was really letting on.

After my shower, I wrapped a towel around myself and reentered the room. Yana had the Barinkoff uniform laid out on the bed for me along with a new pair of boots.

"Do you have underwear I can borrow?" I asked. "Whoever stripped me down at the Medical Wing never returned mine."

Yana glided over to a chest at the foot of the bed. She pulled out a black, see-through number I would have never in a million years picked out for myself. Underwear should cover, not expose! I wiped a hand over my face.

Taking the barely-there underwear, I reentered the bathroom to slip them on. Then I braced myself for the process of getting into the Night Student uniform. How could anyone put it on without help? The corset lacing alone needed an extra pair of hands. But, to my immense relief, dressing took half the time I'd expected. Deidra, the Silent Demitri had introduced to me when I first woke up in Zhamvy City, had treated the process like a ceremony. Yana saw it as an everyday chore. Her quick pulls and tugs had me dressed in no time.

"I take it you're used to this sort of thing," I said with a wince as Yana tightened the corset with a dainty grunt.

"I know how to dress someone, if that's what you're referring to. How do you like your stay in the kingdom so far?"

Her question caught me off guard. It took me a long while to consider my answer. What was I supposed to say? *I like it here, but I have issues with my feelings for the prince?* Or, *Oh, by the way, I just survived a smack down with said prince's fiancée and I was currently his brother's guinea pig?* Put that way, my stay in Zhamvy City resembled a really bad soap opera.

I must have taken too long to speak because Yana said, "I'm guessing you're not comfortable with that question."

"It's not that," I replied. "I think I'm overwhelmed by it all." I sighed, and then proceeded to give her a rundown of what had happened so far. I explained how I'd broken curfew. I told her about Calixta threatening my life and meeting Luka. Then I moved on to Dray asking me to help him with his experiment. I left out the parts about biting Demitri, vomiting blood, the Zhamvy disease, oh, and the whole confession about my mother to Demitri. But I did include my brawl with Calixta. I figured, if she was Luka's sister, and she knew so much already, it was pointless to lie about why I was in Zhamvy City and why I was like them.

Yana laughed. "Thank goodness someone finally stood up to that princess wannabe. Did you really give her a head-butt?"

I nodded ruefully, feeling awkward and proud at the same time. Then I said, "Yana, I've been wondering, how old are you?"

"Not a day over six hundred."

"How old is that in human years?"

She looked impish for a moment. "About twelve."

I laughed, which got Yana laughing, too. I didn't know why I found her age funny, but I did. "What about Luka and Demitri?"

"Oh, they're both about nine hundred, although Luka's older by a year."

I did the math—so eighteen, just a year older than me if they were human. I found it crazy to be around beings that had lived for so long, and yet, they were so similar to humans. Despite their age and their seclusion, the Zhamvy seemed acquainted with technology and human advancements. Demitri could drive. Dray had sophisticated equipment in his lab that rivaled what CERN had. I hated to admit it, but Calixta had a point when she'd said the Zhamvy and humans weren't that different. I chuckled.

~ ☾ ~

"What are we laughing at again?" Yana asked.

I wrapped my arms around my waist as a new bout of chuckles attacked. "The absurdity of it all."

"Always a good choice. How about a tour of the house to pass the time?"

A tour? How normal. I couldn't discount the tickle of happiness her offer caused in me. I didn't have enough friends to actually visit houses, so I never went on tours. Heck, I didn't even know what to expect on a house tour. So, without over thinking it, which I obviously had been doing, I trailed Yana into the hall and down the grand staircase.

The landing had a massive bouquet made up of exotic flowers in a large crystal vase sitting on a hexagonal table. Yana led me into the living room where she pointed out the differences between bentwood and stick furniture. To me, all types of wood meshed into one thought: they came from trees. She babbled on about the rustic theme continuing into the dining room, the kitchen, and the game room.

We stood in the sun room when I couldn't help myself anymore and asked, "Yana, why are you and Luka different from the other Zhamvy?"

She paused looking like a woman far wiser than her six hundred years.

"We are the offspring of the *Superiori*," she finally said. "It is said, and I only know this from my studies, that the Zhamvy come from two clans: the *Superiori* and the *Aperiori*. The differences being the *Superiori* are cold-blooded while the *Aperiori* are hot-blooded. All of the Zhamvy you've encountered are descendants of the *Aperiori* clan. My brother, my aunt, and I are the last of our kind here."

Well, that explained the differences in skin temperature. "What happened to the rest of you?"

A flicker of grief crossed over her face.

I rushed to her side and hovered like a mother hen. "You don't have to answer if you don't want to."

Her cute factor turned me into mush. I didn't quite know how to react. My protective instincts clashed with my need to pummel the cause of her distress, which confused me even more. How could I beat up myself?

~ ☾ ~

Yana blinked away tears before they could fall. "It's not that. Don't feel like you can't ask me things." She squeezed my warm hand with the coolness of her own. "I just recalled something." She closed her eyes, breathed, and opened them again. "I don't really know what happened to the other *Superiori*."

I decided to stop asking questions along those lines. Getting answers didn't merit seeing Yana in tears, so I returned to the topic of touring the house and allowed her to lead me into other rooms. I listened intently to what she had to say. Learning about why the house looked like a manor on the outside and a cabin on the inside made me laugh. Apparently, Yana and Luka couldn't decide if they'd wanted something Victorian or something rustic. Eventually, they'd struck a compromise, but not before they'd driven the builders crazy.

"You mean this is all new?" I asked.

"Oh, yes," she said, marching down a long hallway with barren walls except for a single portrait at the end. "We used to live in the palace."

She started babbling on about how they'd decided on furnishing the house when a question entered my mind.

"Where are your mother and father, Yana?"

Again she stopped, her back ramrod straight.

The feeling of having made another mistake came as spiders running across my skin. "I—"

"You should know," she interrupted my apology. "I'm sure Luka hasn't told you, but he should have."

My heart leapt to my throat. "What do you mean?"

Yana pointed to the end of the hallway. "I think you should see for yourself."

Bewildered, I followed her finger with my gaze and moved forward, drawn by an invisible force toward the lone painting. Soon, a figure in maroon robes sitting on a throne came into focus. A large shield with the profile of a lion on its haunches hung above the throne. One of the lion's paws grasped a sword. Its tip impaled the head of a snake while the serpent's body wrapped around its other front paw. Above the lion's head floated a crown and the words: *fundamenta inconcussa*.

~ ☾ ~

"Unshakable foundation," Yana said from behind me.

My throat muscles constricted.

My gaze traveled to the man. Even in dim lighting, the luminescent tumble of blond curls reminded me of someone. On his forehead, a simple gold circlet kept his unruly locks from taking over his brow. He had classic features: a straight nose, high cheekbones, a stubborn chin, and sensual lips. The same silver crescent scars that covered Darius's skin marked his hands and neck. His eyes captured mine. The lightest shade of blue. Like ice.

"Luka," I whispered as a profound numbness came over me.

"No." Yana stood by my side and gestured to the painting. "Phoenix, this is my father, the exiled King Yaris Orion Visraya of the Visraya Dynasty."

~ ☾ ~

Chapter 18

Fallen

Holy—

I had no words. Surprised couldn't come close to describing what I felt. Goosebumps spread across my arms and legs. Luka's father had been the king, which meant Luka had held the title of crown prince, and Yana had been a princess. What had happened to their father? Why didn't he rule Zhamvy City? Dray's words about the king's exile being unimportant haunted me. Why wouldn't Dray want to elaborate on what really happened after the eating of flesh had been forbidden? And, more importantly, why would Luka hide the fact that he had royal blood? My right eyebrow rose as I thought about my last question. Demitri had been secretive about his status, too. I puffed out my cheeks on the exhale of a huge breath in an effort to calm my nerves.

Things I hadn't noticed before made sense now, like the time in the Solar Garden when Luka made Calixta leave and forced Demitri to kneel before him. And when Luka took me to the market, someone had called out: "Prince." At the time I'd figured Demitri had been near. Now that I thought about it, Luka couldn't get away fast enough from the person who'd spoken.

I shouldn't blame him for keeping his position hidden from me. Everybody had their secrets. But my little introduction to the portrait of a man I didn't know yet recognized, twirled my already chaotic world off its axis. My

~ ☾ ~

mind worked on overtime. A small seed of hope was planted into my heart and it was growing fast. With every beat my heart made, the seed sprouted into a vine that was slowly, surely, wrapping itself around my heart. If I waited any longer, I was sure that vine of hope would end up wrapping all over my insides, spreading through my veins, getting into my stomach, overpowering my resolve.

When I'd pushed Demitri away at the balcony, it was because I thought I was too broken to deserve his feelings along with mine. His duty to his people was also a factor. He was a prince. I had no right to take him away from his ailing father. But with Luka being a crown prince also...I grabbed Yana by the shoulders. I had found the answer I was looking for that would free Demitri.

"Where is he?" I asked, almost manic.

She blinked. "Who?"

"Don't mess with me, Yana," I said. "I don't know what you're playing at here or what you want to accomplish by showing me this portrait, but I need to see Luka."

Yana gave me a devious smile. I never knew someone could have so many different smiles before, making it even more disconcerting because those smiles were on such a young and innocent looking face.

"He's probably in his study going over some reports," she said.

"Right." At the back of my mind, I was right to feel scared of this little six-hundred-year-old Zhamvy. "Care to take me there?"

"Thought you'd never ask." She twisted out of my grasp and skipped away.

I had to stomp down my shock. I kept finding myself in situations where the Zhamvy led the way. No time like the present to learn to let someone take the lead. It wasn't like I could find my way to the study anyway. I gave the portrait of Yaris one last glance. He stared right at me as if to say, *I know what you plan to do.* The thought made me shiver. An exiled king. One who had the power to forbid the consumption of their main food source, yet he'd been banished like a leper.

~ ☾ ~

"Phoenix!" Yana called. "Are you coming or not?"

"Why do I get the feeling you're enjoying this too much?"

"Nothing exciting ever happens anymore."

"Is that your way of saying I'm here to entertain your bored little princess butt?"

She raked her blue gaze over me and goose bumps rose on my arms. She was definitely keeping something from me too, and I was starting to get sick of all the secrets these Zhamvy had.

"That remains to be seen," she said.

I shook my head and followed her lead. We hurried through the house. By the time we'd reached large double doors, my mind went blank. My throat constricted. Standing outside a study had never reminded me of staring at the gates of hell before. I half expected Virgil to say something poetic. Instead, I got a beautiful Gothic Lolita princess who seemed far too mischievous for her own good. Apparently, it ran in the family.

Yana leaned toward me and said, "What now?"

My heart somersaulted and landed in a heap above my stomach. The intricate carvings on the doors of a forest scene with birds, rabbits, foxes, and an owl watching from the branch of an oak tree looked so calm, but what was behind those doors reduced me to a tight ball of nerves. Was I crazy enough to ask for what I wanted? The answer was so simple, it scared me.

"Phoenix?" She pinched me.

"Ow! Geez." I rubbed my arm. "I'm getting to that."

"You asked me to bring you here, and yet you don't know what to do?"

"I'm guessing you're not too sure what to do, either." I gave her a sidelong glance.

"Well, I thought—"

"Shhh!" I pressed my ear to the trunk of the carved oak.

"*What* are you doing?"

"Will you shush? I thought I heard something."

Yana copied my posture.

With my ear against the wood, I made out a few words. My hearing wasn't as acute as the day I'd first woken up with the formula still fresh in my system. I wondered briefly if my lack

~ ☾ ~

of super hearing had anything to do with Dray mentioning whatever he'd injected me with would eventually fade. Could my reduced hearing be a sign?

Luka's voice from behind the doors recaptured my attention.

"Are you sure?" he asked.

A baritone voice answered, "Yes, my prince. We've been keeping watch. According to reports, the Bogatyr under his control are mobilizing."

"How many are allied with him?"

"The numbers are unclear." A pause, then rustling—maybe paper. "Not more than fifty percent of the troops. Many are still loyal to Darius."

My breath hitched. What about Darius? Could this be what Demitri said about their family being in danger? What else was going on besides what Dray had been up to?

"Even less than fifty percent is still too many. We'll have a problem," Luka said.

"Not necessarily, sire. Your troops are ready for any eventuality."

The hair on the back of my neck stood on end.

The double doors opened inward, sending Yana and myself stumbling into the study and falling to the floor on our hands and knees. Busted!

I lifted my head.

A man with long, ice blond hair—wearing a silver breastplate with the lion crest emblazoned on it—stood in front of us. He had eyes so light blue they were almost white. Shallow wrinkles gave his face character.

"I believe we have two spies among us, sire," he said, spreading his lips to a grim line.

I glanced at Luka, who half sat, half leaned on the edge of a large desk carved from the same wood as the doors. It had their family crest on its front panel. He crossed his legs at the ankles while his arms folded across his chest. The spark in his arctic-blue eyes spoke of playfulness. It matched his devilish grin.

"Hello, brother," Yana greeted. "We were just coming to see you."

~ ☾ ~

"Yana, how many times do I have to tell you to stop listening in on my meetings?" Luka displayed mock disappointment. "It's for your own safety, scamp."

Yana beamed at her brother as if she played spy all the time. "But then, where would I get all my information from?"

"You should be out playing or doing what girls like you like to do."

"I like to spy," she said. "That's what I like to do."

Luka glanced at the soldier. "You may leave now."

The man grunted, scowling at me. I grinned. Our eyes locked for another second before he gave Luka a curt nod and strode out of the study in quick strides.

"Now," Luka said, coming before me, "should I be afraid to ask why you are here?"

I stood up and dusted invisible dirt off on my skirt. "Yana took me on a tour of the house. You know, like normal stuff. I discovered nothing about your family at all."

"Luka, won't you help your dearest sister up?" Yana whined.

"I have only one sister, and sadly, she proves to be a constant headache." Luka lifted Yana in the air, eliciting a delighted squeal from the girl.

Yana never seemed younger than right then. She actually looked twelve in human years. And the smile on Luka's face as he swung his sister down was priceless.

Again, memories of my mother invaded my thoughts. Her smile. Her laugh. That cold winter morning she'd taught me how to make snow angels. She kept popping up more often than ever before. Was it because I was helping the Zhamvy find a cure? I pushed images of her away. I needed to concentrate on what I came to Luka's study for.

"Luka, can we talk?" I said.

Concern wrinkled his brow at my tone. He returned his gaze to Yana. "What've you been sharing with this *villyat*?"

"Nothing she doesn't deserve to know." Her blond eyebrows came together in a stubborn line.

He sighed deeply. "Leave us then, scamp." He turned Yana around and smacked her bottom. She giggled all the way out of the room and winked at me before shutting the double doors.

~ ☾ ~

"Why don't you take a seat?" Luka pointed at one of the chairs facing the desk. "I have a feeling this will take a while."

Too restless to sit, I stayed in the middle of the room and crossed my arms. "Who's mobilizing the Bogatyr?"

"That's not what you came here to discuss."

I lifted my chin. "Well, I want to know."

"It's none of your concern."

"For all I know, I'm the cause of all this. Who was that with you?"

"The captain of the Vityas."

"The *what*?"

"They're similar to the Bogatyr, only ..." Luka paused.

"Only?" I stepped forward.

"The Vityas serve the royal family."

"*Your family.*"

He nodded once, sorrow in his eyes. "I shouldn't have agreed when Demitri asked me to keep an eye on you."

My heart picked up its pace. "Tell me about what happened, Luka. Why was your father exiled? Dray brushed it off as unimportant, but I don't think it is."

Luka leaned his shoulder on the side of the leather chair behind his desk and clutched his elbows with his hands.

"The Traditionalists are planning something," he said. "Ever since the eradication of the Black Death, they've continually lobbied for the return to the old ways."

A large lump lodged itself in my throat. "By old ways, you mean ..."

"The consumption of flesh, yes." Luka leveled an even stare at me. "We've been monitoring their movements. They were never happy with Dray's experiments. The sudden outbreak of the plague a few years back, the miscarriages, the inoculations. The Traditionalists believe Dray is hiding something from them."

And then some.

"I'm guessing you already know my secret?"

"Phoenix," Luka shook his head at me, "you underestimate my intelligence. I met you as a human. Now, you're less that and more like us. Don't you think it's obvious you'd want to hide that fact?"

~ ☾ ~

I bit the tip of my tongue to keep from saying it aloud. From the way Luka spoke, he confirmed what Demitri said about the Traditionalists. They were a threat not only to me but to the peace of the kingdom as well. And they were sniffing too close to the secret Dray had kept for centuries. Luka had confirmed my fears. That seed of foreboding in my heart blossomed. If the Traditionalists got wind of the disease then they'd get their way for sure. They'd start eating flesh again. And the closest humans? My abdomen clenched. The Day Students.

"Their suspicion of Dray's activities in the lab is making them proceed with their plans. Demitri believes Dray isn't concerned by these developments. At least, he hardly seems perturbed by the continuing probes and inquests of the Traditionalists into his experiments," Luka continued. "Vladimir—"

Despite my concern for what Luka's words meant, I quickly caught up with what he tried to do. He was trying to distract me away from my original question. Oh, he was good.

"Whoa!" I yelled and ran to the desk, then slammed my hands on the wood. A few sheets of paper fell to the floor. "What do you think you're doing?"

"Answering your question." He shrugged with maddening indifference.

"That's not my question."

"You had several. I simply chose which one to answer."

My muscles tensed amid barely leashed frustration. I wanted to grab his impeccably pressed shirt, yank him across the desk, tie him to a chair, and torture him until he confessed. But I had a sinking feeling Luka would actually enjoy getting physical, so I slumped into a chair and massaged my temples instead.

A couple deep breaths later, I asked, "The prime minister?"

Luka had the gall to snigger at me. "Vladimir has been a staunch Traditionalist since the days of my father." A hint of pain entered his eyes. "He secretly seethes at the thought of Darius taking the throne. Before Darius was the king, he was the prime minister. And he's married to my aunt."

~ ☾ ~

I gaped. Demitri and Luka were first cousins. Huh, who'd have thought? Well, they bickered like family. *Figures.*

"So, Darius became king. And you?"

"Me?"

Irritated, I said, "Vladimir wants the throne."

"Retract the claws, little cat." Luka regarded me with a guarded stare.

"Then stop playing around and answer me directly."

"Yes, Vladimir wants the throne, but he needs just cause to take it."

"What could give him …" The words refused to come out of my mouth. I swallowed. "Me? He wants me."

"What Dray has done can give Vladimir the ammunition he needs to further his ambitions."

"And how much does Vladimir know?"

"He can't prove anything yet. He's just mobilizing." Luka organized the remaining papers on his desk. "Although, this latest inquiry into Dray's experiments has us worried. You coming into the picture changes things drastically. There are too many rumors roaming around already."

"But Darius—"

"You aren't worried about Darius." He moved to where I sat in easy, gliding steps. He grasped the armrests of the chair, hemming me in.

"And why not?" I pushed him away and stood quickly, moving to the center of the room again.

"Because we both know you're worried about a certain crown prince. Am I close?" He followed.

I stared him in the eye as he backed me into one of the floor-to-ceiling bookshelves of one wall. The hairs at the back of my neck and arms rose at his smooth yet hostile tone.

"What if I was?" I challenged.

Luka grinned, but there was something so feral about the movement of his lips that I thought he was going to take a bite out of me. "I would make a better match for you," he said.

"I'm sorry, Luka." My breathing turned shallow.

"He can never be yours."

"And you can?" I laughed at that. "Luka, you're a prince

too, and with more rights to the throne than anyone in this kingdom."

"Then why did you come here?" He placed his hands on my shoulders. Their strong gripping kept me still.

My heart twisted painfully. I cared for Luka, but not in the way he wanted me to. I understood that now.

"I'm being selfish," I said, turning my head to the side.

Cupping my chin with one hand, Luka turned my head back to face him again. "What do you want from me?"

"Take the throne," I whispered, tears flooding my eyes. "Take the throne and release Demitri from his duty."

The sadness in Luka's eyes was heartbreaking, as if he was watching someone he cared about die in front of him and there was nothing he could do. I knew those eyes. My father had that same expression almost every day until my mother died.

"You *are* being selfish, little cat," he said softly. "What makes you think I could?"

Tears fell just as the first sobs came from my throat.

"Because you are *Superiori*," I said. Luka's eyes widened a fraction. "And your father was the king."

"What makes you think I would take it?"

"Because," I swallowed another sob before it had a chance to escape, "you have to."

Helpless laughter came out of Luka. It was a sad laugh. Then his face hardened to an emotionless mask that scared me.

"For a kiss then," he said.

"A what?" I asked, slack-jawed, my brain blacking out.

"A kiss for the throne. You can give me that much, can't you, little cat?"

I had to blink away tears several times to fully understand what Luka was asking me. A kiss? The ice in his eyes melted. A roguish grin replaced the dour line of his lips. Luka may be handsome, and he may have tempted me when we were hiding from the palace guards, but Demitri was...Demitri. No one could compare. I knew it from the night he drove me home to the dorms. The way he made me feel was enough to shatter my world and put it back together again in seconds.

~ ☾ ~

"Luka, not like this," I said, my heart beating in my throat.

"That's my price." He moved away.

Luka's price was too steep. If I kissed him, I'd be betraying what I have with Demitri. But if I didn't kiss him, I might as well say good-bye to Demitri now. Damn Luka for being too complicated.

With a hurried breath, I grabbed Luka's shirt, and pulled him back. He more than willingly obliged. I captured his lips with mine. A soft, feathery touch. Just as I was about to pull away, his hands clasped my waist and plastered my overheated body to the coolness of his.

I barely heard the door open. Suddenly, Luka's lips left mine. And when I opened my eyes, the sight of a fist startled me, followed by a loud crash to my right. Quivering, I turned my head and watched Luka pick himself up from the desk he'd been slammed onto. The heavy piece of furniture had tipped over and papers rained around him.

"Stay away from her," Demitri said, gravel in his voice.

Staggering, I gasped for breath that wouldn't come.

"Ah, the dutiful prince arrives. You should see your face right now. I'd say you've lost that emotionless reputation of yours, cousin," Luka said. The bruise on his cheek healed almost immediately.

Demitri's potent rage had my heart racing. His fiery gaze shifted to me.

"I want her," Luka continued. "Besides, you can never give her the kind of affection she needs."

I clenched my fists and scrambled to think of a way to make things better. My heart beat too fast. My breaths became too shallow. The world around me began to spin. Wait! I said, but the word hadn't come out.

Demitri lunged at Luka.

Moisture dripped from my upper lip to my chin. I lifted my fingers and swiped at it. I brought my hand to eye level. It took me a moment to realize I had a nosebleed. But just as the thought to ask for help entered my mind, my knees gave way.

~ ☾ ~

Chapter 19

Restless

A prick on my arm woke me. I sighed, feeling the needle being pulled out and something soft and moist replacing it, applying pressure to the puncture wound. My eyes fluttered open. I needed a moment to adjust to the dim lighting. The overabundance of frills said I was back in the room Lev led me to in Luka's house.

Bottomless onyx eyes studied me when I turned my head to the side.

"Demitri?" I mumbled, my voice still rough from sleep.

"No," a voice said. "Not Demitri."

It took me a couple more seconds to recognize the messy hair and ashen pallor of the figure sitting by my bed.

"Dray?" I swallowed, attempting to relieve a scratchy throat. "What happened to me?"

"You collapsed. You're growing weaker."

I tried to recall what happened. I'd found out about Luka's father. Yana had led me to the study. I'd confronted Luka. He'd told me about the Traditionalists instead. My eyes widened a fraction, halting my thought process.

"Dray, they're coming for you." I grabbed the sleeve of his lab coat.

"Who's after me?" he asked with a small smile.

"Luka ..." I swallowed again.

"Luka's after me?"

I shook my head. "Water."

~ ☾ ~

Thankfully, he didn't joke about water being after him. He handed me a goblet and supported my shoulders with his arm as I took a sip. The cool spring water brought much needed relief. I took one more gulp before settling into the covers again.

"The Traditionalists," I said after clearing my throat. "Luka told me they're suspicious about the outbreak and the miscarriages and your experiments. They're coming for you."

Dray sighed, folding his hands on his lap. "They've been after me for years, Phoenix."

"But—"

"They won't find anything," he assured me. "I've set up decoys that will put them off the trail. Besides, the Traditionalists are not what I'm worried about right now."

I blinked at him and waited.

His gaze fell to his clasped hands. "Phoenix, I took some blood from you before I gave you another booster shot."

"I'm going through a lot of those, aren't I?" I sounded relaxed, but my insides were jelly.

"More than I would have expected."

"What do you think is causing me to bleed?"

He shook his head and stood up. "I have to examine your blood first. The booster I've given you will probably last a few hours, if my calculations are correct. I'll come back as soon as I know more."

Nothing about what Dray said took away the worry building inside me. In fact, his cryptic words added to my current state of internal agitation. My situation resembled concentric circles. The biggest circle contained the worries caused by the Traditionalists. The middle circle enclosed my concern for my health and safety in connection to the formula Dray had injected me with. And the smallest circle held my feelings for Demitri. Even if I felt energized as a result of the synthesized blood, I didn't want to get out of bed. I watched Dray leave the room without any further words exchanged between us.

A few minutes later, the door creaked open.

"Oh good, you're awake!" Yana entered, carrying a silver tea tray.

~ ☾ ~

She wore a black lace dress with red silk ribbons. Her ensemble reminded me of the bride of Dracula, only blond, blue-eyed, and way peppier. She didn't look like a Zhamvy girl slowly decaying from a disease caused by consuming synthetic flesh.

For a second, I doubted the credibility of Dray's story, but remembering how desiccated Darius looked dissolved all my doubts. I might not see the manifestation of the disease at every waking moment, and those around me seemed to be at the peak of health, yet something affirmed the truth in what Dray had confessed to me.

I pushed aside the morbid thoughts and said, "Dray just left."

Yana deposited the tea on a round table at a corner and clapped twice. The light brightened to a soft glow. She smiled her approval and poured tea into dainty blue cups framed in gold enamel. "I must have missed him. You scared the holy out of us when you passed out."

My heart skipped. I didn't know what to tell her. "I'm sorry?"

Yana stopped arranging the tea-sandwich-shaped *yusha* with purple cucumbers to level a stare at me. My blush felt red hot as I worried the sheets around me.

"Don't worry about it," she said. "After Demitri carried you into this room—"

"He carried me?" I cut her off.

"He seems to like you. Like, a lot." She wiggled her eyebrows at me.

I threw a frilly pillow at her, which she somehow dodged in six-inch heels. The fluffy missile landed with a muffled thud on the wall and bounced to the floor. I ignored how happy Yana's revelation about Demitri made me feel.

"Have some tea," she said.

"Based from experience, I just have to ask, this isn't laced with anything, is it?" I took the cup and saucer she brought me.

Yana crossed her arms and pouted. "It pains me that you would think I'm capable of adding something to your tea."

The floral aroma floating up from the amber liquid

soothed my nerves. I took a tentative sip. Tea slid down my throat and pooled in my stomach like sunlight on a forest floor.

"I wouldn't put it past any of you," I teased.

She shrugged. "You're absolutely right." Taking her own cup, she glided to my bedside and sat at its edge. "But I consider you my friend. I'd never slip anything into your tea. Well...unless I thought it was for your own good." She placed her teacup on the bedside table.

I slid my teacup beside Yana's and reached for her hand. "Yana, why did you show me the portrait? Was it because you wanted me to ask Luka to take the throne?"

"Partly." Her expression grew sheepish. "I didn't think you'd actually go through with it. I was counting on your feelings for Demitri to get you the rest of the way."

I couldn't understand Yana's intentions until my brain figured out what she'd meant. "How do you know about my feelings for Demitri? Actually, it's scary that you know so much."

She sighed. "I like spying. It's the only exciting thing to do around here."

"But why?" I frowned. "I know why I want Luka to take the throne, but what about you?"

"The thing you have to know about my brother is that he may look like he doesn't do anything, by he's actually a very active part in Demitri's plans to stop Vladimir. Everyone thinks he's someone content at being good for nothing. I think Luka believes this about himself too, but I know all he wants is to lead. He's born for it, Phoenix. He wouldn't have set up the surveillance on Vladimir if he didn't want to be proactive in leading this kingdom. Surely you understand that."

Seeing the sadness on Yana's face strengthened my conviction. "Tell me everything that happened with your father's exile," I said.

"Do you already know about the Black Death?" she asked, determination wiping away her sadness.

I nodded.

"And the cannibalism that happened as a result of it?"

"That, too."

"Okay." She took a deep breath. "Because our society was one step away from complete anarchy due to starvation, King Yaris had all the cannibals rounded up and killed while the rest of the population watched. It is taboo for us to taste our own flesh, and the king made sure everyone was reminded of it." Yana stared at a point beyond where I sat. "Once the last of the cannibals were executed, he forbade the tasting of flesh. Shock froze the masses. Flesh-eaters never to eat flesh? The king might as well have asked everyone to commit suicide. Yaris rubbed salt into the wound he'd opened by proclaiming that anyone who broke the forbidden would be exiled."

I let her words sink in. "Why would exile be harsher than death?"

"We're social creatures, Phoenix. The punishment of exile is far more painful than death. To be exiled means isolation. And isolation is enough to drive a being that could live several millennia insane. Can you just imagine living a thousand years without talking to anyone?" Yana raised a hand, killing any questions I had.

I shifted to a more comfortable position and waited.

"Pig flesh, along with certain genetically enhanced vegetables, became the sustenance of a majority of the population. Life returned to normal again. And when *yusha* came along, the Royals turned away from pig flesh entirely."

I had to stop myself from revealing the ramifications of a diet consisting mainly of synthetic materials. I tried to sound casual when I said, "So, you guys munched on pigs. That doesn't sound so—"

"You have to understand that pigs might work as a substitute for a while, but their flesh is not enough to sustain us. Even so, our people considered Yaris a hero. Who would've thought he'd break his own proclamation?"

"The exile."

A bleak phrase. It filled the room with the unsaid.

She nodded without meeting my eyes. "He was found devouring a young girl exactly fifty years after he forbade the tasting of flesh. Luka was the one who found him. He was

~ ☾ ~

only three hundred years old."

Six in human years, my mind calculated—a little kid. Luka, a boy that probably worshiped his father for saving their people, had watched his admiration shatter with every bite the king took of the young girl. The devastation on Yana's face said as much.

Tears flooded her eyes. I reached out and pulled her into a fierce hug. No sobs escaped her lips. I only knew she cried because the blouse I wore soaked up her tears. I didn't know what to say or how to soothe her, so I settled for stroking her hair.

"My mother told me everything before she withdrew from the world," she said.

I trembled.

Yana lifted her head and smiled despite her tears. "It's for the best, Phoenix. Really it is."

"No mother should have put her child through that kind of revelation."

She leaned closer and placed a soft kiss on my cheek. "Thank you."

Embarrassed by her display of affection, I coughed into a fist. "What did Luka do after he discovered Yaris?"

Yana dried the last of her tears with a lace handkerchief she fished out from her cleavage. "A servant was with him at the time."

The heartbreaking sadness on Luka's face when we'd visited the market flashed before my eyes. The Silent who'd broken his vow—the one Luka had told me about—did it for the young prince. And Luka carried that guilt for six hundred years. I couldn't begin to imagine what that must have felt like. Demitri's words that night at the Medical Wing came back to me. I mourned my mother every day, yet Yana's story allowed me to understand what Demitri had meant about my father. Like Luka, my father shut his heart away to keep from getting hurt all over again. It all made sense to me now.

"Phoenix?" Yana bit her lip.

I blinked several times and realized I'd drifted off into my own thoughts. "Sorry. Got sidetracked. So, what happened to Yaris?"

~ ☾ ~

"He was tried by a tribunal and the new king."

"Luka?"

"My brother became the youngest king in the history of our people. He exiled Yaris without showing any remorse, or so our mother told me. But I'm sure it broke him inside."

That I could believe. "But—"

"He abdicated soon afterward."

My eyebrows shot up.

"My mother didn't have a clear answer as to why. I believe it became too much for him. But the Traditionalists would have none of it." Yana reached for her cold teacup and scowled. Without another word, she stood and sashayed to the tray and refreshed her cup.

I scrambled off the bed. "So, wait—how did Darius assume power?"

She made a show of sipping. "Luka proclaimed Darius regent. Since he was married to our father's sister, Darius certainly had a right to become our next ruler. Vladimir didn't like any of it, but a proclamation from the king cannot be questioned without just cause. At the time, he had none. Darius became regent, and Luka remained a solidifying influence. With two *Superiori* backing him, Darius was slowly accepted by the Merks and Serfs, and eventually, the Royals. Luka fully released his hold on the throne about two centuries ago."

"If Luka chose to abdicate, why do you want him to become king?" I asked.

Yana glanced out the window. "I believe it's the only way for him to get over the guilt he feels for exiling our father. Luka needs to forgive himself for what happened."

I heard the truth in Yana's words, but I needed to speak to Luka. I needed him to make me understand why he didn't want the throne. I thought I was being selfish for asking him to release Demitri from his duty, but in reality, Luka was just running away from his people and leaving someone else to take up his rightful role.

"Where can I find Luka?" I asked.

The smile on Yana's lips sent a chill down my back.

Chapter 20

Scars

When Yana told me Luka was in the Weapons Room, I laughed in her face. A house with a Weapons Room? Her face looked so serious that I had to tease her about it. Once she was red-faced, I asked for directions. I had to see this Weapons Room for myself, even if Luka wasn't my main purpose.

After a couple of minutes of brisk walking, following Yana's directions and trying to figure out what I had to say to Luka to convince him to take the throne, I found myself staring up at a sign in bold letters that said: WEAPONS ROOM.

I didn't know what to expect from this particular room, but surprisingly, it had no guns or explosives. Swords of every kind rested on countless racks: long, broad, double-handed, short, slim, double-edged. Some had the exotic slant I recognized as scimitars, like in *One Thousand and One Nights*. Another rack held a selection of bows. Long bows, crossbows, flat bows. Quivers full of arrows hung above each one. Several stands held up maces while others had shields. A variety of nasty looking battleaxes dangled from hooks on one wall alongside an odd assortment of weapons—lances, clubs, spears, and others I didn't recognize. I dubbed those *miscellaneous*.

At the center of the room sat three long tables. The one in the middle had benches. The farthest consisted of rags and an

~ ☾ ~

assortment of tins that contained wax and oils. The one nearest me was covered with several pairs of gloves, chainmail, and leather armbands, wrists-guards, and padding of different sizes. Opposite the battle-axes stood dummies and circular archery targets. On the far wall hung the Visraya crest, its lion sitting regally with the tip of its sword piercing a snake's head.

I'd read enough fantasy novels to be amazed. Luka's Weapons Room was a stunning example of life imitating art. It was way beyond cool.

Below the crest stood the Zhamvy I'd been searching for. I had no idea how to convince him of what I wanted. It had gone oh so well the last time. Begging him became a possibility I didn't relish. I never begged.

I sighed.

Chances were, even if I dropped to my knees, he would laugh at me. Would I risk my dignity for Demitri?

I'd hit a new low. The Phoenix before Barinkoff had never allowed herself to care for a boy, or anyone else for that matter. She could walk away without looking back. But my days in Zhamvy City had transformed me into someone I hardly recognized. I'd agreed to an experiment that could possibly kill me. I'd bitten a Zhamvy prince and instantly created a sexually charged connection between us. And I'd met a sad prince reluctant to own up to his responsibilities to his people. All of them I wanted to help. To save. If I met me now, I wouldn't know whether to slap sense into me or feel sorry for myself. So, teetering on my heels and toes, I studied Luka.

A billowy shirt over pants so tight they hugged his thighs and knee-high boots seemed to be Luka's preferred way to dress outside of the Night Student's uniform. His clothes accentuated his form, enhancing rather than hiding. He held a broad sword with a ruby the size of a baby's fist at its pommel. Its silver blade caught the light as Luka swung and slashed at an imaginary opponent. Then he lifted the sword over his head and slashed down. He repeated this move and several others effortlessly, like a dance that was meticulously timed and choreographed.

~ ☾ ~

Despite his exertion, no sweat gleamed on his brow. His shirt didn't even cling to his body. I couldn't believe Luka was dying. How could someone so magnificent be rotting from the inside out?

"How long are you going to stand there, little cat?"

I blinked twice, unable to process.

"Little cat?"

Luka paused and held the sword at an angle to the floor. "Phoenix?"

"Huh?"

He chuckled, a devilish gleam in his eyes. "I asked how long you were going to stand there."

"Standing? I'm not standing anywhere. I'm not watching you or anything like that."

"Of course not," he said and waved me over.

I moved absentmindedly and stopped a few feet away from him. I snapped my fingers. I needed to ask him something. I had a purpose to this visit. I sure did. But what was it?

"What're you doing?" He dropped his free hand to his side.

"Thinking." I continued snapping my fingers.

"Maybe this will help." Luka closed the gap between us and wrapped his arm around my waist. In one swift tug, he pressed my body against his and leaned in, stealing a kiss. Before a whimper had a chance to leave my mouth, he broke the contact.

Glaring at him, I said, "You weren't supposed to do that."

He shrugged casually. "Why not? When I see you, all I want to do is kiss you."

"No, you don't."

His playful expression changed immediately to guarded weariness. He searched my face with his gaze.

Seeming to find the truth in my expression, Luka asked softy, "What do you know?"

"Yana told me everything," I said.

"I sincerely doubt that." He sheathed his sword.

"I know enough," I answered. "What's the sword for?"

He showed me the flat of the scabbard. It had a gold pin with his family crest etched on it. "This is a ceremonial blade. It's used when performing the Sword Dance."

~ ☾ ~

"Was that what you were doing?"

Turning away, Luka walked to a glass case and placed the sword inside. "Yes, a few steps, nothing more."

The detachment in Luka's voice shattered my restraint. I rushed forward, and without thinking of the consequences, I hugged him from behind. My hands grabbed fistfuls of his shirtfront. His honeysuckle scent wrapped around me like a comforter on a cold day. He, of all people, needed comfort. I knew how it felt to break a little inside every day until only an emptiness filled with sadness remained.

Luka stiffened.

Resting my cheek on his back, I listened to him breathe. "Luka, what happened wasn't your fault. You don't have to bear any guilt for what you had to do."

"You need to stop letting my sister manipulate you into convincing me to take the throne." He covered my trembling fists with his hands. "It's not going to happen."

"I don't care what Yana's motives for wanting you back on the throne are," I said, hoping my voice didn't crack. "What I do know is that she's right. You can't just do nothing with the rest of your life, Luka."

"What if I like doing nothing with my time?" His voice had no humor behind the question.

"Because you wouldn't be spying on Vladimir if you didn't want to do anything. Luka, you were born to be a leader. When I was vomiting all that blood in the market, you took care of me. You even invoked the Silence for me."

"Phoenix."

The way he said my name broke my heart. "I'm sorry you found your father that day."

He trembled. "He was a good king, a just king. He knew how to rule his people. I looked up to him, everyone did. And when he forbade everyone to eat flesh, I knew he did it because he wanted to save us. He was a hero to us all."

"I'm sorry you had to exile him."

He sighed heavily and spoke as if I hadn't said anything. "I was bringing him kikaron the day I found him." His tone changed from sad to grave. "At first, I couldn't open the door. I was so busy balancing the large plate in one hand and opening the door with the other that I didn't hear the sounds from the other side. I called out to him, but he was too busy—"

"Luka, it wasn't your fault," I whispered, tears rising.

He shook his head and cleared his throat. "I called to him, but he was too busy with the girl. She was sprawled on the floor, lifeless. And just as my father turned to look at me, a Silent came into the room and covered my eyes and pulled me away." He shuddered. "The next time I saw my father was while I sat on the throne, him kneeling before me, shackled, head bowed in shame. He couldn't meet my eyes."

"I'm sorry you had to be king at such a young age," I said. "I'm sorry you were forced into something you were too young for." I moved my head so my forehead leaned on his back. "But you're not that child anymore. I've only known you for a short time, but I believe you have a good heart. That you're strong enough to rule your people."

He spun in the circle of my arms and pushed me away.

"How do you know that I would make a good king?" he asked.

I shook my head. "I don't know that, and you can't know unless you try. You can't keep running away from your responsibilities and expecting someone else to take up the slack, Luka. People's lives are in danger."

His gaze hardened. "Admit it, you're only doing this because you want Demitri all for yourself."

My hands had begun to shake, so I fisted them. I searched the floor for answers, for what I had to say next. "What's the harm in you taking your rightful place in your kingdom? You owe it to the Silent who broke his vow. Don't let his sacrifice go to waste."

"Luka!" Yana's sharp voice interrupted our argument.

She stood in the doorway, a wild look in her eyes. "Come quick!"

"Yana, more words, less panting," Luka said.

"Vladimir's asking Demitri for atonement," Yana answered as she gulped air greedily.

My skin turned to ice. Vladimir had Demitri? "Luka?"

"We have to go," he said and ushered me out of the room.

~ ☾ ~

Chapter 21

Atonement

    The once cavernous throne room was now crowded shoulder-to-shoulder with Zhamvy. I should've been used to cramped spaces since I'd been on dance floors in Europe so packed that only jumping in place was possible, yet a sense of claustrophobia crushed my lungs. The women wore expensive gowns to rival any Hollywood red carpet. And the men wore different variations of suits: double-breasted, pinstriped, two-buttoned, three-buttoned—the works. I spotted a tux here and there, too. Why did they gather? What did the Atonement mean? The atmosphere felt more like a ball than a trial. My nose burned from the multitude of scents around me. Some smells seemed stronger than others. I had never needed fresh air more in my life. How the Zhamvy could stand the cloying scents mixing together without passing out amazed me.

    Since Yana was smaller than I was, I figured I'd create space for her to move around. Every time I bumped into Zhamvy, they threw disgusted glances at me. Some protested my bumping into them, but the moment they noticed Yana behind me, their eyes bulged and they let us through with muttered apologies.

    The next time it happened, Yana smacked me and said, "I think you should let me go first. We'll get there faster."

    "Ow! God, you're stronger than you look." I rubbed my arm. "I won't punch you back if you explain why."

~ ☾ ~

"You forget the caste. You resemble a Merk. We're in a room full of Royals. They would definitely take offense to you being here. While I'm—"

"A *Superiori*." Awe washed over me. "This doesn't have anything to do with a rumor floating around that I'm Luka's pet, does it?"

She flinched. "You've heard about that, huh? I don't want to seem elitist, but that's just how it is around here."

"Apology accepted." No point in feeling sorry for myself. I motioned for Yana to lead the way. Then I heard the one voice I dreaded the most rise over the din.

"My ward and I will not stand for this affront," Vladimir said in a high-and-mighty tone. "My family, now *her* family, cannot believe we have been treated with utter disrespect. From the crown prince, no less."

My blood froze.

"Come on." Yana grabbed my hand and maneuvered us to the front of the pack.

A few yards ahead of us knelt Demitri, head bent, hands shackled behind him. Untied and untamed, his hair obscured the sides of his face. Someone had torn his Barinkoff uniform shirt, revealing the silver crescent scar similar to the ones on Darius and Yaris and on other Zhamvy males in the room. The mark at the junction of his neck and shoulder.

My stomach tumbled. Desire, heat, passion, need, want, longing. There weren't enough words to describe what seeing the scar did to my system. I wanted to run to Demitri and kiss him, even in his state of dejection.

"That scar," I said.

Yana squeezed my hand and whispered, "Zhamvy create a connection when a male allows a female to mark him. It is the first stage of mating. To us, allowing to be bitten is the height of vulnerability. The female leaves her mark and a bond is formed. The male and female are drawn to each other's presence afterward, urging them to complete the ritual."

The blood roaring in my ears almost drowned out Yana's words. I had to concentrate just to listen to her. Not that I didn't already know half of it. Demitri warned me about what my biting him would do. I felt it every time I saw him.

~ ☾ ~

"The bond is sealed through the act of consummation," Yana continued. "During that time, the pair can't be apart for more than a few days or they will be driven mad. Seals are only severed through—"

Vladimir's words interrupted Yana.

"When my ward came to me," he said, gesturing to Calixta, who wore a magenta dress with a plunging neckline and a smirk, "I wouldn't allow myself to believe what she had informed me of. She claimed Prince Demitri betrayed the trust of their betrothal." He glanced at the masses for theatrical effect. "Surely the crown prince wouldn't be so reckless."

A wave of murmured disapproval spread through the crowd.

My knees shook. Terror twisted in my gut like a knife. "I did this," I mumbled. "He's here because of me."

"Breathe, Phoenix. Just breathe." Yana clutched my arm with her other hand. "What are you saying?"

"I bit him."

"You *what*?"

I couldn't see Yana's face, but from her tone, I heard her surprise and trepidation. "That mark came from me," I said, my voice low. "When Dray asked me if I bit Demitri, I lied because Demitri didn't want me to admit it. But when I encountered Calixta in Dray's garden, I let it slip that I bit him."

Yana pulled me closer to her. Whether she held me back or gave support didn't matter to me. My focus was on Demitri.

"Explain yourself, my son," Darius said.

I only noticed the monarch when he'd spoken. He sat on the throne like a statue in robes—a hint of concern in his eyes. It must have been difficult for him to sit there and question his son. As king, his people came first. Objectivity must be enforced for order to be maintained.

To his right stood a fair-haired goddess who could have easily been Luka's and Yana's mother. She wore a Grecian gown the color of Darius's robes. Her curls fell loose and elegant over her shoulders. She wore large gold armbands studded with sapphires. One hand rested on the king's shoulder while the other clutched her hip. Statuesque. Apart from her livid eyes, glaring at Demitri with intermingled love, concern, and reproach, she hardly moved.

Demitri lifted his head and said, "It is true, father. I have allowed myself to be marked."

A collective gasp sucked all the air from the room.

"I hardly believe—" Vladimir swallowed the rest of his words when Darius interrupted. A look of contempt flitted across his face.

"Continue, my son."

"I am drawn to her, father. Is that not how we find our partners? We answer the call from deep within us for another."

Happiness underscored my worry. My heart wanted me to run to Demitri's side then and confirm what he was saying. I wanted to defend him, to shield him from persecution. But Yana's tight grip kept me in place. I couldn't move even if I wanted to. And a small voice inside me warned that if I said anything I might make this experience worse for Demitri.

"But you willingly entered a betrothal with Calixta." Darius stated.

Demitri nodded. "I did it for my people. I believed I would not be fortunate enough to meet the one who could change my world with one glance, one word, one kiss." He paused. "But I have. I am fortunate. Like you, Father. Like you, Mother." He looked at the woman beside Darius. Her face softened.

"I will not question your choice, my son," the queen said in a throaty voice that exuded power and grace. "I know what it means to be marked. I know the pleasure of it." She gave Darius a sidelong glance.

"But, your highness." Vladimir hid none of his fake shock. "It's not your place to decide—"

The queen gave Vladimir a withering glare that could cause the strongest of men to wilt.

"You forget your place, Vladimir," she said. "You may be prime minister, but *I* am still your queen."

A chorus of "bless her beauty" resounded throughout the room.

~ ☾ ~

"But, also," she said, "I may not be making decisions here, but where my son is concerned, I have the right to speak."

Vladimir placed his right hand on the center of his chest and bowed slightly. "Yes, my queen."

"Bless her beauty!" Everyone cheered in perfect unison.

"How shall we proceed?" Darius asked impatiently.

"The betrothal is broken." Vladimir hushed Calixta's protest with a curt wave. Then he addressed the crowd, arms wide, his voice booming to the far corners of the room. "No female would take a marked male."

Many heads nodded. Whispers buzzed.

"Even if this is so," Vladimir scanned the crowd, and when he saw me, his eyes widened then narrowed, "we, my family and I, demand atonement for our honor."

His snake-eyed stare sent tingling dread all over my skin. A wild rage seethed inside me. Only Yana's whispered warning in my ear to keep still prevented me from flying forward and ripping him a new one.

Darius glanced at Vladimir. "Name your atonement."

Vladimir conferred with the group of Zhamvy Calixta stood with. Eli was with them, a smug look on his face. He hadn't noticed me yet, or if he had, he wasn't showing any signs of it.

"Where's Luka?" Yana asked through her teeth.

Halfway to the throne room, Luka had whispered he needed to take care of something. He promised to join us as soon as he could. I wanted to question him, but he'd already hurried down a different hallway.

Vladimir nodded once and addressed the king, "Your highness."

"Your atonement?" Darius inclined his head.

"My family and I have come to ask one thousand lashes for breaking the betrothal."

Frantic whispers erupted.

Could anyone—Zhamvy or not—survive a thousand lashes? I felt nothing from my waist down.

The king's impassive expression hardened.

The curtains to the right wall parted and a hush swept swiftly over the crowd as everyone turned their heads.

~ ☾ ~

Yana sighed in relief.

I tore my attention away from Demitri long enough to watch Luka stride into the throne room flanked by six Vityas—all ice blond, all impossibly tall, and all smelling faintly of the forest. He wore an immaculate gray suit with a maroon tie. Robes similar to what Darius wore were draped over his suit. He had his usually unruly curls slicked back. A gold circlet gleamed on his forehead. He looked so much like his father that it was eerie.

Luka held up his hand and the Vityas stopped. A second later, they moved to form a loose semi-circle behind him. Each one had his left hand resting on the pommel of his sword. They may seem relaxed, but the way they stared straight on belayed concentration honed by years of hard training.

Vladimir paled, hiding his surprised expression by bowing. "Prince Visraya, what an honor that you could join us today," he said.

Luka inclined his head and said, "It is my pleasure to be here when my cousin is facing atonement. In fact, I wondered why I was never informed of this." He stared pointedly at Vladimir.

The seriousness and air of formality that surrounded Luka reached inside me and clutched my heart. So this was what he could be as king. I liked his playful nature, but his powerful aura now inspired admiration. I shivered. He was glorious in full regalia. All he needed was to sit on the throne Darius occupied and the ensemble would be complete. I was right—he lived to be king.

"It was so sudden, Prince Visraya." Vladimir pulled at the lapels of his jacket self-consciously as he straightened. "And with your ne'er do well ways, I didn't think you would find a gathering such as this worth your time."

"Barinkoff Majesty." Luka tilted his head at Darius, shifting his gaze away from Vladimir.

"Visraya Majesty," Darius greeted, lifting his right hand to his chest.

Luka turned to the queen and bowed. "Aunt Yalena, lovely as always."

~ ☾ ~

"You flatter me, nephew." Yalena smiled.

"Now." Luka slid his frosty-blue eyes to a more composed Vladimir. "What atonement did you ask from my cousin?"

"One thousand lashes, my prince." Vladimir smirked.

"That is excessive, considering he is the crown prince and was only following the urges he felt for the one who had marked him."

"But—"

"*Urges*, Vladimir, you remember them, I suppose. Urges rule the way we live. They are what make us who we are. Seeing as you are not marked, could it be that your own urges are impotent to find a female?"

Vladimir flushed scarlet.

Darius defused the situation before the prime minister blew a gasket by saying, "Show respect for our *beloved* prime minister, young Visraya."

Luka blinked. "Your majesty, I merely state a fact, for our *beloved* prime minister does not show marks."

"State your case, Luka." The king's manner held a mix of exasperation and affection.

"I request to lower the lashes to five hundred. My cousin will perform the Sword Dance with me tomorrow at the Winter Solstice Festival and I need him fit for the task."

The queen gasped. "Luka, you cannot be serious!"

He shrugged. "He has already made the arrangements with me, aunt."

Demitri growled in protest.

"I am sorry for spoiling the surprise, cousin," Luka said. "Five hundred lashes and no more, Prime Minister."

An expression of sheer malice formed on Vladimir's face. "Then I request the use of the Lightning Rod."

The Zhamvy around me cried out in outrage. Yana, in her lilting voice, cursed a blue streak; shocking on a girl who looked so young. Demitri shuddered. Darius gripped the arms of the throne. Yalena looked sick. While Luka's brows knotted.

"What's a lightning rod?" I asked Yana.

She rubbed her forehead. "It's a special whip."

"What's so freaking special about it?"

~ ☾ ~

Yana held my hand with both of hers and gave me the kind of look people attending funerals give the loved ones of the recently deceased. "The Lightning Rod is made of a special alloy that burns Zhamvy skin," she clarified. "We heal slower that way. After being hit several times, we stop healing all together during the whipping."

"How many times?"

"A hundred, a hundred fifty at most." Panic mixed with sadness shadowed her pretty face. "But it really depends on the strength of the one being whipped."

"That still leaves three hundred fifty lashes that Demitri has to endure without the possibility of healing. God, I think I'm going to be sick." I doubled over.

"So be it," said Luka with noticeable reluctance.

"Brilliant!" Vladimir clapped once. "Bring in the implements."

"Phoenix, you can't show any weakness now." Yana yanked me up.

My world spun. I took a deep breath and braced myself for the whipping. I'd never seen anyone punished in person before. My lungs couldn't seem to take in enough air. I felt woozy. Never had I wanted to kick serious Zhamvy butt more than I did in that instant, even more so than during my catfight with Calixta.

"Phoenix, breathe." Yana slapped my hand.

Four Bogatyr entered. Two carried poles with rings at the top. Another brought rope while the last one held a silver horsewhip that crackled from an electric charge running through it.

A deathly hush fell over the room. Vladimir smiled and rubbed his hands together in excitement. Darius and his wife held hands. Luka's lips were in a hard line, while his guards all remained impassive. Yana and I huddled together, holding each other's hands for strength.

The soldiers carrying the poles positioned themselves on either side of Demitri. The one with the rope kneeled behind Demitri, turned him to face the crowd, and removed his shackles. Then he tied the rope around each of Demitri's wrists and tossed one end each to the Bogatyr on either side of them. They threaded the ends into the rings at the top of the poles, raising Demitri's arms. In a swift plunging motion, they planted the poles into the floor. The Bogatyr who had brought the rope ripped the rest of Demitri's shirt away, leaving him naked from the waist up. A hard tug on the ropes suspended Demitri a foot off the ground.

Demitri lifted his head, and our eyes met. I clutched Yana's hands tighter. He mouthed something to me, but I couldn't quite get it at first. I shook my head at him. My gaze focused on his lips.

What? I mouthed back. When he'd repeated himself a third time, I felt all the blood in me rush to the pads of my feet.

His lips formed the words: *Look away.*

Chapter 22

Wounds

    I stood frozen, unable to feel, barely able to breathe. Demitri hung suspended in the air by ropes tied to his wrists. The air crackled with electricity. The hairs on the back of my neck and arms stood up from the static.

    When my mother had wasted away, it frustrated me that the doctors could do nothing for her. I would watch her chest move up and down as the respirator kept her alive. I would sit by her bed and stare at her peaceful face, wondering if she felt any pain. Eventually, an empty void grew inside me, sucking up all my happiness and ability to live a normal, everyday life. Everything seemed like an out of body experience.

    Now, in the throne room, I couldn't summon the void that kept me from breaking during those days at the hospital. Demitri took the "atonement" asked of him. I felt every lash as if I'd been the one being whipped.

    Anxiety coiled inside me like a rubber band with no way for release. Demitri stared at me with determined eyes, silently begging me to do as he'd mouthed before the whipping started, but I couldn't look away. I needed to hang on to what connected us. If I couldn't prevent the whipping, the least I could do was bear it with him. The only time he betrayed any sign of pain started about a few minutes into the whipping. The muscle twitching along his jaw gave him away. Seconds later, he pulled back his lips and bared all his teeth. But never did he cry out.

~ ☾ ~

I didn't know how he managed to remain conscious for so long, but when he finally fainted, a part of me felt glad he didn't feel the pain anymore. Another part of me wanted his eyes to keep staring at my face. With his eyes closed, I couldn't tell if he was still breathing. No one checked his vital signs. The Bogatyr with the whip just kept going, his face expressionless.

The sound was the worst part.

As the ordeal continued, my knees weakened with every resounding *whapack*. My legs, arms, and hands went dead. Yana gripped my fingers as hard as I clutched hers. She called my name at one point, but I ignored her, concentrating on Demitri while trying to remain aware of everything else around me.

Luka stared stone-faced at the proceedings, hardly moving. His guards barely shifted their legs to balance the weight of their bodies. Uncanny.

Vladimir relished every whip crack, his hands clasped as if in reverent prayer. His eyes sparkled with unabashed joy. On the other hand, hellfire burned in Calixta's eyes. She stared at me the whole time, blame and hatred in those molten obsidian orbs. I actually thought she'd charge me based on the rage contorting her face. And Eli. He enjoyed the proceedings immensely. I sensed this was payback for when Demitri saved me from his clutches and ordering the Silence.

The crowd displayed a mix of emotions. Some flinched. Others remained still. Women turned away. Men placed bets on how long Demitri would stay awake. Some, I noticed, inhaled deeply then exhaled slowly—a classic sign of healing. The disease continued to ravage the Zhamvy even as their crown prince endured five hundred lashes.

Another portion of my mind—the more rational side—discovered something new about the Zhamvy. They bled blue. The blue of the Mediterranean Sea, shimmering in the morning sun. Then my thoughts moved on to another revelation concerning bleeding. No wonder rumors of a human surfaced after I had vomited blood all over the deli floor. I may resemble them in skin, hair, and eye perfection. I may have my own scent signature. I may have been as strong.

~ ☾ ~

But, fundamentally, I still stayed human. I still bled red.

The blood pool beneath Demitri grew so large, I wondered if he had any left inside.

"Just fifty more lashes," Yana said.

"Blood." My throat felt drier than autumn leaves. I trembled, exhausted. "There's so much blood."

"I know," she said. "But at least he's still alive."

I shook my head in complete desolation. My hearing had returned to normal. I could no longer pick out Demitri's heartbeat the way I used to. "How can you be so sure?"

Her gaze fell. "I'm not. I can only hope he is."

If only my heart could beat for the both of us. Staring at the ocean of blue blood spreading beneath him made it hard to continue hoping. I wanted to cry out, "Demitri, open your eyes!" But my tongue refused to move.

The final lash became the longest few seconds of my life. I wanted to yell at the Bogatyr to get on with it. I wanted to beat up the Bogatyr. I wanted to strangle Vladimir. I wanted many things, but all those thoughts stopped the moment the last *whapack* bounced off the walls.

Luka ran to Demitri. "Let him down—*now*!" he ordered. He slipped on the blood, but managed to regain his balance before he fell. The bottom of his robes turned a vivid shade of violet as the fabric soaked in the blood.

Four Vityas crowded around them, treading carefully on the blood-slicked floor. His other guards left and returned with a stretcher. Two replaced the Bogatyrs holding the ropes, slowly lowering Demitri. The other two freed his wrists while Luka bore his weight. Then they carried him onto the stretcher, his decimated back parallel to the ceiling.

Demitri groaned and my heart stopped. My legs collapsed underneath me. My palms flat on the freezing stone surface. Yana encouraged me to stand, but I kept staring at the floor. He was alive. Oh God, he was alive.

"Not so fast, Prince Visraya," Vladimir said.

Luka said, "For all that we believe is holy, do not come near him or else—"

"Yes, my prince." Vladimir paused. "May I enquire as to where you're taking Prince Demitrius?"

~ ☾ ~

"My home, prime minister. With your permission, Barinkoff Majesty." Luka's tone froze anything in its path. Darius nodded once. Then Luka said to Vladimir, "You have taken your five hundred lashes. Now, I will take Demitri to recover. Someone look for Prince Andrayus and apprise him of what has happened here. Dray will want to tend to his brother."

"What about—"

"You will get your Sword Dance tomorrow, *Prime Minister*. Now, let us leave this room in peace."

Leave. They were leaving? Without me? I needed to go with them. My legs refused to carry my weight as I struggled to stand.

Yana poked my shoulder. "Phoenix, if you can't get up on your own, I'll be forced to carry you," she said. "At the risk of sounding prissy, I don't want to rip the lacing of my dress, so get up. We have to go!"

Somehow—the details of *how* escaped me—I stood on shaky legs and followed the retreating party that accompanied Demitri. All the gory movies in the world could never prepare anyone for the actual thing. I personally thought of myself as tough, but what I'd been through—made to watch Demitri take five hundred lashes—had stolen all my strength. Only by the force of my remaining will was I able to manage to make it to the Weapons Room without hurling. The last thing I needed was complete access to sharp weapons when a vendetta simmered in my mind.

"Why aren't you bringing him to a room?" I asked.

"The best place to operate is on a flat surface, and the only tables sturdy enough to support Demitri are in this room," Luka explained as he cleared the table closest to the double doors by shoving everything on top onto the floor in a clatter of chainmail and a heap of gloves. He instructed the Vityas to gently place their unconscious load face down on its surface. "Dray's lab along with the Medical Wing is currently crawling with Traditionalists because of the inquest."

Demitri's groan made my stomach flip. He felt pain. I wanted to move, I wanted to do something other than stand there, but I didn't know what I could do to help. The skin on

~ ☾ ~

his back resembled blue ground meat. I gagged. The slashes overlapped with each other so much that I couldn't differentiate between individual wounds. To say he looked bad only mocked the situation.

Dray and a team of assistants in matching lab coats—carrying bags of equipment—arrived just as Luka barked out new instructions. Yana went off to gather towels. A few Vityas picked up the mess Luka had made. And I stood frozen in a corner.

Dray took in the scene and said, "I want this room cleared of unnecessary personnel and sterilized before we begin."

Luka ordered the Vityas to drop whatever they were doing and leave the room. The sliver breastplate clad soldiers filed out without protest. Soon, only Dray, his assistants, Luka, and I remained.

"Dray, I want to stay," I said.

"If you can handle hearing Demitri scream, then fine." He glared at me then returned his attention to his assistants as they frantically built a clear plastic tent around the table.

Luka came to my side and placed a hand on my shoulder.

"Don't!" I stepped away from his touch.

"It might be best if you leave," he said.

"I want to stay."

"There's nothing you can do here."

"I caused *this*. If I hadn't told Calixta that I bit him, he wouldn't be lying on that table." I wrapped my arms around myself and clutched my arms until my nails dug into my skin. "And if you say it isn't my fault, I swear—"

"But you aren't at fault here."

"God, I should've known this would happen!"

"How could you? He should have stopped you, but he didn't. Demitri knew what he was doing by letting you mark him."

"Phoenix," Demitri moaned.

Without thinking, I ran to him, shoving aside the Zhamvy hooking an IV into his arm. I kneeled in front of Demitri and cupped his face with shaking hands.

"I'm here, Demitri, I'm here," I said.

He opened one eye. "How bad do I look?"

~ ☾ ~

"You have time to joke around even when you're bleeding to death? You've got to be kidding me!" Before relief could blossom in my chest, I noticed Demitri's skin shrivel. "Dray!"

He rushed to my side, examining Demitri's arm that now resembled a lufa. "His shot is wearing off. The healing he needed during the whipping seemed to have aggravated the disease."

"Dray, what's happening to him?" Luka asked.

I'd forgotten that Luka still stood in the corner I'd vacated. I quickly whispered to Dray, "Help him. Please. I'll take care of Luka."

He frowned. "Hurry."

I stood up and approached Luka, putting a wobble in my step. He caught me before I faked a fall, blocking his view of Demitri's rapidly desiccating body. I clutched at Luka's arms and looked at him beseechingly.

"I'm not feeling well. Can you bring me to my room?"

He searched my face for a second then nodded. He wrapped his arm around me to support my weight. Outside the makeshift operating room, Luka picked me up and carried me the rest of the way, his robes flowing around us like red wings with purple tips. He nudged the door to my room open, strode in, and placed me on the bed. He pulled the covers over my body and sat next to me.

"Are you alright?" he asked, tucking a strand of my hair behind my ear.

A creeping blush heated my face at his tender touch. Guilt suffused my chest. I had to force myself to speak coherently. "I'm fine now."

"Are you sure?"

"Really, I'm fine." I squeezed his hand. "I'm a little hungry though," I lied.

He didn't want to leave me. I saw it in the tightening of his lips. But his quick glance at the door showed his unease. He worried for Demitri as much, maybe even more, than I did.

He turned back to me, his brows knotted. "Are you *sure* you're alright?"

"Just get some *yusha* in me and I'll be fine," I assured him with a smile.

~ ☾ ~

He stared at me skeptically before he stood up. "I'll send Yana with lunch."

"Thank you, Luka," I whispered as he stepped out of the room. As soon as the door closed behind him, I counted to ten, then leapt off the bed and succumbed to pacing. I never paced, but I had too much energy to stay prone. I strode to the door, turned around, and marched to the French windows. Before long, I had worn a path in the carpet. I hated not being part of the action. I hated feeling so helpless.

"Will you be pacing while having lunch?" Yana asked, her sudden presence in my room a surprise.

"I didn't hear you come in."

"You were too busy clomping around to notice." She set the tray on the table at the corner.

"Any news?"

"From the sound he's making, he's still alive."

"The *sound*?"

"Why not wait for Dray?"

"Spit it out, Goth Girl!"

Her jaw tightened. "The screams. Demitri's screams."

My body sagged into a chair as my nervous energy dissipated. I buried my head in my hands and moaned.

"See?" she said. "I told you to wait for Dray. Blaming yourself isn't healthy, Phoenix."

I sighed. "Too late."

"Fine, whatever. Blame yourself."

The door opened, and I leapt to my feet. Dray staggered in. He closed the door and leaned against it, head bowed, resting his chin on his chest. His hair stood on end, the collar of his lab coat askew.

"How did it go?"

He lifted a finger. "Let me breathe for a second. I didn't expect that patching him up would take half my soul with it."

"Oh, come on. Don't make me wait."

Dray lifted his head and gave me a blistering glare. "You try scraping away dead skin and applying a skin graft on your own brother while he's screaming and let's see if you want to talk about it."

I ignored Dray's sarcasm. "You have to tell me how he is."

"Damn it! This is because of you!" He rushed me and grabbed the front of my blouse. "How could you!"

"What?" I blinked at him.

Gritting his teeth, Dray let me go and ran his fingers through his unruly hair. "Do I have to spell it out for you? I thought you were smarter than that."

"I didn't know Calixta would go running to her guardian or whatever Vladimir is to her."

"You should've told me you bit him when I asked you."

I shoved him. "Demitri didn't want me to tell you."

Dray stepped back. His gaze fell as he combed a hand through his hair again. "I made a mess of things."

"Understatement of the Zhamvy year." I crossed my arms. "So, how is he?"

"Recovering."

One word. One word that erased all my previous annoyance at Dray. We all had a slice of the blame pie. I'd decided to break curfew a second time. Dray had injected me with his formula. Demitri had let me bite him. Luka...well, I couldn't think of anything specific, but still, he seemed like the underhanded sort. In the end, none of it really mattered. Demitri would live. No matter how screwed up the situation seemed, he would live.

Chapter 23

Confessions

    With Demitri still healing from the operation, I decided to take a shower, letting the hot water wash away the tension in my muscles, before I went to see him. My mind calmed. The rush of adrenaline ebbed. As I finished dressing in a sundress Yana had left for me, I heard a loud crash, followed by a door slamming shut, then Dray's voice muttering to himself. No threat, then, but what?
    I came out of the bathroom and gaped. In the time it had taken for me to finish my shower, Dray had transformed the room of frills into a mini-lab. Which meant more tests for me. Beeping equipment stood in one corner. A microscope along with test tubes sat on the table. When the guy said he had some tests to perform, I didn't expect that he'd bring his entire lab with him. I squinted, noticing the teapot, which lay in a sad broken pile that no super glue could put back together.
    I looked at Dray. "What happened to you? Where's Yana?"
    He rubbed a red welt on his cheek. "She threw the teapot at me and stormed off."
    "Knowing you, I'm sure you deserved it."
    "What do you mean I *deserved* it?"
    "Dray, the only reason you're still alive is because you're useful."
    "I resent that!"
    "Admit it. When it comes to your precious experiments, nothing else matters."

~ ☾ ~

"I don't understand."

I sighed. "Do I have to spell it out for you? I thought you were smarter than that."

The answering growl said he didn't appreciate having his words thrown back at him. I laughed.

"You're selfish when it comes to needing results," I said. "And it's because of those results that you're still alive." I wrapped my wet hair in the towel and looked at Dray, who stared into space. Could he actually be more emotionally stunted than all of us combined?

"Why was Demitri screaming during the procedure? Didn't you have anesthetic?" I asked, wanting to return the topic to what was important.

He snapped out of his daze. "Sedation wasn't an option. For the skin grafts to adhere, he needed to be awake." He massaged his eyelids with his thumb and index finger. "With the booster shot, healing is faster when the subject is lucid. If he wants to be able to perform the Sword Dance tomorrow, he needs to stay conscious all night to heal enough. Damn Luka for even suggesting it."

I winced. "I don't think he had a choice. Vladimir was out for blood."

Dray said something under his breath in their language, which sounded like rocks rubbing together.

"What did you just say?" I slipped on the ballet flats Yana had left for me by the bed.

"Believe me, ignorance in this case is bliss." He looked at me, considering.

"What?" I felt self-conscious with Dray silently staring at me.

Then he shook his head. "I still can't believe he allowed you to bite him."

"What do you mean?"

"Remember when I asked you if you tried to take a bite out of Demitri and you said no? Thanks for lying about that, by the way."

I sighed and rolled my eyes. "Demitri didn't want me to tell you. I don't know why he wanted to keep it a secret. I didn't think it'd be an issue."

~ ☾ ~

He rubbed his chin. "I assumed that since I injected you with the formula you'd wake up driven by the hunger caused by the id. You would have taken a bite out of anyone in that room. It could have been anyone. What baffles me is why Demitri let you bite him, knowing the consequences of that action."

My skin chilled, as if a sudden draft flew through the room. "Are you saying it's coincidence that I bit him?"

He nodded. "But," he added before I could say another word, "the connection you have with him because of that bite is real."

"If the connection is real, then why did I still feel attraction for Luka after biting Demitri?"

Dray blinked. "That's new. Normally, once a connection is forged, you're devoted to one another. Feeling attraction for another shouldn't be a factor. Maybe it has something to do with your body still being fundamentally human. Do you still feel attracted to Luka?"

I thought about it for a second. I shook my head. "Not since I woke up in the Medical Wing."

"Do you feel lust when you are near Demitri?"

"Excuse me?" I spat out.

"I'm asking this for purely scientific reasons."

"Sure you are."

"Just answer the question, Phoenix."

My skin went from chilled to warm in a split second, especially my cheeks. I stared at the carpet when I nodded an affirmative.

"Do you feel drawn to his presence?" he asked.

Again, I nodded.

"Do you feel euphoric when you touch? I assume you've kissed. It's impossible not to. It's like defying gravity."

"Assume all you want."

"Do you feel the need to copulate with him?"

I laughed nervously at the term he used. Dray really did look at things from a scientific point of view. He and Preya would get along. If only I could introduce them. With my luck, Dray would offer to make Preya a test subject and Preya would actually say yes. A scientific marriage made in Petri

dish heaven. I lifted my gaze until our eyes met.

"None of your business," I said with a smirk.

"I'll take that as a yes." His face lit up. "This is totally an unexpected result. I didn't think a connection could be formed since you're still fundamentally human. But from your answers...this is brilliant! Just brilliant! Your attraction to Luka was just a glitch caused by your overactive hormones. What you have with Demitri is more real."

I didn't know what to make of Dray's excitement, and something told me I shouldn't try. Then, as if the bubble of his elation had burst, Dray sobered. His gaze traveled the room, resting briefly on his equipment before landing on me again. That sense of foreboding I'd been feeling since I'd found out about the disease had returned.

"What is it, Dray?"

"Shall we begin the tests?" he said.

"Seriously? Do we have to?"

He answered my whine by pointing at the chair beside his.

Hours later, groggy and grumpy, I continued to endure Dray's tests. He drew my blood, made me dip my fingers in several solutions that stank like rotting meat, and attached me to a heart monitor. He'd been quiet the whole time. I tried making conversation, but he refused to engage in it. I gave up after he detached me from the monitor. He then took a slide with a drop of my blood and examined it on his microscope. He sat up and faced me as I sat cross-legged on the bed.

"I'm sorry, Phoenix," he said. "I really am."

I cocked my head to the side and asked, "What's with the sudden apology?"

"You're dying."

He words jolted me out of my calm. "What? Wait! *What?*"

"The formula is slowly eating you." Dray glanced at a clipboard with notes scribbled on it. "It seems the reason for your bleeding has to do with the formula consuming the parts of you that remain human."

"You're joking, right?" I couldn't breathe. It felt like a bear sat on my chest.

"I'm afraid not," he said.

"Then get it out of me," I yelled. "Get it out! Get it out!"

~ ☾ ~

"Phoenix." He stood up and put his hands on my shoulders. "You need to calm down."

"How can you ask me to calm down when you just said I'm dying? I thought you said there was no permanent damage when I woke up from puking all that blood."

"I didn't know at the time what the formula was doing to your system. I only started seeing signs of degeneration when I tested you at the lab. I thought another dose of the booster would stabilize the formula. But you bled out again. And when I tested your blood a second time…"

"What?" I grabbed his wrists. "What!"

"The only thing keeping you alive right now is the last booster shot I gave you." He held my stare. "I don't know if the formula will fade before it completely ravages your body."

"Then what's the plan?" I asked, panic reaching a painful peak inside my chest.

"I have a possible way of flushing out the formula from your—"

"Do it," I said. "Give it to me."

"Phoenix," he said, shaking me, "it's dangerous."

I had no words left. My chest continued to inflate and deflate, but it no longer felt like breathing. I waited for what he had to say next. And he didn't disappoint.

"In order to flush out the formula, I need to inject you with my strain of the bubonic plague," he explained.

I slumped forward, unable to believe what Dray had told me. He let go of my shoulders and moved to the table and sat down. I vaguely heard him sigh. A sad, remorseful sound. The rational side of my brain saw the truth in his words. The formula transformed my body to mimic that of a Zhamvy, but fundamentally, I remained human. And what did Zhamvy eat? It seemed plausible that the formula would begin consuming me from the inside out. The emotional side of my brain screamed in panic. My heart rate picked up. My survival instincts kicked in, making me want to run and never look back. It wanted the formula out of my body quick. It wanted me to live.

I rubbed my palms together and closed my eyes. Then I rested the heels of my hands on my eyelids, attempting to soothe the sudden, piercing throbbing that gathered within. I breathed. In and out. In and out, trying to calm the emotional and think with the rational. I couldn't gather the strength to be pissed at Dray. He couldn't have known what the formula would do. I'd agreed to help him. Unfortunately, that decision had backfired on the both of us. Now, the formula was ravaging my body and I had two choices: ride it out until it faded or let Dray inject me with his version of the bubonic plague. Both put me in a dangerous situation. Both held the possibility of killing me.

I dropped my hands, opened my eyes, and looked at Dray. For the first time since he'd injected me with the formula, true remorse marred his features.

"I'm sorry for doing this to you, Phoenix," he said.

The once unapologetic mad scientist was apologizing. I must really be worse off than I could ever think I was. My heart shrank into itself. I didn't know what to say to Dray. Saying I was fine was a blatant lie. Saying it was okay would send the wrong message. I wanted him to be sorry. I really did. Then the smiling face of my mother flashed before my eyes.

I smiled through the tears welling in my eyes. "When my mother got sick, we all thought it was just the flu. She got a check-up and the doctor sent her home with a prescription. Two weeks later, she was still sick and getting worse. They confined her for tests. My father told me everything was going to be fine. She never left the hospital since they brought her in."

"Phoenix," Dray whispered.

"Every night I prayed the doctors would find what was wrong with her." I wiped away the tear that escaped. "When you came to me asking for help, I really wanted to say no, but then I realized you were fighting to save your people the way I wanted the doctors to fight for my mother. Maybe they did fight their hardest. I don't know." I looked into Dray's eyes then. "But this I do know, no matter how scared I am about dying right now, I don't regret saying yes to helping you."

"Phoenix, the death of your mother wasn't anybody's fault." Dray's raised hand stopped what I was about to say. "I cannot tell you what happened with the doctors because I wasn't there. But based on everything I've read about your mother's case, no one could have done anything. Maybe even I couldn't have saved her if I was her physician."

I heard the truth in his words. I spent months of my life being angry at the doctors for being able to do nothing for my mom. Like what I told Luka about forgiving his father, maybe I should forgive the doctors. It wasn't their fault my mother got sick. And I said yes to helping the Zhamvy. I would see this thing through to the end.

"I want to see Demitri," I said. "Before I make my decision, I want to talk to him."

"Alright." Dray nodded. "He should be up and about. You can go now."

I stood up and headed for the door, feeling a sudden high that propelled me forward. Anticipation curled my insides. I needed to see him. I needed it so badly.

"Phoenix?" Dray called just as I twisted the doorknob.

I glanced at him over my shoulder. "Yes?"

He hesitated. "If you happen to see Luka, will you send him here?"

A small smile spread across my lips. "Finally telling someone else?" I asked.

"I figured it's about time." He shrugged. "He saw what happened to Demitri. He should know."

I left Dray in a daze. The realization that I was dying didn't seem real. I wondered if this was how terminally ill patients felt right after the doctor told them they had six months to live. Did Mom feel the same way when the doctors told her they didn't know what was wrong with her, just days before she'd slipped into a coma?

I walked, yet my feet didn't feel like they touched the ground. In fact, I felt nothing from my chest down. The need to see Demitri kept me going though. I wanted to...what? I had no idea what I wanted to tell him. Should I tell him about the disease? Should I tell him about what the formula was doing to my body? I had no clue.

The same questions kept recycling inside my head until I reached the Weapons Room. Demitri wasn't lying on the table anymore and the plastic tent had been dismantled. Only a lone Vityas remained in the room, mopping blood off the floor.

I grabbed his sleeve. "Where is he?"

"Who?" He blinked at me.

"Prince Demitri."

"With Visraya Majesty, but—"

I didn't wait for him to finish. I turned and ran for Luka's study.

Chapter 24

Precipice

    Breathing hard and more than a little nervous, I stared up at the double doors. The carved owl glared down as if judging me. Should I go in? Should I knock? Would they let me in? Before I could make up my mind, one of the doors opened. I jumped in surprise. Luka slid out and yanked the door shut.
    "Little cat," he greeted.
    "Geez! Don't do that."
    A wide grin erased his worried expression. "I knew you wouldn't be able to resist coming to me. Come, give us a kiss."
    I put my hands up. "Not when Demitri's behind those doors."
    "So you're saying if Demitri wasn't in my study right now you'd kiss me?"
    "Stop being a jerk, Luka."
    He looked away, smile disappearing. My heart broke in half. I closed the gap between us and touched his cheek. He leaned into the contact, covering my hand with his.
    "I shouldn't let you go in there," he whispered.
    I pulled my hand from his cheek and stepped closer until I stood inches from the tall, blonde Zhamvy prince. Shifting my weight, I planted a soft kiss on his jaw.
    "Thank you for saving him," I said. "I owe you one."
    Luka regarded me with an icy-blue stare. "If you had bitten me first, would things be different? Would you have considered me over him?"

~ ☾ ~

"I don't have an answer for you, Luka."

Many unsaid words floated between us, choking the air. We stood still, gazes locked, searching for answers in each other's faces. I wondered what it would have been like if I'd bitten Luka. Would I have felt the same connection? The same physical pull? From what Yana and Dray had told me, they found partners by first forging a connection. Not the other way around. I stopped myself. I couldn't let myself dwell on the "what ifs." As Darius said, what was done was done. There was no use hoping the past would change because it never would. All I could do now was move forward.

"Are you sure he's the one you want?" Luka asked.

"Yes," I said.

With a sad sigh, Luka stepped aside. "He's still recovering. Don't do *anything* to aggravate him."

My face smoldered. "Geez. I won't—"

A golden eyebrow arched. "I doubt that."

I punched his arm playfully. "Dray has something to tell you."

He nodded and left.

An overwhelming sense of sadness I couldn't explain gripped my chest while I watched him turn a corner. My shoulders slumped. If Dray thought he'd made a mess of things, what about me? I'd just clawed Luka's heart out and stomped on it with my ballet flat. I was the worst person in the world right now.

After a huff, I faced the doors again. My knuckles hadn't even touched the wood when Demitri said, "Come in."

Hand trembling, I twisted the knob and went in. I pushed the door shut with a soft click and leaned on its surface, my head bowed, afraid to see what stood in front of me. No point in denying Yana's words. My body reacted the moment I entered the room. My skin tingled. My heart raced. The pull of him had similarities to a magnetic field. If I moved away from the door, I knew I'd catapult toward him. A burning thirst that needed quenching by pouring rain ravaged me. A primitive urge swelled inside me. Its beats came from the most ancient of times, leaving me craving for some sort of release. My heart contracted when I remembered Demitri almost died today. He'd allowed himself to get whipped because of what I'd done to him. All this time, he'd been saving me, acting as my shield against anything that posed a threat. No matter what was happening between us, he managed to wrap me in his warmth and make me feel safe. I couldn't ask for more, and yet, I had a feeling if I did, he would give everything he had. It was enough to make me cry. I couldn't lose him. Not now.

"How long do you plan on staying there?" Demitri asked. His deep voice touched my skin, sending a delicious shiver all the way to my toes.

Lifting my head, I looked up, then gasped.

Demitri stood by the massive desk in his usual pirate's attire, except his shirt was white, like Luka's. Something told me Luka relished the fact that he had to lend his cousin clothes. Demitri's hair was tied back with a white ribbon. Probably Luka's doing, as well. Despite seeming paler than usual, Demitri looked like he had never been whipped five hundred times. I approached him carefully. I was afraid he'd disappear if I hurried myself. I wanted to feel him, to know he was really standing there.

Demitri gathered me close. I hesitated at first and he waited patiently until I stepped into his arms. He sat on the desk's edge and leaned me against him. His groan reverberated from his chest into mine.

"Does it hurt much?" I asked, pulling away slightly.

"Hurt? No."

Despite his features barely showing any expression, I saw desire blazing within the infinite blackness of his eyes. A smoldering blush blossomed on my cheeks and climbed up the bridge of my nose. My heart raced like a hamster on a wheel.

"I thought you were going to die," I whispered.

He searched my eyes. "Not now."

"But you *could have*. You shouldn't have let me bite you."

"Are you saying you made a mistake in marking me?"

"Whoa! Where is this coming from?"

"No matter, the end justified the means," he said.

I squinted. "You wanted to get whipped?"

~ ☾ ~

Demitri met my accusing stare with a stubborn one of his own. "Vladimir needed to feel he was in a place of power. Having me humiliated in public would make him complacent. It would push him to move forward with his plans."

His words flew over me. "I don't understand."

"Luka told you as much," Demitri said. "Vladimir has been planning on stealing power from my father the moment Luka abdicated. He wants to return to the old ways, to lift the forbidden. Having me whipped shows his party members how much power he holds, hopefully inspiring them to act. And when they do, we will be ready for them."

I couldn't believe it. Did he just tell me that he'd planned the whole thing so that he could corner the man who wanted to take his father's throne? Anger and disgust left me cold and alone.

"That's sick! You sacrificed yourself. You had me worrying just because you wanted that vile man to act on his plans?" I clenched my fists until my fingernails bit into my palm. "I hate you! I really do!" No sooner did those words leave my mouth did arms wrap me in a strong embrace. "Let me go," I whispered with enough venom to kill everyone in Zhamvy City.

"No," Demitri said. "You have to understand."

"What exactly don't I understand? You used me, plain and simple. And to think I…"

"You what?"

I shook my head in defeat. "It doesn't matter anymore. Dray says the formula is killing me. If I don't let him inject me with his version of the plague, I'm gonna die."

"Phoenix, look at me," he said urgently. I didn't, so he shook me, and commanded, "Look at me!"

I did then, but with all the hatred I felt in my heart.

Demitri's eyes narrowed. "I do not believe you."

"Ask him then," I challenged. "Better yet, let me go and wait for him to tell you. The less I see you the better." I struggled, but it was useless. His grip was too strong.

In seconds his lips were on mine, claiming, taking, forcing his way in. I tried to keep my lips rigid, unresponsive, but it was a losing battle. I hated how weak I was against Demitri's kisses. No matter how used I felt, I was still melting in his arms, asking for more, responding as if nothing was wrong.

Without much struggle coming from me, Demitri turned us around and moved toward the desk, not once breaking the kiss. I whimpered when my back hit the desk's edge. Demitri's lips swallowed the sound. He hooked his hands behind my thighs, and in one swift lift had me sitting on top of the desk, positioning himself between my legs. I didn't care at that point, lost as I was in the drug of his lips. All I could do was cling to his neck in the hopes of living through the heat burning inside me.

Before I could protest, Demitri's lips left mine and moved to my ear. While he was kissing a line down to my shoulder, he pulled my hands free from their death grip behind his neck and pinned them at my sides, palms flat on the table. I wanted to hold him, but he wouldn't let me. It was torture to have his lips touch me and I couldn't touch him. I moaned my frustration.

His kisses stopped. I opened my eyes and saw him staring at me with hot intensity. I felt the burn of his eyes all over my body.

"Listen to me," he said almost like a threat. I nodded even if my mind was still muddled from his kisses. "I did not use you. I would never think of using you."

"Then why did you say so?" I accused more than asked.

"Because ..." he started, but turned his face away.

I wished he wasn't pinning my hands then, so I could use them to turn his face back to mine. "Because?"

The muscle on his jaw jumped. He returned his gaze, but his eyes were strangely guarded. "Because you are only responding to the change. Because you do not feel the same way I do for you."

His words made no sense. Me? Not feel the same way? It was crazy. How could he ever think...?

"Let go of my hands," I said, meeting his stare with one of my own.

Reluctantly, Demitri released my hands.

I cupped his face and pulled him down until his lips met mine. His palms slammed on the tabletop as he received my kiss. I put every feeling I had in the kiss, but it was my eyes he was looking at when I broke free to catch my breath. Granted, my kisses weren't as earth shattering, but they were honest.

"How can you be so dense to think that I don't feel the same way you do?" I clapped his right cheek with my hand. Not really a full on slap, but I was sure he felt the force of it.

"But you said as much when I asked you about marking me." He had the face of a lost puppy when he spoke. If I wasn't so angry at him, I would have laughed.

"I didn't know what I was doing, Demitri," I said. "You've got to understand that, but it doesn't mean I don't feel anything for you."

"Before I met you, Phoenix, I was ..."

"A robot," I finished. All I saw of his annoyance at the word I used was the furrowing of his brow. "Hey, just speaking the truth," I said defensively.

"Appropriate in many ways." He paused a moment, then said, "Luka and I are working together to keep Vladimir off the throne. We have been monitoring him. I hardly cared before. I was helping because it was my duty as prince."

At some level, I understood what he said.

"But when I saw you backing away from Eli that night, something in me screamed to save you. Maybe it was the way you faced him head-on. Or maybe it was your innocence. I was going to walk away, but I found myself running toward you instead." His eyes focused on my face, but I was sure he wasn't seeing me. He was remembering the night I had broken curfew. The night everything changed.

Demitri continued. "After that, all I wanted was to keep you safe. As a Zhamvy Royal, a crown prince, I could not be under the spell of a human like you. Humans and Zhamvy do not mix. Ever." He took my right hand and kissed my palm. I felt the heat of his lips all the way to my toes. "Dray, bless and curse him at the same time, gave me what I wanted."

"The formula," I blurted out.

Demitri nodded.

"Demitri, I asked Luka to take the throne back," I said before I lost my nerve. Now was my chance to show him what

I'd been planning since Yana showed me the portrait of King Yaris.

The look in his eyes hardened. "You what?"

"Okay, not the reaction I was looking for." I pulled back. "That time you found me kissing Luka."

Demitri's breathing quickened.

"It's not what you think," I quickly said before he stopped thinking clearly. "I asked Luka to take the throne and he said he would if I kissed him. Don't you see? You're free. You can travel the world—"

"Do you think just because you kissed Luka that he would take the throne?" he said, ice in his voice. "Phoenix, what you heard me telling my father about travelling is irrelevant."

The first stab of betrayal went into my heart. "What are you saying?"

"I will be the next king after my father relinquishes the throne."

The second stab joined the first.

"It is my destiny to lead my people."

Words failed me. How could I argue with the determination in Demitri's eyes? He practically said we couldn't ever be together. That his feelings for me weren't enough to accept that Luka would take back the throne. Each beat of my heart sent the knives of betrayal deeper in, killing me slowly.

"Listen," he said, then was interrupted when the doors slammed open. Luka's sudden entrance prevented Demitri from continuing. The urgent energy surrounding him as he strode to his work desk zinged over my skin, causing electric goose bumps to rise.

"We have a problem," he said, the strong lines of his shoulders tense. "Phoenix, I think you should go back to your room."

Demitri moved from between my legs and helped me down from the desk. I pulled the dress that had ridden up back down to a more conservative length.

"I'm staying," I said.

"I think he is right," Demitri said. "I think it would be better if you returned to your room, Phoenix." He touched my cheek.

~ ☾ ~

I moved away from his touch and focused my gaze on Luka. "Whatever you two need to talk about, I'm staying for all of it. I'm already in waist deep. The least you can do is let me help."

Luka shook his head in defeat while Demitri loosened the tension on his shoulders by popping his vertebrae. In case they still thought off convincing me to leave, I crossed my arms and widened my stance. Nothing was moving me from the room.

"You were right," Luka began, settling his gaze on Demitri. "Vladimir plans to mobilize tomorrow during the festival."

"Do we have contingencies in place?" Demitri asked.

Luka shuffled through the wrinkled papers on the table, searching for something. I refused to blush when the memory of what we were doing to cause the desk's disarray flashed through my mind.

Finding what he was looking for, Luka said, "I have everything in place."

"What about the time?" Demitri took the paper from Luka and scanned its contents. "Do we know when he will strike?"

"That's what we are trying to find out. We get the sense that he's waiting for something."

I put all the events together in my head. "He wants me," I said.

"What?" Luka and Demitri said in unison.

"When I was found tied up in that room," I said to Luka instead of Demitri, "you guys already knew who was behind it."

From my periphery, I saw anger color Demitri's face. "What are you saying?"

I crushed the need to sooth Demitri. He'd made his choice and I wasn't it. I needed to focus before the thoughts slipped from my mind. "I'm just saying that Calixta finding me in Dray's garden seems a little too convenient. Someone did knock me out when I got her pinned down. Since she's Vladimir's ward, or whatever, wouldn't he use her to get what he wanted?" I kept my gaze on Luka. "You did say Vladimir was looking for just cause. Isn't that me?"

"I don't like where this is going, Phoenix," Luka said, his face growing pale.

~ ☾ ~

"Use me as bait. It's the only way."

"Absolutely not!" Demitri bellowed. "I am not putting you in any more danger than you already are in, Phoenix. With the formula killing you, who knows what could happen."

I looked at Luka beseechingly. "Surely Dray already told you about me."

He nodded reluctantly.

"Then back me up here," I said.

"Phoenix!" Demitri was beyond livid.

Luka held up his hand to stop Demitri's advance toward me. "Demitri, this might be the only way."

Demitri shuddered. He turned his back on us and breathed several times. When he turned around again, he had renewed resolve in his eyes. "As the crown prince, I do not condone this plan." He leveled his intense gaze at me. "You will be confined to your quarters until after the Festival."

"Demitri—"

"Guards will be posted outside your door at all times," he said, cutting off anything I was about to say.

"Demitri," Luka said. "Don't do this."

Demitri pointed at Luka. "Stay out of this. You abdicated of your own will. Now, let those in power rule for the good of the Zhamvy."

I saw the hurt form on Luka's face a second before he hid it behind a blank mask.

"I will send two Bogatyr to escort you back to your room. I suggest you go with them." Demitri didn't look at me when he left the room.

I rushed to Luka's side. "You can't let him do this," I said.

"You heard him." He looked into my eyes, the same sadness I'd seen before had returned. "Demitri is crown prince now. I have no right to overrule him."

I grabbed Luka's arms and shook him. "Snap out of it."

Luka twisted out of my grip and faced his desk, leaning his hands on its edge. "I'm no king, Phoenix."

"That's not what I saw when you asked Demitri to kneel before you in the Solar Garden or when you stormed into the throne room wearing your father's robes and crown forcing Vladimir to lower Demitri's sentence." I moved closer to him

but didn't touch him. "You are every bit the king I know you are, Luka. Now, do what's best for your people."

A tense silence settled between us.

I opened my mouth to speak again, but closed it immediately when I heard Luka breathe in and out. I knew in that moment he'd made his decision.

He glanced at me over his shoulder, a steely glint replacing his sadness. "When the Bogatyr arrive, go with them."

"And then what?"

He stood up straighter than I'd ever seen him stand and faced me. The aura I felt radiating from him in the throne room during the atonement had returned. "I'll make sure everything goes as planned."

Chapter 25

Trapped

    I struggled against the chains that suspended me above the floor from a hook on the ceiling by my wrists. The plan Luka and I had concocted after Demitri left had worked too well. The last thing I remembered was lying down on my bed. The guards who were supposed to be posted outside my room were pulled out. We needed to make Vladimir believe I was being left unattended. I just didn't think he would pounce on the chance to capture me so quickly. Then again, Luka did say Vladimir had something planned for the Winter Solstice Festival and all he needed was me, so here I was, hanging from the ceiling. The ache from my suspended arms marched like an army of fire ants biting their way down my skin. I bit down hard, holding in a scream of pain and frustration.

    To pass the time and to ignore the pain, I tried to figure out how I had ended up smack dab in the middle of another empty room, all tied up without Demitri knowing. I wondered how Luka managed to pull it all off. On the bright side, this time the room had a lit sconce on the wall. It cast sputtering yellow light all around. The musty smell told me I'd been the first occupant within these four walls in quite a while. I briefly wished for the tied-up-on-a-chair scenario like last time, but I had to admit that having me dangling was far more ingenious. I didn't have enough super strength left to free myself.

    Just as my arms had gone blessedly numb, the only door

~ ☾ ~

opened. Its hinges squeaked. The gray suit that came into view caused my blood to freeze for a moment. Then I reminded myself that this was all part of the plan. The snake-like smirk on the lips of the Zhamvy Prime Minister didn't help matters, though.

"Welcome, my dear. I'm so glad you could join me today," Vladimir said. He came closer, clapping his hands once and holding the pose.

I grimaced, his gag-worthy stench unforgiving. "How did I get here?" I asked, playing along.

"We have ways." He spread his arms wide. "To think, no one was there to guard you as you slept so peacefully. It's a show of their incompetence that you're here with me now. And I assure you, there is no escaping this time."

"This time?" I faked. I already knew what was coming, but I had to continue the charade of being a helpless captive. "The chair, the ropes, the gag."

"Yes. If Demitri hadn't come along...anyway, you're here now. That's all that matters."

I had to keep him talking. I needed to get to the bottom of his plans, so I asked, "What do you want from me?"

Vladimir's frosty smile warmed a fraction. Eagerness sparkled in his eyes. "Ah, my dear, you're a guest. I merely wanted for us to meet. I knew from the moment I saw you that you were different. Now we're here to find out just how different you are. We can do this the easy way or the hard way. Lady's choice."

I wanted to kick him in the shins, but he stood far beyond my reach, as if he knew what I had in mind. "I'd hate to see what you do to your prisoners."

The corner of his right eye twitched. "What do you think of your accommodations?"

"Kinky."

The slap came hard and fast. The sting erased the ache in my arms. Instead of spitting, I swallowed—iron and salt, the taste of blood and fear. I needed to gain some modicum of control over the situation or it would be all over faster than I could blink.

"I will not tolerate disrespect from any of my guests."

~ ☾ ~

Vladimir moved away, hands fisted at his sides.

I chuckled, masking my trepidation with false bravado. "For someone who looks like he's all put together, you're very high-strung."

The taunt got him to take a deep breath and piece together a mask of self-assurance. He smoothed the lapels of his jacket and tilted his chin up. Even though I dangled off the floor, he still stood an inch or two taller, which allowed him to sneer down at me.

"Who are you?" he asked.

"An exchange student from the north."

He dismissed my answer with a careless wave. "Spare me the lies."

"If you already know, then why do you need me to tell you?"

"The hard way it is, then." With a grin, he sauntered to the door. "Let him in."

Eli entered. All the boredom left his expression when our eyes locked. The same hawk-meets-prey attitude he displayed the first time we'd met had returned.

Vladimir rested a hand on Eli's shoulder. Eli, breathing heavily, didn't take his hungry gaze from me. He cracked his knuckles by flexing his fingers in eager anticipation. Of what, I had no idea.

"Can you tell me about this girl?" Vladimir asked while he hovered like a scavenger eyeing a carcass.

Eli shook his head.

"Bound by the Silence, I see. We'll keep it to a yes or no line of questioning then."

Well, that was convenient. The Silence prevented Eli from speaking, but it didn't mean he couldn't answer questions by nodding or shaking his head. Why hadn't anyone thought to share this little piece of information with me?

"Is she a student?" Vladimir glanced at me.

Eli nodded.

"Brilliant!" The vulture clapped his hands. "Is she from the north?"

At Eli's "no" shake, Vladimir's grin grew wider. My heart hammered against my ribs. Sweat beaded my brow. No more

secrets. Now they'd probably eat me. No. After witnessing what Vladimir had done to Demitri, I wouldn't be surprised if they didn't play with their food first. Despite the breath in my lungs and the pulse in my veins, I was officially a goner.

"Ah, wonderful." Vladimir paused, relishing the moment, "Is she human?"

Eli raked his eyes over my body and dipped his chin. Even in the sundress, I might as well have been naked from the way he leered at me. I clamped my jaw and endured the scrutiny. Somehow, volunteering as bait didn't seem as noble as it did a few hours ago.

"There it is." Vladimir's expression contorted into mock surprise. "We'll have to verify, of course. Come Eli, take a bite."

"No!" I squirmed, which brought fresh pain coursing through my body.

Vladimir ignored me. "Where would you like to bite her, Eli?"

"Anywhere," Eli said and swallowed.

"What about the word 'no' don't you understand?" I said.

"My dear, you wanted to do things the hard way." Vladimir tsked. "This *is* the hard way. But I'm not as cruel as you think. I'll give you the choice. Where do you want the bite?"

"You can bite my a—"

Vladimir wagged a finger. "Ah, ah, ah. Be careful what you say. I'm sure Eli can oblige."

So no matter what, I was screwed.

"Where, my dear?" Vladimir restrained Eli as he pressed eagerly toward me.

I thought about all the possible places a Zhamvy could bite me. If I lived through this day, I needed to make sure no one would see the scar. But, then again, why worry about a scar when my life hung in the balance?

I didn't know if I wanted to laugh or cry, so instead I said, "Thigh."

"Very good. Eli, if you please."

Eli needed no other encouragement. He stood in front of me before I could even inhale. He reached up and ran his hands down my arms. Not once did he stop staring at my face, stop licking his lips. I cringed. He leaned in. I turned away and grimaced as his wet lips touched my cheek. His hands roamed my body, squeezing, groping.

I bared my teeth. "Get on with it."

"Oh, but why?" Eli's hot breath made my skin crawl.

"Because I'll kick you so hard your future children will feel it."

"I like my girls fiery."

I took hold of the chain, pulled up, and lifted both my feet, kicking him in the stomach. Wide-eyed, Eli slammed into the wall. Bits of plaster fell on him from the ceiling.

"She certainly has fight in her," Vladimir said as he clutched his elbows. "What a pity. I was hoping for a more submissive human."

"Bite me!" I spat.

"We'll leave that to Eli."

The instant his shock wore off, Eli had his hands all over me again. I didn't even notice he'd moved away from the wall. He lifted the hem of my dress and bit my thigh. I screamed until my throat hurt. My skin tore like paper. Eli stumbled back, spitting out my blood.

"She tastes like …" His voice broke.

Vladimir rushed forward and swiped at the blood trickling down my leg. He lifted his fingers to his nose and took a tentative whiff. Shock contorted his face into a demented mask.

"What kind of an abomination are you?" He turned to Eli. "You may leave."

Eli straightened. "But—"

"I said leave!"

Eli scrambled out of the room like a dog with his tail between his legs.

The pain from the bleeding wound sapped all my strength. I couldn't even find it in me to whimper.

Vladimir lifted the hem of my dress with two fingers, watching the wound mend into a silver scar. "You heal like us, yet your blood is red. What has Dray been up to in that infantile lab of his?"

Vladimir slapped me. My head whipped to the side. The

sting of his hand jerked me from my pain-induced stupor. I glared at him and snarled. No one slapped me a second time and lived to tell about it. He currently topped my "To Murder" list.

"Just wanted to make sure you hadn't fainted. And from the looks of it, you haven't." He stepped out of reach. "You've come at a perfect time, my dear."

"I know," I mumbled.

He lifted an inquiring eyebrow.

"You have plans to overthrow the king. I know all about it."

"Hail the king," he said absentmindedly. "Go on."

"You've been rallying supporters, and it's only a matter of time before you try to take the throne. But it won't work."

"And why is that?"

The mild amusement in Vladimir's expression unnerved me. "Because Demitri and Luka will make sure you're stopped."

I'd never actually heard real diabolical laughter before; however, Vladimir's came close. The harsh melodious sound bounced off the walls, making all the hairs on my arms stand up.

"You are, by far, the most entertaining female I've ever encountered," he said after he regained his composure. "I like you. Too bad you're off the mark."

"They'll kill you when they find out what you've done to me, you sick, conniving bastard."

He showed all his teeth in a sinister smile. "Not if I kill them first."

Cheering roared from the outside.

Vladimir whirled in a tight circle with his arms raised and said, "It's time." He walked to the door and called out again.

Two Bogatyr marched into the room.

"Untie her," he ordered flippantly. "Then follow me. Oh," he said, throwing me a glance, "there's no use struggling, my dear. They can snap your neck faster than you can inhale. So if I were you, stay still and let them do their job."

In seconds, the Bogatyr had released me from my bindings. I moaned as blood rushed back to my limbs—the

~ ☾ ~

worst case of pins and needles I'd ever experienced. They dragged me without mercy down a long tunnel, its darkness punctuated by a small dot of light at the end. Vladimir's silhouette moved a few steps ahead, shoulders squared, head held high. The crowd's roar grew louder with every measured step. The image of a gladiator about to meet death at the coliseum flashed before me. And, unfortunately, in this scenario, I was that gladiator.

The tunnel opened to a large balcony overlooking the courtyard. I blinked several times to clear the white blindness. The Silent and the Bogatyr had transformed the quad into a staging ground similar to the ones for jousting matches during medieval games, except without the fence running down the middle. Bleachers spanned three sides: one for the Serfs, one for the Merks, and the last side for the Royals. Countless Bogatyr stood in lines dividing the spectators and the activity area. I could see Darius and Yalena watching the festivities from a canopied box. Several Vityas, in silver armor, stood guard around the royal couple. Dray and Yana sat close to the king and queen. No one noticed me.

The masses cheered again, sending my attention to the court grounds.

Luka, in silver armor, and Demitri, in black armor, faced off like knights on opposite sides of a chessboard. Luka grasped his ceremonial sword with its ruby pommel while Demitri held a sapphire-pommeled blade.

I'd never seen anything like the Sword Dance before. The synchronized movements of Luka and Demitri mimicked a combination of gymnastics and martial arts. Every lunge, slash, jump, and stretch were perfectly timed to the music. The audience cheered for the complicated routines they executed. Demitri whirled in a tight circle, his weapon only a hair's-breadth from Luka's neck. Luka countered with a lunge, sending his blade across Demitri's left cheek close enough to graze skin. One mistake, one wrong move would result in a cut or worse.

I flinched. My human brain tried to grasp how Luka and Demitri made it look so easy. The armor they wore looked heavy at the very least, yet they moved as if they weren't wearing anything. After a couple more moves, I noticed Demitri's movements were stiffer than Luka's regardless of their grace. His back must still be in bad shape if he couldn't move as freely as he wanted to. Even from a distance, I could tell he was struggling based on the tightness of his lips and the set of his jaw. He was concentrating too hard.

"Wonderful, isn't it?" Vladimir said above the cheers. "This is the first time the Sword Dance has been performed by two princes. A spectacle worthy of beginning my rule, don't you think?" He gave to me the wickedest smile.

I spat on his shoes.

"I deserved that."

I hated him unlike anything I'd ever hated in my life. He ranked above poachers, weapons dealers, and baby seal killers. I struggled against the hold of the Bogatyr. But Vladimir was right, it was useless. My two guards stood solidly at my side, keeping me in place.

"Here we are." Vladimir sighed. "The finale."

I glared at Vladimir. He nodded once. The cheers turned into gasps and cries. My attention snapped back to the quad. Demitri and Luka were now kneeling on the ground, surrounded by Bogatyr with swords drawn.

"What's the meaning of this?" Darius bellowed from the canopy.

Vladimir waved away the king's question and said, "My people, my friends." He spread his arms wide as if to hug someone. "I have come before all of you today to present a most troubling discovery. One that would change the way we see ourselves forever."

I wanted to take a sword from one of my guards and stab him with it.

"On this day," he continued, "the day we celebrate our abstinence from flesh, I bring you a secret the royal family has been keeping from all of us. Yaris, our exiled king, once declared we must refrain from consuming flesh. He did this to save us. We must thank him for his thoughtfulness." Vladimir placed his hand over his heart. "I regret that he needed to be exiled. And because of this, his son abdicated. As replacement, we were given someone who cares more about progress than the welfare of our people." He pointed at Darius. "The plague among the humans is no more. We no longer need to consume synthetic flesh when we have an abundant source of the real thing. This is why I have fought long and hard for us to return to the old ways. Humans have multiplied in number since the days of the Black Death. We can have our fill, yet we continue to waste away eating *yusha*."

Rapid questions of "what" and "how" filled the air from the increasingly agitated crowd.

"Sources close to me say that the experiments Prince Andrayus is conducting are actually making us sick." Vladimir pointed his finger at Dray, who sat between his father and Yana. "That the plague outbreak a few years ago was caused by him."

Vladimir paused as gasps spread through the crowd.

"And the miscarriages," he began again. "It has been decades since we have had young ones running around. I am told that we can no longer reproduce because of *yusha*. And those bi-yearly injections. What could they be doing to our bodies? We should not stand for what he does to us, using us as his experimental subjects."

With every word that came out of Vladimir's mouth, the royal family became paler and paler. Darius glanced at Dray with an incredulous expression on his face while Yalena covered her mouth with her hands, shaking her head in disbelief. Luka kept his face blank while Demitri stared up at me with barely leashed anger on his handsome features. I didn't crumble at the weight of his stare. What Luka and I were doing was the right thing, regardless of what Demitri might think. I was dying anyway. It might as well be for the good of the Zhamvy.

"The worst has yet to be revealed," Vladimir said.

Someone from the crowd shouted, "What could be worse?"

"I, as a loyal citizen of this great kingdom, cannot condone what has happened. Imagine a human being turned into one of us."

The cries of horror reverberated from the masses.

"You see, among us is an imposter," Vladimir said, raising

his voice. "For whatever reason, Prince Andrayus was able to turn a human into Zhamvy. What could this mean for our future? What could he be planning?" He punctuated his words by slapping the balcony balustrade.

The crowd shifted in growing panic.

"What proof do you have?" This question sent a chorus of others like it.

Vladimir savored every second of his speech.

"Proof?" He scanned the throng. "I have proof right here."

On cue, the Bogatyr released me into Vladimir's hold. His death grip on my hair threatened to pull out several clumps if I struggled. I didn't care. I squirmed, clawing at his hand, trying to break free using what little Zhamvy strength I had left.

"You want proof?" Vladimir goaded, and the crowd responded with angry jeers.

In my peripheral vision, I noticed Yana melting into the crowd, leaving a wide-eyed Dray behind. One of my guards handed Vladimir a dagger.

"What does this girl look like to you?" Vladimir wiggled his grip on my hair, causing me to cry out.

"One of us!" they shouted.

An ugly shiver crawled down my body. I wasn't one of them. Not by a long shot.

Vladimir scoffed and said, "That's where you're all wrong—"

And with his words, pain exploded along my collarbone.

~ ☾ ~

Chapter 26

Flight

Chaos.

Utter confusion.

The world around me shifted into complete disarray.

Black and blue spots exploded before my eyes from the pain on my collarbone. The front of my sundress suddenly felt wet and sticky. Vladimir shouted something, but the crowd didn't pay him any attention anymore. Screams rang in my ears. So much movement. Lacquered armor closed in on the Zhamvy surrounding me. Demitri and Luka had disappeared.

"Time to let her go, Prime Minister. She's no longer of use to you."

"Ah, Princess Visraya, so nice of you to join us," Vladimir said as he spun us away from the balcony's edge to face Yana. "You don't mind if I hold on to her a little longer, do you?"

My head swam at the sudden movement. My stomach roiled, wanting to unload its meager contents onto a floor that seemed to melt and swirl beneath us. I lifted my head and saw two of Yana standing by the balcony entrance.

"I'm afraid I mind very much. I believe you've made your point." Yana gestured at the mayhem.

"You're wrong, princess. She's valuable to my bid for the throne."

"I command you, as a *Superiori*, to hand her over."

Vladimir laughed. "I believe I'll have to decline."

~ ☾ ~

Yana's eyes grew wide. "How dare you disobey!"

"Oh, just for now," Vladimir responded dismissively. "You won't be alive long enough to be obeyed anyway."

The two Bogatyr who previously stood as my guard lunged at Yana, swords drawn.

"No," I mumbled. What was up? Why did I feel woozy?

"Don't fret, my dear. It will be over soon."

I cringed at Vladimir's breath on my ear. My chin dropped, and I finally noticed the bleeding gash along the line of my collarbone. I no longer healed fast enough. The blood gushing out of my body had a strange euphoric effect. Dude, I was so up in the clouds right now, high wasn't even the word. Yeah! I shook my head to try and clear it, but only managed to make myself dizzier.

The scuffle between Yana and the Bogatyr distracted me. They were a whirl of lace and ribbons versus a tangle of armor and swords. Yana had something sharp in her hands. A dagger, maybe. It flashed, catching the light.

With my rescue party preoccupied, Vladimir bolted, dragging me along. I struggled, but my head refused to communicate with my arms and legs. I flailed helplessly instead. My fingers felt like rubber and my blood like oil, weighing me down.

"Stop moving or I'll drop you," Vladimir said.

"Drop me and go, you scum," I snapped back.

"It's not that easy, my dear." He stopped, which sent a new wave of nausea through me.

"Let her go, Vladimir."

I concentrated so hard on not puking that I failed to recognize who spoke at first. Purple joined the blue and black fireworks exploding before my eyes, magnified by the white walls that surrounded us on all sides. I couldn't tell which route Vladimir had taken, and at the moment, I hardly cared. I just wanted him to put me down so I could close my eyes and sleep for a year.

"Glad you could join us, Visraya Majesty," Vladimir said.

"Give her to me," Luka commanded.

"As I explained to your sister, I think not."

"Luka," I called out weakly.

~ ☾ ~

"Everything's going to be fine, Phoenix," he reassured. "Hang in there."

"How touching." Vladimir tsked. "The reluctant ruler caring for an abomination like her."

Rage colored Luka's features before he charged, sword in hand. Vladimir raised his dagger in time to block the coming blow. I flinched at the clash of steel against steel. It grated at my nerves like teeth on stone.

Vladimir dropped me to better defend himself against Luka's fierce attack.

My knees and palms cushioned my fall badly, sending rattling pain up my arms and legs. My stomach protested again. The floor beneath me felt like jelly as I clutched my wound. The blood only trickled as opposed to gushed. The formula still had some healing effects.

"Phoenix, run!" Luka yelled. He managed to get between Vladimir and me.

"No," I mumbled.

"This isn't the time to be stubborn. You've done your part, now let us do ours." He grunted as he pushed Vladimir against a wall. He aimed his blade at the throat of the other Zhamvy, but Vladimir lifted his dagger and barred the blow from going any further. "Yana, a little help here please!"

"You're going to have to do better than that to stop me," Vladimir spat.

Small hands gripped my arms.

"Get up," Yana urged. "Come on, Phoenix! We need to get you out of here."

I scrambled and lost my footing, unable to keep my eyes on Luka and Vladimir.

"*Geez*, Yana, pushy much?" I muttered. "If you haven't noticed, I'm injured here."

"We don't have time for this. Would you rather be alive and injured or dead?"

She had a point. "Alive."

"Then get up! I'm not ruining my dress by picking you up."

She tugged at me, sending a jolt of pain all the way to my open wound. I yelped, which Yana ignored. She was too busy leading us down the hall. I glanced over my shoulder, and the last image I saw was of Vladimir's dagger slipping between the metal plates of Luka's armor.

"Luka!" I stopped and turned.

"Phoenix, no." Yana grabbed my arm and propelled me onward.

"We can't just leave Luka," I screamed. Running rattled my insides further. My brain bounced like a basketball in my head.

"He's a big boy," she said, then cursed.

Slamming into her, I stumbled. "What the—oh, no!"

At the end of the hall, Calixta blocked our way like the hounds of hell in a shift dress and high heels. If I ever had a better reason to run, I couldn't think of one. And yet, the urge to pound Calixta to the ground kept me in place. We had a score to settle.

"I trust you'll let us through?" Yana lifted her dagger, blade at the ready.

"Good luck with that." Calixta smirked.

I opened my mouth to speak, but Yana stepped forward, chin tilted up, and said, "Follow my command. Kneel."

Calixta trembled. Her fingers curled into tight fists until her knuckles lost all their color.

Yana repeated the command.

At first, Calixta fought the urge, scowling at the both of us. She shook like a minutes-old colt attempting to remain standing. But, eventually, her knees bent. Yana relaxed, flipping the knife so the blade didn't point at Calixta anymore.

Calixta glared and ground out, "This all happened because of you. If you hadn't come along, our lives would never have been disturbed."

"Then you're naïve," I said.

Calixta frowned. "What are you trying to say?"

"That you don't know Vladimir well enough to actually think I caused all of this."

"You're taking too long, Phoenix," Yana interjected. "We don't have all day, you know."

If I continued to explain to Calixta her mental inadequacies we'd get nowhere. The formula was entering its final stages. My slow healing told me so. If I didn't take advantage of what little strength I had left, I wouldn't be able to get away.

"I'm working on it," I said.

An arm wrapped around my waist and carried me away just as Calixta lunged at Yana. The jolt sent my stomach reeling. I swallowed the bile that climbed up my throat. Everything was a blur around me. Whoever had me ran fast. My hair whipped in my face. I looked up to see who was stealing me away and my blood froze.

If I thought I'd never encounter Eli again, I was totally wrong. He held a broad sword in one hand, poised for attack should anyone or anything stand in his way, and me in the other. How could I have thought of him as handsome the first time we'd met? Now, he looked sinister. His face was a mix of concentration and giddy anticipation. Periodically, he licked his lips. I didn't want to know what he was thinking about to prompt him to do so. The harsh chill of dread filled my lungs when I realized what was happening.

I slammed an elbow on Eli's cheek. He barely tilted his head from the blow. I had no strength left.

"Vladimir's been looking for you," Eli said.

"We'll have to see about that," I said, but all my bravado had no basis now. I couldn't lift my arms anymore and I couldn't feel my legs.

Eli moved so fast that I had no idea where in the palace we were. Then a clash of steel jarred any thoughts of escape. He cursed and let me go. The floor broke my fall and stole all the air from my lungs. I shifted to my side, coughing to catch my breath.

I looked up and recognized the suit. "Lev?" I croaked

Lev didn't acknowledge my presence and instead focused all his attention on Eli.

A new set of hands grabbed my shoulders. I flailed but stopped myself the moment I recognized Deidra, the maid Demitri introduced me to. She hooked her hands under my armpits and pulled me away from the fighting. She pushed curtains aside and settled me into one of those niches that Luka had hidden me in during our sneaky tour of the castle. I wanted to thank her, but I didn't have enough strength to speak again. She knelt down and raised her finger to her lips before shutting the curtain.

 I breathed in and out, in and out, working to get my heart rate to settle. Thankfully, the nausea had left and the blood from my wound only trickled now. My sundress no longer was white in front. If someone saw me, they'd think I'd stepped out of a horror movie set. I blinked once, twice, and by the third time, my eyes refused to open. I drifted. The sounds of clashing swords, screaming Zhamvy, and slamming bodies faded into muffled twangs and grunts.

 Within seconds, heat pulsed from my heart to spread throughout my body. Sweat beaded my forehead. I grit my teeth against crying out and grabbed fistfuls of my dress. My feet kicked out, pushing me further into the alcove.

 My skin sizzled. I clawed at my chest, smoldering from the inside out. Every beat of my heart sent a new jolt of pain. Powerful shivers racked my body. My lips and tongue went numb. Calling out for help stopped being an option.

 Even if I could call for help, the fighting just beyond where I hid didn't make me feel like I would be safe if discovered. Vladimir wanted me for some reason or the other, none of them good ones. I needed to keep a low profile and Deidra had given me that chance. But hiding also meant Dray, Yana, Demitri, or Luka couldn't help me since they didn't know where I was. What a sad way to go.

 I slowly closed my eyes and let the darkness slide over me.

"Phoenix."

Demitri's voice.

 But as soon as I took a deep breath to answer him, the heat turned into ice. In seconds, I went from burning to freezing. My teeth were chattering so badly I thought they would fall out. Speaking wasn't going to happen anytime soon. I couldn't even move from the intense shivering rolling through my body.

"Where is she?" Yana asked, panic in her voice.

 I wanted to say I was in the niche, but I couldn't. My lips and tongue had gone numb. My voice box wasn't functioning.

~ ☾ ~

"Her last booster must be wearing off by now," Dray said anxiously.

By sheer force of will, I managed a small whimper.

Suddenly, the navy curtains were yanked aside. Demitri, with an expression a cross between panic and relief, fell to his knees in front of my shaking body. He was still in full armor. He cast aside his sword and reached out, gathering me into his arms like I was an infant. I willingly let him take me, even if every movement my body made shot pain everywhere.

I screamed the moment my skin touched Demitri's armor.

"What is the matter with her?" Demitri spat at Dray.

Hardly flinching from his brother's venom, Dray bent over me and touched my forehead. "The formula is ravaging her system. Her body is entering a hypothermic state to stabilize her core temperature. I need to inject her with the plague now or risk the formula killing her."

"Is there another way?" Demitri asked, a slight tremor in his voice. He settled his eyes on me, gentleness instead of intensity within those obsidian orbs. He reached out and rubbed my arms, doing his best to transfer some of his body heat to me. "The plague might kill her, Dray."

"She dies anyway if we don't take this chance, Demitri," Dray said.

Demitri kept his gaze on my face. I couldn't nod from all the shaking, so I blinked instead and hoped he got my message. His lips tightened for a second before he turned to Dray and nodded.

Dray removed a syringe from his pocket. "Hold her still."

I felt Demitri's grip tighten around my arms. I was shaking so badly that I thought the needle Dray plunged into my arm would snap off. I didn't even feel the needle go in because of the amount of pain rolling through my body.

Demitri leaned me back into the niche carefully. "Why does she keep screaming when I touch her?"

Dray thought for a second. "She screamed when her skin touched your armor."

"Then get me out of it!" Demitri commanded, grappling with the straps holding his chest plate in place. "Get it off me!"

~ ☾ ~

Yana and Dray knelt beside him, scrambling to unbuckle the straps and remove the pieces of metal from his twisting, lunging body.

"Stop moving!" Dray shouted at his brother. "We can't help you if you're too anxious."

Demitri froze, staring at my face. I held his stare for as long as I could without blinking. Watching me in pain hurt him just as I hurt when I watched him get whipped. With the force of sheer willpower, I reached out a shaking hand to him. He grabbed it like a lifeline during a storm, placing my clammy palm on his horribly warm cheek. I grimaced, but I wasn't about to scream. I didn't want him worrying more than he already was.

As the last of his armor was removed, Demitri wasted no time in gathering me into the soft cloth of his shirt. Thankfully, no pain greeted the touch of my skin. I was still shaking like a mad woman, but there was no pain. I would have sighed if I could manage it.

"How long will this take?" Demitri asked in a more settled tone. Holding me close was calming him down. I leaned my head on his chest and watched his face. The strong lines and plains became my anchor.

His words when we were together in Luka's study came back to me. He said he had feelings for me, but I didn't believe him because he chose his duty over me. The way he held me close in this moment, like he wouldn't let anything come between us, told me more than his words ever could. All this time, he'd done nothing but keep me safe. My heart swelled at the realization. The desperation I saw in his eyes when he parted the curtain to find me was real. If I died tonight, I would go knowing someone like Demitri loved me. He may not know how to say it, but he definitely knew how to show his feelings. I saw them in his eyes now as he looked down on me, checking if I was still alive. Demitri had the eyes my father did when he held my mother's hand in the doctor's office when we got the news about her sickness. The kind of eyes that held fear beneath the love. Fear of losing the one he loved. Demitri had that in his eyes now, clearer than ever.

~ ☾ ~

"Not long now." Dray took my hand and lifted my fingers to his nose, inhaling deeply. "She smells more human now, but we need to get her to a human hospital soon or else the plague in her system would end up killing her too."

Shouts and sword clashes came from the end of the hallway.

Yana turned to the sound and said, "I don't think we have the time to stay here anyway."

In one smooth motion, Demitri stood, holding me in his arms. "We need to get her to the academy. Alek can take it from there."

No protest came. I wanted to say no, but my teeth were still chattering too much for me to speak clearly. All I could manage were little moans.

"Shhh, shhh, breathe," Demitri murmured. He was already walking swiftly away from the sounds of fighting. I couldn't see Yana and Dray, but I was sure they were nearby. "You will be good as new in no time."

Somehow, even if his face looked worried, I believed Demitri. There couldn't be that much pain without something good happening at the end of it, right? I needed to believe something good would happen. I needed to.

A small groan left my lips. A dull ache pulsed on my collarbone. I took a deep breath, which hurt, but the scent of morning dew—of Demitri—made me forget the pain. I exhaled slowly. So, the sense of smell was the last to go of my superpowers.

Even in dim light I had a perfect view of Demitri's face. His gaze fell to mine. He watched me, a mix of relief and sadness on his face. How long would it be before I would see his face again? How long until I felt the strength of his arms around me or the softness of his lips on mine?

Demitri smiled. A smile so slow, so deliberate, that I forgot what I was thinking of for a second. He bent his head and took my lips with his, never stopping his easy stride forward. I touched his face and felt the feverish heat of his skin. I was human again, I knew it deep down, but his kisses affected me profoundly just the same. I thought my feelings would be different when I'd changed back to human, but I was wrong.

~ ☾ ~

The shivers alone were heaven, coating the little aches and pains of my body with divine pleasure.

The kiss ended when Dray caught up to Demitri and touched my cheek. "How are you feeling?"

"Like I'm a guest waiting for Death to open the door to the house of Hell," I said, my voice raspy. My throat felt raw.

Dray smiled. "Then you'll be fine. But we still need to hurry. We aren't safe yet."

I felt a sudden chill go down my back. "Yana? Luka?" I whispered, my worry bubbling over.

Again, it was Dray who answered, "Yana is right behind us, and Luka is with the Vityas, trying to restore order."

I let myself exhale in relief. Vladimir hadn't killed Luka. He was alright.

"Demitri?" I said, touching the jumping muscle on his jaw. "Put me down."

"What do you mean?" he asked.

"I can walk. Put me down."

His grumbling was like boulders rolling down a mountain.

"I will not put you down," Demitri finally said.

I struggled in his arms, pushing at his chest with my hands and thrashing my legs. He had no choice but to put me down. My feet touched the cold ground. I held on to him until I regained my balance. His arms were around me protectively while his eyes attempted to bore a hole into my face. I smiled, making him snort in disgust.

Leaning to the side so I could see Dray and Yana, I said, "Can you give us a minute?"

Dray was about to protest, but Yana took the hint and started dragging him back down the way we came.

"Now," I said, turning back to Demitri, "take me back."

"I *am* taking you back," he said, his face going from stoic to confused.

"Not to the academy. Take me back to Zhamvy City."

"I will not return you there in your condition." His brows came together. "You are not safe there anymore."

"It was never safe, but I was with you," I argued. "I was with Dray, with Yana, with Luka. You all kept me safe." My hoarse throat fought my attempt to raise my voice. "Back at the academy, I will be alone. I don't want to be alone, Demitri." Angry tears welled up my eyes. I'd been alone for eighteen months. Preya had been a good friend, but in the world of the humans, no one loved me. Not like I was loved here.

In a swift move, I was in Demitri's sweltering embrace. But I wasn't thinking about the heat. I was too angry and frustrated.

"Do you think this is easy for me?" Demitri challenged. "You must be somewhere safe, and the only place I know is at the academy."

"Dray must still have the formula. He can turn me into one of you again. If I'm one of you, I'll be safe here"

My shoulder grew wet. It took me a moment to realize the wetness were tears on my shoulder...Demitri's tears.

I felt him swallow hard. "He already injected you with the plague. If you do not get medical attention, you will die." His own anger and frustration was palpable. "I cannot let that happen to you."

I couldn't see his face. I wanted to turn and look at him, but Demitri was hiding behind a curtain of my hair. I reached up and squeezed the back of his neck.

"I don't want to leave you," I said, tears in my voice too.

We stood in each other's embrace, no longer sure who was holding whom. All I knew was I didn't want to leave this Zhamvy who held me tight. But I was at my wits end when it came to finding excuses to stay. All I had left was my stubbornness. I wasn't budging. He would have to forcibly separate me from him if he wanted me to go.

After another heartbeat of silence, I spoke. "Demitri, I—"

"Demitri!" Dray's yell echoed in the hall, followed by the sounds of running. "Take her away. They're coming!"

"No!" I said. "I'm not going back to the academy."

I was already in Demitri's arms when the last of what I said intermingled with the sounds of countless feet stomping on the tunnel floor. I called Demitri's name as loud as I could, but he wasn't listening to me. His attention was in running as fast as he could. I kept asking him to take me back, but my panicked requests met deaf ears.

~ ☾ ~

In seconds, we reached the tunnel, and at the end of it was the elevator. Dray took out a key card and slipped it into a slot beside the doors. He quickly punched in the code on the number pad below the slot and the doors opened. Yana ran into the elevator before anyone could say anything. Dray joined her.

"Take her," Demitri said to Dray, handing me off like luggage.

"What about you?" I asked.

He ignored me when he said, "My sword."

Yana handed him the ceremonial sword he used for the Sword Dance. Demitri checked the blade before turning his back on the elevator.

"No! I won't leave without you!" I screamed, wiggling out of Dray's hold. I jumped out of the elevator and ran to Demitri.

He growled at me. "You have to go. I have to stay and help my people."

Demitri shoved me into the elevator. The sounds of our pursuers grew louder, bouncing off the tunnel walls, making it impossible to determine how many were after us. I struggled to get out of the elevator, but Demitri's grip was too strong.

He bent his head until his lips claimed mine in a hard kiss. Time stopped. The sounds of our pursuers and the yells of Yana and Dray to hurry disappeared. All that mattered was that kiss. And just as quickly, Demitri leaned away.

"Forgive me," he whispered before he knocked me out.

Chapter 27

Limbo

I glanced at the clock on the wall by the door. According to my count, it had been seven days, ten hours, twenty-seven minutes, and so on seconds since the night I woke up in a hospital room screaming Demitri's name. Aleksander Kiev, who currently sat on a stool beside my bed, had his heavy eyebrows knitted in concentration. Apparently, my screams had prompted a nurse to rush in and sedate me. I didn't know why I'd woken up screaming. And I didn't have any answers for Kiev when he'd asked me why. I couldn't even remember what I'd been dreaming of. Everything mixed together in one black, drug-induced blur. I did know I wanted to go back into my dream, whatever it was about. If dreaming was my way of seeing Demitri again then I'd rather be asleep than sit and chat with the headmaster. I stared at the closed blinds to my right, ignoring the ache in my chest.

"Where am I?" I rasped out.

"The European Medical Center in Moscow," he said in his rolling Russian-accented English. "You will need to stay another week for observation."

"What for?"

"They found traces of the bubonic plague in your system, which they are now treating with doses of antibiotics. They cannot figure out how you contracted it. Between you and me, let us keep it that way. You also have a long cut just above your collarbone, but they say it is healing nicely. Some bumps

~ ☾ ~

and bruises, a bite mark on your thigh, but no internal bleeding. It took a lot of arm-twisting to dissuade them from calling the authorities. Luckily, I am friends with the chief of surgery."

"Of course you are," I mumbled under my breath. I already knew everything he told me. I'd live through the wounds. After a brief pause, I tore my gaze away from the nothing I was staring at and looked Kiev in the eye. "Any news?"

From the way Kiev shook his head, I could tell he knew what I meant. My heart fell. I tried to convince myself that no news was good news. If something had happened to Demitri then Kiev would tell me. Wouldn't he?

"Demitri—"

"I would tell you, Phoenix."

I didn't believe him. I'd have to find my own answers. Dray and Yana must have filled him in on what had happened because not once did Kiev ask me about my time with the Zhamvy. He was keeping something from me. I was sure of it now.

"So." I looked back at the blinds. "Does this mean I'm expelled? Like, for real this time?"

Kiev heaved a weighty sigh. "I do not see the point of depriving you of an education. You already know the secret of Barinkoff, and I will trust that you are not foolhardy enough to involve anyone in the dangers you have experienced. Am I making myself clear?"

I exhaled a sigh of my own. "Absolutely."

I needed to be back in school if I wanted to find a way back to Zhamvy City. This wasn't over. If Demitri thought knocking me out and putting Kiev on babysitting duty would keep me away, then he was dead wrong. I'd broken curfew before for less.

"Here." Kiev handed me a black rectangular device.

I stared at it, my brain taking a few seconds to recognize it. "My phone," I said. "Huh. I thought I'd lost it."

"I charged it for you." Kiev stood up and headed for the door. He paused and looked at me over his shoulder. "I will be back in one week to pick you up. And I thought you should know, your father has been informed of your stay here."

~ ☾ ~

Dropping his bomb, he opened the door and walked out without waiting for a reaction from me. It wasn't much of a reaction anyway. All I felt was numb. My father knew about my hospital stay, and yet he didn't even bother sending word to me. Not even a call.

I stared at my phone for the longest time after Kiev left. I thought about what Demitri had said to me when I sat in a different hospital room. Thinking of him hurt, but I wanted to test his theory about my father. If he was wrong then the worst that could happen was my father would continue ignoring me. But if he was right...I didn't even want to go there. If I started to hope now, a let-down would irreparably shatter me.

I took a deep breath and scanned my contacts list for the number I hadn't used in almost a year. I tapped the green call button and prayed the person on the other line wouldn't pick up. After the third ring, my prayer wasn't answered.

"Hello," said the coldest voice in the history of cold voices.

My heart constricted for a painful second. I couldn't back down now even if it was all too easy to tap the red call-end button. I reminded myself to breathe.

"Dad," I said, my voice was a touch shaky. I blamed it on the meds when really it was because of my fear.

Complete silence on the other line. I checked the screen in case the call got cut, but the seconds counting up the call duration said otherwise. I bit my lip and waited.

Then a long suffering sigh stopped my heart, followed by, "Phoenix, I'm just about to walk into—"

A sense of urgency gave me the courage I needed. "I'll make it quick, I promise." I inhaled. "Someone really important to me once said that maybe the reason you push me away is because you're afraid, that if you don't love me then you won't have to lose me. I didn't believe him at first. But the more I think about it now, the more I think he makes sense."

"Phoenix—"

"I just wanted to tell you that I understand," I interrupted him, my fear gave me wings. "Please, just think about what I said. When you're ready to talk, you know where to find me. I love—"

~ ☾ ~

I heard the line cut before I could finish the last of my sentence. I stared at the words "Call Ended" on the screen. I managed to say what I needed to say, but I didn't feel any better. I hugged my phone to my chest and curled up into the smallest ball I could possibly make on my hospital bed. I wished Demitri hadn't knocked me out when he did. I wanted to be with him so badly that I'd give anything to find out if he was okay. He could be so selfish when it came to doing what he thought was best for my safety. It frightened me to think what could have happened to him in the tunnel. But I held on to my faith in his strength. It was all I had left to keep me sane. For the first time since I met the Zhamvy, I'd never felt more unsure of my safety. Without Demitri by my side, I was vulnerable and alone.

The only time I'd felt important was when I was in Zhamvy City, helping Dray find a cure for his people. Did he have enough data to succeed? My blood felt like ice in my veins. I needed warmth. I needed...sleep. I called for the nurse and complained about the pain. She gave me what I needed to go under.

The next day, Preya arrived. She seemed uncomfortable and nervous. She arranged the flowers she brought in a pitcher of water since my room didn't have a vase. I was happy to see her, but the emotion didn't quite reach my heart. Each beat still felt broken, like a vital piece was missing.

"You know, I didn't believe you were on retreat when the headmaster told me," she said cautiously. "But when he explained that you needed the time to get away so the rumors about your probation would die down, I thought he was right."

Her words held no meaning for me anymore. Who cared if the rumors of my probation still floated around?

I shrugged, staring at the whiteness of my bed sheet. It reminded me of the ultra-white walls of the palace. The one place I would rather be.

"I'm sorry, Preya. Really. Thank you so much for coming, but I don't think this is the best time for a visit." I fisted the sheet in my hands. "I'm still feeling really tired."

"They said you were injured on your retreat—and were in a

coma for a week! You have to tell me what happened," she said all wide-eyed. "I nearly had a stroke when I found out from Kiev."

I shrugged again, my shoulders feeling heavier now. "Not much to tell." I concentrated on breathing. "I fell on a hike. I don't remember much after that."

She blushed beet red. "If you weren't injured, I'd smack you, Phoenix McKay."

I wished she would. Maybe she would knock me out and I would wake up from this reality into my dream.

After Preya left, I was even more unsettled. I felt bad that I wouldn't engage in the conversation she started. Somehow, knowing I had returned to something familiar didn't help. My life was forever changed and I couldn't quite tell if I would ever fit into my old one ever again.

A day after Preya's visit, my phone buzzed. I reached for it, winced at the pain that came with the stretch, and tapped the screen.

Before I could say hello, my father said, "Why am I getting billed by the European Medical Center? Is there something I should know?"

"Wow," I answered. "They must have me on some pretty cool drugs. You sound just like my father."

"Phoenix, stop joking and answer my question."

He didn't have any concern in his voice. Just the same ice he'd treated me to for months. But, I knew better now. I understood him more. Whether the revelation could be a good thing or not still remained up in the air.

I realized in that moment that I hated lying to him despite the way he treated me. He was still my father. The only family I had left.

I set aside my sudden attack of moral scruples and said, "I thought Kiev told you."

"My assistant neglected to inform me until today."

Someone was getting fired. I heard it in his voice. "I got into a minor accident during a retreat."

"What accident?"

Maybe I'd been wrong about the lack of concern. Or maybe the painkillers they had me on messed with my head. Either

~ ☾ ~

way, a small smile stretched my lips. "We were on this hike and I wasn't paying attention," I explained. "I rolled down a hill."

"Are you alright?"

"Recovering."

"Good."

A long pause stretched out between us. I thought how much I had changed since surviving Zhamvy City. It gave me the courage to take a chance.

"Dad?" I said.

No answer at first. I actually thought he'd hung up on me. I checked the screen. It indicated the call was still in progress.

My father cleared his throat and said, "Yes?"

"Do you remember the time I woke up from a nightmare and you were the one who came into my room instead of Mom?"

"Yes."

I blinked away unexpected tears. "You said you would never let the monsters eat me. Is that still true?"

A deep shuddering breath came from the other line then my father said, "Phoenix, you will always be my little girl. I may not be the best father in the world, but I'm trying."

My tears fell then. "Thanks, Dad."

He cleared his throat again, but his voice was still thick with emotion. "How long will you be there? Do you need me to fly out?"

"A few more days," I managed to say through a tight throat. "And you don't have to. I'm fine. Really." What I left unsaid was that I wasn't ready to see him yet. Phone calls were all I could handle right now.

"Alright. I'll have my assistant take care of it."

The icy tone had returned. I didn't mind. He'd called. A step forward. A move away from the stagnant place we'd been mired in for so many months. I tapped the screen to end the call. My heart pinched. Demitri had been right after all. He'd given me hope that things with my father would be alright.

The week passed quickly. The plague was fully out of my system and most of my strength had returned. After I left the hospital, my first week in school was spent in a total daze. I walked down hallways without a care as to who I bumped into. I just kept going, plowing through anything and anyone. My classmates quickly learned to get out of the way when they saw me. My uniform chafed. The cotton, button-down shirt irritated my skin. The blazer felt heavy on my body. The ribbon choked. I longed for the floor-length skirts, the soft blouse; even the corset seemed more tolerable than the sweater vest I had on.

Classrooms once so familiar became as alien as the surface of Mars. My teachers' monotone lectures jarred my ears. The lessons they taught flew over my head. I never answered any of the questions asked, even if I knew the answers. I'd reached a new emotional low I hadn't known I was capable of.

The crazy part had to be hanging out with Preya. Her peppy, bouncy, mental rollercoaster state grated on my nerves like nails on a chalkboard. Like she was trying too hard to be happy around me. I couldn't keep up.

The Coffee Bar's bustling activity remained the same, too. Brewing coffee awakened the senses. The Mathletes still argued over theorems. The Physics jocks still huddled together, whispering. The one-liter soda bottle and air pump was now replaced by a water hose, goggles, ball bearings, and ten packs of plaster of Paris. The artists and non-science students still chilled like the world contained purple clouds and pink bunnies. Just because my world had imploded, it didn't mean the United Nations of Barinkoff Academy stopped living. *Still, still, still.*

Everything stayed sickeningly normal. The sun shone. Birds flew across the ever blue sky. Friends greeted each other. I should have been happy to be free of the responsibility of keeping all of humanity alive. But I wasn't. Everything may be the same all around me, but I wasn't the same girl anymore. I'd fallen in love with a flesh-eating member of a superior race currently living beneath our feet. A guy who put his duty for his people above me. The jerk. He couldn't let go of his one-track sense of responsibility.

By the next week, I felt more in control of my senses. Well, controlled enough to want to sneak back into Zhamvy City

~ ☾ ~

again. I wanted to return to a place that could potentially kill me because I needed to see Demitri, to make sure he was still alive and possibly knock some sense into him. I'd make him see that there were other ways he could serve his people. Ways that involved having me in his life.

    The first time I tried, I stayed late in the library with the thought of climbing the secret steps leading to the Chem lab. It was a simple enough plan that had worked before. Why wouldn't it work a second time? I hid in my secluded corner, sitting on the floor with my e-reader. When the last bell tolled, Kiev materialized in front of me. Silently, he walked me to the parking lot, then drove me back to the dorms.

    For my second attempt, I snuck into the solarium to wait, no matter how heartbreaking it felt to be among the greenery encased in glass. But I stayed anyway. Unfortunately, Kiev found me five minutes before curfew. His brow knotted together in annoyance, but like my previous attempt, he had said nothing.

    A week passed before I tried a third time. I had cut my last class and headed for the edge of the Solar Garden, constantly checking if anyone followed me. The bell clanged six times. I anxiously waited, peeking from the side of the large pine I hid behind. No headmaster. Not that walking in a campus filled with flesh-eating Zhamvy could be any safer than getting caught by Kiev.

    I let another thirty minutes pass before leaving my hiding place and heading for the tower. I fiddled around with the number pad, but soon gave up since I obviously needed a key card to activate it. I'd decided to roam around until I bumped into anyone who could bring me to Zhamvy City. That was, if I convinced them not to eat me.

    My heart beat in my throat. The campus stayed eerily quiet. My boots on marble sounded too loud for comfort. Empty hallways. Deserted classrooms. Maybe the Night Students were still on their way? I sighed. Here was to hoping.

    An hour passed, then two. I walked around like a lost girl.

    My resolve wavered. I couldn't find anyone. Not a soul. But just as I felt hopeless, I realized I'd completely forgotten to check one place. So, with renewed energy, I took the stairs to the second floor two at a time. When I reached the Chem lab, I had a stitch on my side. I doubled over to catch my breath. One breath. Two breaths. Three. I straightened and entered the room. Clean tables greeted me. No beakers. No test tubes. No microscopes. No nothing.

My knees gave way beneath me and I fell to the floor. Something told me no matter how hard I tried I would never see Zhamvy City again. My insides sank. Then large hands closed around my arms and pulled me to my feet. I looked up.

"Kiev?" I said in a desolate whisper.

"Enough, Phoenix," he said.

"They're not here." My eyes filled with tears. "He's not here."

Kiev pulled me out of the Chem lab and kept his hold on me until we reached the entrance where his car was parked. Funny thing, I didn't struggle. I couldn't feel my legs even if I wanted to struggle. I let him take me away. I didn't expect how badly the separation would hurt me. I stayed mute during the entire drive, staring at the dark night outside the car window. Like they never existed, the Zhamvy were gone. What could have happened? Dray said Luka was regaining order. If that was true, then they should all be back in school by now. But they weren't. Would they ever come back? From the way campus looked, maybe not. I wiped away a stray tear.

When we arrived at the dorms, Kiev asked, "Will I expect more attempts from you?"

I leaned back into the seat and shut my eyes. I shook my head. The emptiness of the campus was heartbreaking. I couldn't stand another night knowing no one would be there.

~ ☾ ~

Chapter 28

Truth

The next few days had been the hardest on poor Preya. She practically put me on suicide watch, brought on by the night I'd returned from the last time I had broken curfew. She'd found me fully submerged in the bathtub. She thought I was trying to kill myself.

"Are you crazy?" Preya scolded after saving me from my so-called drowning. "What the hell were you thinking?"

I shrugged on the robe she handed me.

"So, you're not answering that question either." Preya reached the edge of her patience, sounding more Indian than British.

I lifted my gaze to meet hers. She gasped and wrapped her arms around me. I allowed the hug without returning it, resting my forehead on her shoulder.

She rubbed my back. "What's happening to you, Phoenix?" Her voice faltered. "Please. Tell me."

"I can't." Simple words. No tears.

"But why?" She cried for the both of us. "It's obviously tearing you apart."

"Then let it." I paused. "I really wish all of it made sense."

Preya dried her tears and regarded me with a new resolve. I liked that. Her stubbornness anchored me. For the first time in my life, I appreciated what having a friend I could count on meant. I still felt lost, but with Preya by my side, I didn't feel hopeless.

~ ☾ ~

A month after my last attempt at returning to Zhamvy City, I was called to a professor's office really early. I entered without knocking. Too early to knock. I currently had no caffeine in my system to blunt my grumpy mood. The night before had been a nightmare of epic proportions. No matter how hard I tried, I couldn't sleep. Preya had been out the moment her head hit the pillow. How she managed to sleep in a snap remained a mystery to me. My brain wouldn't turn off, so I started reading one of her science textbooks, thinking the academic language would lull me to sleep. The experiment managed to make me more restless. Reading about the different ways to contract the Bird Flu only got me so far.

My skin crawled. My fingers twitched. And my feet itched in a way that made me want to keep moving, so I wandered the dorms for hours. I had to dodge the dorm master, a few maids, and three guards playing poker. Getting tired of walking aimlessly, I shuffled back to the room I shared with Preya, got into bed, tossed and turned, and by the time I got a wink of sleep, my alarm clock blared and I had to get dressed for school. If it weren't for the appointment, I didn't really need to be up so early.

On the other end of the receiving area, a brunette sat behind a desk reading a book. A classmate of mine, but for the life of me, I couldn't recall her name. I mentally kicked myself for not grabbing coffee.

Lips pressed together, I dragged my feet over to her. "I'm here to—"

"Good morning, Phoenix!" She glanced up from her book as if a VIP had walked in.

I hustled for an appropriate response. "Right. Uh, sure...Sta...Pa...Eri...Tam...?"

"Brittney, silly. We have European History together."

"Right, *Brittney*."

"Are you going to the assembly?"

I blinked at Brittney, completely forgetting my appointment. "What?"

She stared at me. "The assembly? A new student's being introduced today. You should see how cute he is. I'd never

seen black hair like that ..."

Her voice faded into the background as I ran out of the office and into the hallway. I turned in a quick circle to get my bearings then headed in the direction of the multipurpose hall. I dashed forward at full tilt through empty corridors.

A new student. A new student on Assembly Day. Cute and with black hair. My heart pounded in my chest. Hope coursed through my veins faster than any caffeine boost ever could. I needed to know. I needed to make sure.

I reached the closed double doors of the room and stopped. My lungs staged a mass protest against me. I bent over, and with every breath, tried not to heave. Adrenaline plus desperation—not a great combination for a body hardly used in months.

Kiev's muffled voice ushered me onward. Trembling hand and all, I reached for the knob and lurched my way inside. A rush of air greeted my damp face. Kiev stood on stage behind a podium with the Barinkoff crest on it.

"As you all know," he said, "Barinkoff Academy has a proud history of gathering the best and the brightest from around the world. A school that stands for invention, reinvention, and innovation. *Scientia est lux lucis.*"

"Knowledge is enlightenment," the students said in unison.

I craned my neck and searched. My horribly shaking knees had me standing by the door, unable to move anymore. The seated students paid close attention to Kiev's speech. Professors sat on the front row. I couldn't find the new student. He shouldn't be hard to spot. Impatience clamored in my throat like an angry mob storming the gates of a fortress. I needed to move forward, to do something, but my legs stayed rooted to where I stood.

"Let me introduce," Kiev motioned to the crowd, "Charles Worthington III."

My heart stopped. The name meant nothing to me.

A polite round of applause broke the tension within me as a boy about twelve-years-old with curly, black hair and glasses stood up from the front row and climbed the steps to the stage in an ambling stride. Kiev shook the new student's

~ ☾ ~

hand and gave him a few minutes to address everyone. I almost laughed hysterically, running my fingers through my tangled hair. In my desperation, I had misunderstood Brittney's words. The one I expected was more than cute. If he was here, everyone would surely know.

The devastation hadn't come yet. Maybe later, maybe never, but one thing happened for sure, I found myself back at square one, and I didn't know if I wanted to be.

"Phoenix."

I lifted my bowed head.

"Over here," Preya said.

Her voice sounded like it came from my left. I glanced left then right. Nothing.

"Center aisle, you ninny." She waved her hands in the air.

Her smile had me recoiling instead of moving forward. I couldn't be here. I just couldn't. I shook my head at her, twisted the knob poking my lower back, and stumbled backward into the empty corridor. Each breath was like ice going in and fire coming out. I couldn't think. I couldn't bring myself to focus.

Of their own volition, my feet moved.

Eyes on the ground, I kept going without really thinking of where I'd end up. I didn't care. Soon, I found myself on the second floor. I ran my hand along the wall as I walked. Once I neared the Chem lab, its automatic door opened with that familiar *whoosh*. I hesitated just outside, my gaze on the small gutter the door slid on. Was I strong enough to enter?

I avoided the Chem lab for a reason, but today my feet took me there without any help from my brain. Maybe it was a sign that I was strong enough to enter the room again. So, after a deep breath of courage, I lifted my foot and stepped inside. A second later, the door *whooshed* closed.

"There you are."

My head whipped up so fast, I thought I would fall from the dizzy spell it caused.

The morning light dimmed. A cloud must have covered the sun. I saw him in stages. The long, lustrous blue-black hair. The solid shoulders. The intense presence. The impeccable way he wore a simple suit with a navy tie, as if born in it. My

~ ☾ ~

breath hitched. My heart raced. My palms grew damp. I swallowed and waited, standing by the sliding door. I stopped breathing for a second. Demitri.

"Phoenix," he said.

"You're here." I stepped forward. "You're really here."

Carefully, like he would disappear if I moved too fast, I weaved through the empty laboratory tables and closed the gap between us.

He started to wrap his arms around me, but I shook my head.

Silently, he complied, letting his arms fall to his sides again. I lifted my hand, reaching for his hair and running my fingers through the black silk. The strands were still as luxurious as I remembered.

My fingers moved from his hair to his brow, tracing the dark archest that rose when I said something particularly interesting, annoying, or appealing. Then I moved on to his straight nose, the lines of his cheekbones, his strong jaw, and ending with the sensual curves of his lips. But I still refused to meet his eyes. My knees were trembling so badly, I thought I'd topple over.

Turning around, I walked away a few steps. I couldn't be that close to him. I closed my eyes and breathed.

"Phoenix?"

His voice, deep and melodic, sent the hairs on the backs of my neck and arms standing on end. A voice I missed so much it actually hurt.

"I'm dreaming," I whispered.

"I have to explain," he said. "Before you, I had no breath. No heart. No life. I walked around like those your world call zombies. When I allowed you to bite me, I was confident I would feel nothing since you were still fundamentally human. I was wrong. Because of your bite, I felt urges I had not paid attention to in centuries. You have no idea how much effort I need to exert just to stop myself from crossing this room and holding you in my arms when I saw you enter. Being away from you is my personal version of hell. But you must understand that the welfare of my people comes first. Always."

~ ☾ ~

Anger rose inside of me. "You don't have to explain yourself."

"I want you to know." His gaze became earnest. "Please, Phoenix, let me explain."

Nothing had changed. I opened my eyes and turned around to confront him. I waited for what he had to say.

Uncertainty entered Demitri's eyes, but he continued. "At first, I thought all my feelings were governed by our connection. I told myself I could control those urges, that I could keep myself from loving you. But, as the days passed, I slipped from carrying out our plans to caring for you. All I wanted was to keep you safe. More than anything, you needed to be safe. I, Zhamvy Royalty, a crown prince, under the spell of a human like you. It was frustrating, yet thrilling."

"Yet you managed to focus on keeping Vladimir from the throne."

"As I said, my people—"

"Yes, your people must come first," I interrupted, no longer able to listen. "I understand."

"Do you?" His lips quirked downward. "Do you really?"

"What's not to understand?"

"Phoenix, I am here. That should count for something."

I crossed my arms. I was skeptical about the reason he was in the lab, but I had to know. "What about your kingdom? Shouldn't you be ruling it?"

Demitri dropped his gaze. He squeezed the back of his neck and said, "Luka said this was not going to be easy. I should have listened to him."

"Luka?" My brows rose. "What about him?"

"He said something about how an annoying human girl convinced him to stop running away from his responsibilities."

My jaw dropped. Then I covered my mouth with both my hands. I couldn't believe it. Could Luka have really listened to me? Could he have taken the throne?

"What happened?" I asked through my hands.

"After Vladimir and everyone affiliated with him were captured, Luka took charge. My father was more than happy to give him back what has rightfully his. I still have not forgiven him for putting you in danger with Vladimir the way he did."

In my giddy happiness, I ran toward Demitri. This time he engulfed me in his embrace. I breathed in the scent of him, trembling uncontrollably.

"Demitri," I sobbed out.

I kept repeating his name the way I had all those nights I woke up in the hospital, screaming.

"Tears?" Demitri whispered into my ear. "Are you not happy to see me?"

I shook my head, rubbing my face on his shirt. My voice had disappeared for a moment. All I could do was sob and whimper and relish the warmth of his strong embrace.

Like a light bulb turning on in my head, I thought, warmth? Demitri's body temperature was always feverishly hot. I stood back a step and cupped his face with both my hands. His skin was warm, but not like he was running a fever. It was a normal warm. I was not a doctor, but I certainly knew how to tell the difference between a fever and normal body heat. I pulled out of his embrace to look at him properly.

The first words out of my mouth were, "You're warm."

Demitri chuckled. "As opposed to what?" He wiped away my tears with his thumbs.

"But...but ..." I couldn't wrap my head around it.

He smiled at my speechlessness. "Phoenix, I'm—"

"Human," I blurted out.

"Almost," he said.

"But how?" I asked, taking a step back.

Demitri pulled me into his arms again before I was out of his reach completely and rubbed the tension out of my back and shoulders.

"Dray," he said like a secret.

One word. One name that explained everything. For the first time in my life, pummeling Demitri's brother to the ground was the last thing I wanted to do.

"He finally did it," I whispered, proud and full of gratitude at the same time.

~ ☾ ~

"You did it," Demitri said. "Without you allowing Dray to experiment on you, he'd never have figured out how to make Zhamvy human. Our people would have continued to die. Our race would have ended. You did this, Phoenix."

I'd done this. I'd served a purpose. My life had value. I wasn't an invisible nothing. I was the girl who'd saved the Zhamvy from extinction. The girl a prince loved. A girl whose father would come back to her someday.

"I really did it, didn't I?" I said.

With a low growl, one I knew so well, Demitri tilted my head up with his hands and kissed me. Its force felt like waves hitting the breakwater during a storm. Fierce. Unstoppable. I felt it all the way to my core, quenching a thirst I never realized I had. Stirring a hunger I'd been ignoring for so long. My skin tingled as if tiny fireworks exploded underneath the surface. Without any hesitation, I reached up and wrapped my arms around his neck. One of his hands moved to the small of my back, crushing me closer. I melted into his new warmth. My heart beat in my ears by the time he broke the kiss.

"Still think this is a dream?" he asked with a voice so husky I felt his words touch me like a caress.

I shook my head.

The next kiss was gentler than the first, giving rather than taking, but it still scorched me with its heat. He gave what I was asking for with such tenderness that it broke my heart and put it back together again. It was a kiss that said he was real, that he was there with me in the Chem lab.

As hard as it was, I pulled back. I looked into his eyes and found my answers. Those intense black orbs stared back at me unfailingly, peeling away all the hurt, all the loneliness, and replacing them with warmth and truth.

"What now?" I whispered more than asked, afraid of the answer.

Demitri leaned in and gave me a quick kiss before he said so softly that it was like a prayer, "With the formula nearing completion, the Zhamvy need homes. You are looking at the one responsible for making that transition happen. I basically

~ ☾ ~

get to travel the world looking for places for the Zhamvy to start a new life in."

His words sent life rushing back into my body. "What about me?"

Heat sparked in his eyes. "What are you doing for winter break?"

I smiled. I guess I was packing my bags.

Kate Evangelista

When Kate Evangelista was told she had a knack for writing stories, she did the next best thing: entered medical school. After realizing she wasn't going to be the next Doogie Howser, M.D., Kate wandered into the Literature department of her university and never looked back. Today, she is in possession of a piece of paper that says to the world she owns a Literature degree. To make matters worse, she took Master's courses in creative writing. In the end, she realized, to be a writer, none of what she had mattered. What really mattered? Writing. Plain and simple, honest to God, sitting in front of her computer, writing. Today, she has four completed YA novels to watch out for. To learn more about Kate, visit her at: www.kateevangelista.com

Acknowledgements

First and foremost, I would like to thank my parents for letting me quit my day job to pursue my wildest dreams. Mom, thank you for reminding me (daily) to always be humble and to keep working. Dad, thank you for continuing to be proud of me even after I told you I wasn't going to be a doctor. I love you both deeply.

Second of all, I would like to thank Rochelle, editor extraordinaire, for seeing the potential in Taste and showing me how to make it better. Your statue is being unveiled as you read this.

Kathryn, thank you for taking care of the rest and guiding me toward a soft landing. Your insight into this project is priceless. Thank you for routing for Luka even if Phoenix was meant for a different Zhamvy prince.

And Taste would not be what it is today without the help of Angie, dedicated critique partner and writing sister from another mother. The dedication up front isn't enough. Love you, sis! The next WIP is in your inbox. *winks*

A special thanks also goes to Steph and Marlene for giving Taste a home at Crescent Moon Press and the gift of an awesome cover. You gals rock!

Noey, thank you for breathing life into Hunger and sticking by me through the mood swings and insanity. Plus, the trailer would never have happened without you. Shine bright. Show them what you can do. Conquer the world, girl!

Thank you also to Sherry, my first ever critique partner, and all the other critique partners that have seen Taste through its many incarnations. You all have taught me much.

And thank you E for letting go. This wouldn't have happened if you hadn't.

To Samantha Sotto, thank you for showing me I wasn't alone. Thank you for showing me how it's done with such grace and poise. You are my golden standard.

To MB Nave, for your gracious heart and courageous spirit, you teach me what it means to be strong.

To Jane, Mel, Shaun, thank you for your continued support. The hours spent just talking and laughing means a lot to me. We will always have Starbucks.

To Liliana Sanches, if you're reading this, I am in awe of your talent as an artist. Thank you for crafting an image so striking, it captures the imagination. Taste would be missing a key component without your vision.

To Sophie, I have one word: Ireland!

To Ms. Filip, thank you for telling me I could write. I wouldn't be here without you opening the door for me. And to all my HS classmates who lined up to read my badly written, poorly edited, riddled with grammatical errors short stories, thank you.

To the wonderful writers of CMP, thank you for welcoming me into the fold. Funny, tenacious, determined, and absolutely gorgeous—all this and more.

To all the amazing bloggers who helped get the word about Taste out there. I know I say awesome a lot, but you guys and gals really are the epitome of the word. Keep on blogging! We writers wouldn't know what to do without you.

And most of all, to the readers of this book, thank you so much for letting Phoenix and the gang in. It is my pleasure to share their story with you. If you have a dream, don't be afraid to chase it. Life's way too short. :-)